TAKING WHAT I LIKE

LINDA BAMBER

TAKING WHAT I LIKE

SHORT STORIES

A BLACK SPARROW BOOK

DAVID R. GODINE, PUBLISHER

BOSTON

This is
A Black Sparrow Book
Published in 2013 by
DAVID R. GODINE, PUBLISHER
Post Office Box 450
Jaffrey, New Hampshire 03452
www.blacksparrowbooks.com

For information contact Permissions, David R. Godine, Publisher, Fifteen Court Square, Suite 320, Boston, Massachusetts, 02108.

The Black Sparrow Books pressmark is by Julian Waters
www.waterslettering.com

LIBRARY OF CONGRESS CATALOGING-IN-PUBLICATION DATA

Bamber, Linda.
Taking what I like : stories / Linda Bamber.
    p. cm.
"A Black Sparrow book."
Includes bibliographical references.
ISBN 978-1-57423-223-3
I. Title.
PS3602.A6345T35 2013
813'.6—dc23
2012033952

First Edition
PRINTED IN THE UNITED STATES

For Liz

Contents

CASTING CALL

The word "post-racial" gets thrown around a lot these days, but I'm not sure what it means, exactly. Whose world does it describe? Not mine, that's for sure. Although I used to be married to an African, most of the people around me these days are "white," the "non-whites" having been earnestly recruited for the sake of diversity. This process is insulting all around. As I was once sharply told, if white people really wanted what black people have, they'd just go where black people are. White people, meanwhile, are seething with resentment over selection procedures that get stranger and stranger. But I'm the chair of a department with exactly one black member; we have a position to fill, and I'm going to fill it with someone diverse or die trying.

The one black member is Othello, and he's not much help. First of all, of course, relations between us have been strained since he strangled me to death with a pillow. Yes, it's me, Desdemona, at the helm of this story, and I'm here with the other members of the cast. To put it as simply as possible, we used to be characters in a play by Shakespeare, but now we're members of an English department in a small university in the northeastern United States. Something similar happened to the *dramatis personae* of two other plays that I know of, although there may be more. *Measure for Measure* is a political science department in Ontario, and *A Midsummer Night's Dream* is a philosophy department in New Delhi. But we are in a special position, because English, after all, is the discipline in which Shakespeare is studied and taught. Now, for the first time, one of us is leaving for another job, and it's his position I'm determined to fill with a person of color or ethnicity or *something*.

As for Othello strangling me, that was very bad; but at the time I was quite the codependent myself. When they asked me who had done the deed, I said with my last breath, *Nobody. I myself.* Can you believe that? I was so in love with him then I couldn't see straight. *Nobody. I myself.*

Well, I'm a different person now—at least I hope I am—and Othello definitely is. He's still intense, but nothing makes him crazy anymore. My problem with Othello these days is professional, not personal. He *will not help* with the affirmative action search, and since the rest of the department is either undermotivated or resentful, I really need him to lend a hand. Of course, nobody says, let's *not* hire a person of color. They just put lots of energy into complaining about the procedures and very little into the recruitment process itself.

The process, as I've said, is awful. We scrutinize applications for signs of a candidate's "diversity" with the color consciousness of the Ku Klux Klan. This one went to a mostly black college, that one belonged to a fraternity one member of the committee thinks is black but another one doesn't. A third candidate is named Tam, which might mean she's Amerasian, but it might be short for Tamara. Should we interview her or not? As chair I'm not allowed to ask candidates directly if they're diverse; but I have to attest to the diversity of the candidate pool anyway, and God help me if I'm wrong.

I need Othello's help. If he'd put his clout behind this, the others would fall in line. But, as one of the very few black faculty members, Othello has too many responsibilities, and I guess his plate is full. He runs the African Diaspora Program, for instance, and he heads every group having anything to do with equal opportunity or the Africana House or the student initiative on racism and justice. He's a superb administrator, so he must get something out of it; but he gives off waves of desperation, exhaustion, and anger when he's asked to do one more thing. So mostly I don't ask.

Recently, I saw Othello in action on a student committee. A Caribbean woman wearing basketball sneakers and a lime green camisole had used the term "incognegro."

"Incognegro," said a fellow student incredulously. "That's racist!" The word refers to what used to be called "passing." I don't know if it's racist or it's not, but when people on a committee start taking positions on something like the word "incognegro," they lose sight of their goal, which in this case was to make life bearable for black students at a university like ours. So Othello moved in. Lightly, quickly, he summarized most of what there was to be said on both sides of the issue, condensing twenty-five years of scholarly and popular thinking on language and political correctness in three minutes flat. Impressed and outclassed, the students subsided and got back to work.

I'm not in love with Othello anymore. He's great and he's awful, like anyone else. When I saw him in the committee, however, it stirred the parts of me that used to think otherwise.

"Oh, yeah," I thought, "the Big Guy. Mr. Cool." I keep wishing he would do that kind of thing in department meetings, but he won't. Last week, when Brabantio started to rant about the hypocrisy of the search process, I kept looking at Othello, but he just hunched down in his molded orange chair. He's quite large, so the writing arm sort of bit into his middle. I wanted him to say, "Listen, you racist windbag, you wouldn't want to hire someone black if he'd won the Nobel Prize. We don't want to hear another word out of you about *merit* and *excellence*."

Instead, Roderigo answered – Roderigo, the lamest, most pointless member of the department, gullible, foolish, spineless, and none too bright. We're always looking for low-level intro courses he might be able to teach without completely insulting the students. Of course, he loves me. Or, he "loves" me. In any case, he wants me, he's always wanted me, he's completely fixated on me. Nothing I do can make him give me up. It's embarrassing.

We were working on the delicate task of advertising Lodovico's position. The goal was to maximize our chances of hearing from "underrepresented" candidates without actually saying, don't apply if you're not diverse.

"How about '*Othello* Studies, colon, African Shakespeare and Shakespeare's Africa'?" suggested Iago. In spite of his unspeakable behavior in the old days, Iago is still a member of the cast. Believe it or not, he positions himself as the champion of the injured and oppressed, waiting for his chance to nail us all for prejudice. I'm suspicious of everything he says, but in this case I didn't see a problem.

"That could work," I said cautiously. The emphasis on Africa, whether real or imagined, could signal our hopes of making an affirmative action appointment. Iago turned to Othello.

"As our legal specialist," he said sardonically, "would you care to opine?"

We all caught our breath. When we first got here, Othello spent months in the law library, looking for ways to have Iago incarcerated or committed for what he had done in the play. It turned out a total amnesty had taken effect, and there was nothing to be done. Now Iago seizes every chance to gloat. "What does the Chief Justice think?" he asks whenever a legal issue is under discussion. Bianca claims she once heard him say, "Ask Clarence Thomas here," which would have been breathtaking whoever said it, but truly incredible coming from Iago.

Othello flashed briefly with rage and contempt but rapidly composed himself.

"Sounds good to me," he said mildly, and we all let out our breath.

"But what do we mean by 'Shakespeare's Africa'?" asked Montano. "Does Shakespeare deal with Africa anywhere *other* than in *Othello*?" This was a reasonable question, so we discussed "Shakespeare's Africa" for a few minutes to see if it worked; but then I glanced at Brabantio and saw he was about to blow.

"Not again!" I thought in alarm. In the old days, Brabantio sometimes got angry, but not like this. When I eloped with Othello, for instance, he simmered down when the Duke told him to.

I here do give thee that with all my heart, he told Othello sulkily, *which, but thou hast already, with all my heart I would keep from thee.* That wasn't great, but okay. Now he just never gives up.

"We're not in Venice anymore," he growled when I reminded him once of his former restraint. Venice at the time was a world capital at the peak of its powers, its wealth and fame and pride in the rule of law. Venice, La Serenissima, self-conscious, exploitative, international, proud. But for a woman, it had its drawbacks. It was a small world, and at every fountain where two streets came together someone was watching what you did and who you did it with. Although in some ways worldly and expansive, Venice for me was claustrophobic; and when Othello came along—an *extravagant and wheeling stranger,* as Roderigo called him—I thought this was my chance. I got as far as Cyprus that time. Now I'm in this suburb of an American city where the shopping mall is anchored at one end by Home Depot and at the other by Toys"R"Us.

Brabantio was in full form.

"By what authority," he shouted, "do you teach? Does that matter? Or are you telling me that authority comes, authority comes, not from qualifications, hmm? But from whether you're black, yellow, or blue; or transsexual, God save the mark! Or sleep with billy goats! Is that what you're telling me? Hmm? Because if it is, just say so and be done with it. Don't talk to me about diversity!"

We were in a spare, windowless classroom. My heart was pounding.

"Dad," I said. "Dad. Dad." I sounded like an embarrassed teenager, not the department chair. Not that being a department chair is a position of much authority (speaking of authority), but at least it's a kind of mom job, not a role for a child. I must be the only department chair in America with her own father in her department.

Brabantio ignored my feeble bleat. "The fact of the matter is," he shouted, "there *are* no notable African redactions of Shakespeare, and you know it! Name me one great Shakespeare text by an African! Just name me one!"

At that I drew a breath of relief. Once the question is naming things, the namers in the department can be counted on to drop dozens if not hundreds of names, and indeed they did. My colleagues named authors from Kenya, South Africa, Nigeria, and the Sudan. They named self-consciously post-colonial authors and authors who had never gotten over the charismatic, domineering dons they studied with at Oxford. They named poems, plays, novels, stories, and essays. Iago did the lion's share of the naming, but Cassio, Emilia, Montano, and Bianca did their parts. By the time they got through, it was clear that African Shakespeare was not only a field, it was practically a discipline all by itself.

Poor Brabantio. He wanted to say, "Yes, but it's all crap! Is there one thing in all that crap that's any good? I'm not talking about genius, I'm just talking about something first class, like, like, like…Wallace Stevens. Hmm? Is there one writer among all those you've mentioned as good as Wallace Stevens? Is there?"

That's what he wanted to say, and he looked as if he might explode if he didn't. Purple face, bulging eyes, winged eyebrows ready to fly off his face and bomb us all. But it's TOO LATE IN THE DAY for that kind of thing, thank God, and even Brabantio knows it.

"That's right, Dad," I thought. "That's right. Shut up now." He did, but then Roderigo piped up. Casting anxious glances at Iago (of whom he's afraid), Brabantio (whose permission he still thinks he needs to be with me), and me (the obsessional object), Roderigo proposed the lamest, stupidest compromise imaginable. Instead of African Shakespeare, he said, why didn't we ask for expertise in "Alternative Shakespeares." Wouldn't that broaden the field? He made this suggestion in a brave, decided voice intended to conceal, mostly from himself, his own insignificance in the group.

"Roderigo, you idiot," I raged later—not to Roderigo, but to Cassio, who was lending a sympathetic ear in my office. "Roderigo, you cretin, 'Alternative Shakespeares' includes every smart-aleck postgrad who's ever done a parody of *Hamlet*. It has nothing to do with diversity!" But at the meeting people took it up, and soon we were involved in an interminable conversation about what constitutes alternativity. At one point Bianca delivered a mini-lecture on the history of Poland as, if I understood her correctly, a *function* of its uses of Shakespeare. That's the kind of thing Bianca does, reversing cause and effect. It's a kind of intellectual parlor trick that makes you feel alternately dazzled and confused, like an intermittently brilliant, drizzly day. Bianca has black hair cut in bangs over clear, dark eyes. She wears dark red lipstick and tiny tight black skirts. I don't approve, but there's something perfect about Bianca, like a soprano hitting the killer high notes every time. Moreover, she has the best professional reputation of anyone in the department, except, of course, Iago himself.

"'Alternative Shakespeares' it is," I finally said, exhausted. And good luck to us, I angrily thought.

"What's the *story* with Bianca?" I raged at Cassio. "Whose side is she on?" Cassio, thank God, is on my side, although he's so genial and laid-back that everyone thinks he's their friend. He was leaning comfortably against my desk while I paced and shouted.

"Well, you know," said Cassio, "Bianca doesn't like identity politics."

"Fine," I raged, "but if you can't take a little identity politics, you end up with an all-white English department. Is that okay with her?"

"Chill, girl," said Cassio easily. "We'll make this work somehow."

I wish Cassio and I...I mean, sometimes I wish there were something between us. There was, in the old days, which was why Othello was so jealous; but now I think Cassio prefers men. That's fine for him, but I'm sick of being alone. So is Emilia. Unbelievably, she sometimes thinks of Iago.

"He could be amazing," she said in a recent fit of nostalgia. "He's so smart."

"Emilia!" I said. "Iago's the pits!"

"I know," she said quickly. "I know."

"And now with that comb-over…!" I said. In addition to being a truly evil person, Iago has aged badly, the comb-over being by no means the worst of the physical issues. But who am I to wonder at Emilia? I get so lonely, once I got drunk enough to go to bed with Roderigo. It was fine, but whatever made it possible that one time never recurred, and when he messed up in the meeting, I let him have it. He ran after me later to make up.

"I just meant…" he said guiltily. "I was only…"

"Nitwit!" I shouted, storming down the hall. It felt good at the time, but the afterimage of his stricken face gave me a sleepless night. Now I'll have to go to the movies with him or something to clear my conscience. Nuisance upon nuisance!

* * *

At the beginning of *Othello* everything in Venice is at sixes and sevens. Although it is late at night, the Duke has called an emergency meeting of the Senate to discuss state affairs. The Turks, it seems, are attacking Cyprus; their fleet, says one senator, is at least a hundred and forty strong.

I've heard two hundred, says another senator. Whatever the strength of its force, the Empire-Next-Door clearly means war. Whom should they send to deal with the threat? Meanwhile, Desdemona has just then eloped with Othello, and Iago can't wait to tell her father.

Wake up, wake up! he shouts outside Brabantio's bedroom window. You've been robbed, you old coot! *Even now an old black ram is tupping your white ewe!* Wake the neighbors, get off your duff!

Iago has a way of putting things. It's not clear why he wishes everyone ill, but he's certainly good at eliciting poor behavior when he wants to.

Up, up! he shouts to Brabantio, *or else the devil will make a grandsire of you.* Brabantio comes to the window, annoyed.

This is Venice, he says. It can't happen here.

Your daughter and the Moor, Iago repulsively insists, *are now making the beast with two backs.* Soon Brabantio caves.

Call up all my people, he suddenly shouts, and runs downstairs in his nightgown. A posse is organized to confront his new son-in-law; with any luck there will be some "accident" in which Othello can be disposed of. Meanwhile, the Duke has sent Cassio, Othello's lieutenant, to bring him to the Senate chamber on urgent business, so now there are two groups of men searching him out in the night.

What's up? Othello asks when Cassio finds him. What's on the Duke's mind?

Something from Cyprus, no doubt, says Cassio. Othello is a great general; the Duke may want him to lead the expedition to Cyprus. Just then, Brabantio arrives with officers and torches.

O thou foul thief, shouts Brabantio, *where hast thou stowed my daughter?* With little more ado, he and his men reach for their swords.

Down with him, thief! shouts Brabantio. Suddenly things are out of control as Cassio and *his* men draw their weapons to defend their leader.

Othello swiftly takes command. Hold on, he says calmly, stepping between the angry men. *Keep up your bright swords, for the dew will rust them.* This is a swoon line: Othello to die for.

Put up your toys, kids, he might as well have said. I wouldn't want anyone hurt.

That works, and things straighten out. The men troop off to the Senate chamber; Desdemona is summoned and movingly testifies to her love for Othello; the Duke acquits Othello of using "black magic" to seduce her and deploys him to Cyprus. Iago is unruffled by the failure of his first attempt to destroy Othello and excitedly looking forward to his next.

How? How? he says at the end of act 1. *I have it!* Cassio's good-looking, *framed to make women false. After some time, I'll abuse Othello's ear that he is too familiar with his wife.* That'll drive him nuts!

What is Iago's problem? Why does he hate Othello? Shakespeare does provide some motives, but they are contradictory, and nothing sticks. Finally, Iago's just a troublemaker, like Shakespeare himself. Without him there would be no plot.

* * *

After the department meeting, Desdemona teaches a class, meets with a university committee on faculty salaries, interviews a candidate for department assistant, and has a discussion with a long-winded administrator from human resources who showed up to supervise the interview.

"That's it now!" thinks Desdemona, closing the door behind the long-winded administrator. "I'm done!" Her apartment is close to campus, and soon she is climbing the three flights to her top-story condo. On days like today there isn't enough distance between her work and the rest of her life.

"*What* rest of my life?" Desdemona wonders, trudging up the stairs. Her condo has large, north-facing windows from which she has a full view of the downhill houses, converted three-deckers like her own. The houses are pale green, brown, and gray, regularly spaced on the hill. She likes them well enough, but she is glad her windows mostly frame sky. A flock of geese goes back and forth daily, making its way from the campus lake to a river nearby. On bad days they represent her own futility.

"Back and forth, back and forth," she thinks, "honking, self-important, and busy." On the answering machine are two marketing calls and a message from her optometrist. Desdemona stands by the humming microwave, considering her options. Although she likes "civilians," as she calls them, well enough, she can only really be herself with other people who once were characters in Shakespeare's plays.

"That's so interesting!" says her therapist, but Desdemona suspects she means, "That's so weird!" Weird or not, it severely limits her options. Roderigo's a fool; Cassio likes men; Lodovico's leaving; Othello? Been there, done that. Whom does that leave? Montano?

"I don't think so," she says sadly to her cat. The cat is orange and beige, like orange juice in crème anglaise. Last year Desdemona had a four-month affair with one of the kings in the history plays; but she had to keep flying to Cleveland to see him, and he wasn't much fun when she got there.

"Too focused on his career," Desdemona told Emilia when it was over.

"Well," said Emilia. "That's to be expected in a king."

"What if someone joined your department?" Desdemona's therapist asked. "Would that do?"

"Someone who *hadn't* been a character in Shakespeare?"

"Exactly," said the therapist. Desdemona considered the question.

"I don't know," she said. "Maybe." She takes her pea soup from the microwave and eats it with yogurt and a day-old chocolate chip muffin. The cat likes yogurt, so she gives him the bowl to lick.

Yesterday was Black Solidarity Day, and we were asked to wear black in support. I had forgotten all about it, but by coincidence I was wearing black anyway.

"Are you going to the rally?" asked Emilia.

"What rally?" I said.

"Some diversity advocate you are," scoffed Emilia. "There's a rally at noon."

"Why not?" I thought; but when I got there I was sorry I had come. The students were standing in the hot September sun, desultory and uncertain. The speakers couldn't find the right note, cycling between bluster, incoherence, and a kind of wince-making irony. Some bejowled ex-city councilor, black, stepped up to the mike to relive a rent strike he'd organized thirty years ago.

"Get over yourself," I uncharitably thought from the sidelines. "No one cares about your glory days."

Suddenly there was a little stir among the rally's organizers. What was up? To my surprise, Othello had arrived and would give the keynote speech. The microphone was adjusted to his height.

"You're looking good," Othello told the students wholeheartedly. "It's good to be together here." By turns rabble-rousing and erudite, he flattered and praised the students, exhorted them, threw them tidbits from black scholars and artists, scolded, teased, and made them laugh. He made *me* laugh. What a speech. Suddenly the day seemed bright instead of hot and dull. I watched Othello at full swing, his whole body charged, and thought of him hunched in his seat at the department meeting. Why can't he do this for us? I wondered. He couldn't stay for the rest of the rally, but after that it didn't matter. The students milled around, laughing and hugging each other, encouraged.

I didn't know if Othello had seen me there or not. I wanted him to know I had attended, so later in the day I sought him out. It was hot in his office, and through the open window you could smell a vine that was foaming with blossoms all over campus.

"You were great at the rally," I said.

"Oh," he said, closing a drawer. "Pfff."

"No, really," I said. I never know whether Othello really doesn't like being praised or just behaves that way.

"How's your father?" he asked. Othello knows Brabantio has high blood pressure when he's stressed.

"Oh, Dad's okay," I said lightly. "He's coming around to the prospect of another sooty bosom in our midst."

"What?!?" said Othello in disbelief. How could anyone think, Brabantio had asked Othello before we were married, that unless I were drugged or enchanted I would leave my father's house for *the sooty bosom of such a one as thou*? We had thought the phrase hilarious. "Come to my sooty bosom," Othello would say to me, sometimes as an invitation to sex. But now he just looked at me in astonishment, and I blushed in shame. Where did I think we were? And in what part of the story? After an awkward minute Othello straightened his long legs and hoisted himself up from the seat of his chair.

"It's really hot," he said, extracting a handkerchief out of his pants pocket so he could wipe his face. Of course, it was the famous one he murdered me for losing. I was amazed to see it reappear like this.

"You're just using that now to blow your nose?" I said.

"Huh?" said Othello. Then he looked at the hanky and quickly stuffed it back in his pocket. After that, I got out fast. Do you remember what that hanky looked like? It was linen white with three red strawberries on it, like little drops of blood.

* * *

In the beginning of the play, racism is on the surface and looks bad. Iago says racist things about Othello to push Brabantio's buttons; Brabantio, to mix metaphors, takes the bait. Bad, bad. Then, before the Duke and Senate, Brabantio accuses Othello of having used black magic—*foul charms*—to seduce Desdemona. Without his forbidden *drugs or minerals* she would have chosen from among the *curled darlings* of her own race, not someone so dark. Othello shakes his head.

I told her the story of my life, he says, unafraid. *This is the only witchcraft I have used.* When Desdemona movingly supports Othello's claim, the whole black magic thing falls apart. The authorities see it for exactly what it's worth and, instead of sanctioning Othello, designate him head of the Cyprus campaign. In the next movement of the play, however, it turns out that Othello *does* have some allegiance to magic, or superstition, or something. He has been given a handkerchief by his mother, who had it from an Egyptian *charmer;* "Egyptians" being gypsies, and gypsies being dark.

When you get married, his mother told him, you must give this to your wife. It is a guarantee of marital fidelity—which is at risk if the hanky is lost. Othello doesn't question this nonsense.

There's magic in the web of it, he tells Desdemona. Desdemona is very sorry to hear it, since the hanky is already gone when she does. Unbeknownst to her, Iago has long pestered his wife to steal it, and Emilia, to please him, has obliged.

What's the big deal with the handkerchief? wonders Desdemona when Othello starts ranting and raving about its loss. In fact, Iago has arranged to plant the hanky on Cassio—with disastrous results.

She's having an affair with Cassio? asks Othello, incredulous.

No way, says wily Iago. No worries, dude! It's just a hanky!

Oh, yeah? says Othello angrily. And what about her honor? Is that no big deal, too? Things go from bad to worse until he gets so jealous and confused he kills his lovely wife. Imperceptibly, the play has slipped into the very premise it began by discrediting. The black guy may not practice forbidden magic, but he believes in it; and the more sophisticated white guy is jerking him around by his "primitive" beliefs.

Idiot! shouts Emilia after Desdemona is dead. I stole the handkerchief myself and gave it to Iago! You're *ignorant as dirt!* Dirt, of course, is black, or at least dark. In spite of the play's early commitment to expose racism, there's racism *in the web of it,* we might say. An African-American prison inmate who participated in a prison seminar on "Shakespeare and Race" put it this way: "What I took from *Othello* was the message that all you've got to do is dig at a black man, dig at a black man, and you'll get him to self-destruct."

* * *

Our best candidate so far is named Lesimba Falana, and he works on Leo Africanus.

"Who was Leo Africanus again?" asked Lodovico. He and Emilia and I were sitting in the lounge after classes.

"Um, a travel writer?" said Emilia uncertainly. All we knew was that Leo was a "Moor" and served Shakespeare as a model for Othello.

"Captured by pirates," Lodovico remembered.

"Ask Bianca," said Emilia, because Bianca knows everything. I ran up to her office and brought her to the lounge.

"Leo Africanus," said Bianca, the way a child in a spelling bee will repeat the word to be spelled before spelling it. "His real name was al-Hassan ibn Muhammed al-Wazzan al-Zayyati, and he was born in Grenada, Spain, in 1495. Noble, prosperous, and intellectual, his family fled the Catholic *reconquistada,* moving to Fez while he was still a child. His immensely popular work on his diplomatic travels around Africa was translated into English in 1600, three years before Shakespeare writes *Othello.* Leo Africanus."

"Shakespeare *writes?*" I said. "What's with the historical present?" Bianca is smarter than I am, as well as better-published, so sometimes I take a jab.

"Like Othello," Bianca went on, ignoring me, "he's an insider/outsider. Captured by Christian pirates and delivered to the Pope, he was a valuable exotic who converted and worked for 'us,' i.e., Christian Europe."

"You don't say 'i.e.' in spoken English," I said flatly. Bianca barely glanced my way.

"Like Othello," she went on, "he was all over the Mediterranean."

"Lesimba spent a year following in Leo's footsteps," I said. "He sent in a chunk of travel narrative as part of his writing sample."

"He sent in a chunk of travel narrative?" said Bianca, suddenly looking straight at me.

"Yes," I said.

"I see," said Bianca, snorting.

"Why?" I said, annoyed. "What's wrong with that?"

"Oh, nothing," said Bianca. "From your point of view, really nothing!"

"You're being obnoxious, Bee," said Lodovico. "What's your point?"

"Oh, come on," said Bianca. "Everyone knows Desdemona's got a little adventure-travel fetish!"

"Are you implying that I have designs on this Lesimba?" I said.

"Is the Pope Catholic?" said Bianca. "Of course you do!"

"Bianca, please!"

"Oh my, Little Miss Innocent, Little Miss Affirmative Action! Now I get it! Of course! Leo Africanus!" She burst out laughing and ran out the door.

Emilia, Lodovico, and I sat in silence. We could hear the drone of a leaf blower cleaning up the greensward outside the building. The two of them looked at me.

"What!?" I said. "Oh, for Christ's sake!" I made an angry gesture, knocking some files on the floor. But in fact the thought of Lesimba *had* crossed my mind. I do go for the adventure thing; it's how Othello won me. His stories *of the Cannibals that each other eat, and men whose heads do grow beneath their shoulders,* however far-fetched, were a longed-for escape from boring Venice. I drifted through its enclosed spaces, dreaming of weird places, while the pigeons flew up from my feet. Now here was this Lesimba with his stories of rocky plateaus, dry riverbeds, and abandoned villages. I admit I was stirred.

Iago came into the lounge.

"We may have someone," Lodovico told him.

"Don't tell Iago!" I thought. But Lodovico had handed him the dossier, so there was nothing to be done.

"What do you think?" I had to ask when he'd looked through it.

"Looks good," said Iago mildly. "If he's black."

"If he's black!" said Emilia. "His name's Lesimba!"

"Anyone can name their kid Lesimba," said Iago. "It might just mean his parents met in Africa. Maybe in the Peace Corps."

"Iago!" said Lodovico. "Did you read the dossier? He had a W.E.B. Du Bois Fellowship, for one thing!"

"Is the Du Bois limited to minority scholars?" asked Iago. "I'm not sure." So we scurried off to our computers to look up all the signs that Lesimba is really black. Clearly he *is*. Iago just wants to make the point that he cares more than we do, as usual.

"More-affirmative-than-thou," Emilia calls him. What a pain he is.

* * *

Last night I went to the movies with Roderigo to make up for calling him a nitwit. I let him choose, so we saw some *Animal House* knockoff, and of course he loved it. He laughed at every politically incorrect joke, until I didn't know which I dreaded more, the tiresome, hateful jokes or the grating bark of laughter from the seat next to mine. We were at the multiplex. As we came out, we ran into Iago on his way to a Japanese anime I would love to have seen. Iago acted cool, but I could see his eyes go square with this piece of new information.

"Desdemona with Roderigo," he visibly thought. "What can I do with that?"

"Totally great," Roderigo enthused stupidly. "You'd love it." Right, I thought, my eyes on the filthy red carpet. Iago would just love the frat-house crap you go in for. Later I told Cassio about the encounter.

"It's not great here," I complained, "but at least there should be some anonymity. Instead I run into Iago at the goddamn mall." I was hoping Cassio would laugh, but he didn't.

"Too bad," he said fervently. "Too bad." And it is. Iago uses every scrap of damaging information he can glean. This will come back to haunt me, I can be sure.

* * *

I've found another good one. Her name is Barbara something, and she's writing about Barbary, my mother's maid. Barbary wasn't her real name, of course. She came from the Barbary Shore, and we called black people by their place of origin, as people here might call a burly guy "Texas" or "Montana." Barbary was in love, but *he she loved proved mad and did forsake her.* Barbara, thank God, is black.

"And you can take that to the bank," I told Emilia.

"How do you know?" she asked.

"One of her recommendation letters says so," I gloated. "In so many words."

"Hallelujah," said Emilia. "I wish they all did that."

"Amen," I said. But what about Lesimba? I have been getting to know him on e-mail, and to tell the truth, I like him a lot.

"Remember," I couldn't help saying. "There's still Lesimba."

"Yeah," said Emilia, puzzled. "And all the others, too."

"I just meant…" I said, blushing. That got her attention.

"Desdemona!" she said. "What's going on?"

"Nothing," I protested; but eventually I confessed.

"Nothing can come of it," I assured her. "Hooking up with a job candidate would be sexual harassment."

"And don't you forget it!" warned Emilia sternly. I told her Lesimba had found an essay I published anonymously titled "This Would Not Be Believed in Venice."

"Oh, my God," said Emilia. "He read *that*?" The essay is about a time in Cyprus when Othello slapped me in a jealous rage.

This would not be believed in Venice, Lodovico had said in the play. Everyone was shocked. In Venice Othello was an honorary white guy, but on Cyprus, fifty short miles from infidel Ottoman Turkey, the Moor came apart. More racism on Shakespeare's part; or Orientalism, or something. But my essay was an exploration of sexual masochism, since I was such a little masochist where Othello was concerned. I published it in a now-defunct journal, and have regretted doing so ever since.

"I have no idea how he found it," I said.

"Maybe it has an underground reputation," said Emilia unfeelingly. "Maybe it's a cult piece."

"Perish the thought!" I cried, burying my head in my hands. "Perish the thought!"

* * *

Desdemona's correspondence with Lesimba had begun as nothing more than the usual back-and-forth about documents, procedures, and arrangements. The first bits of personal information seemed like nothing more than e-mail amiability, an effort at cordiality from a potential colleague.

"I leave Tuesday for a conference in Tunis," Lesimba might say; but then from Tunis there'd be a quick description of some people at the conference. It would have been rude of Desdemona wholly to ignore such witty friendliness.

"Sounds familiar!" she might wryly reply. After Tunis, Lesimba went to Granada, where Leo was born. It was Lesimba's description of the Kasbah, its narrow, winding streets and its hilltop view of the Alhambra, that was the turning point.

"I wish I were there!" thought Desdemona when she read it. On second thought, she didn't want to be there at all; she wanted to hear about it from Lesimba, preferably in bed.

"You're starting up," she told herself in alarm. "Stop it!" But she thought about him more and more.

But is Lesimba really black? Iago won't let the question die, and Desdemona herself has doubts.

"Based on what?" asks Emilia.

"Well, for one thing, he's from Vermont," says Desdemona.

"White state," agrees Emilia. Race apart, opposition is growing in the department to Lesimba's candidacy.

"I don't get it," Desdemona tells Cassio one day over drinks. "What's going on?"

"I'll have another Jack," Cassio tells the bartender.

"You will?" says Desdemona sharply. In her opinion, Cassio drinks too much.

"Hard to say," says Cassio, ignoring her second question. In a meeting Othello has complained about Lesimba's work.

"It's glib," he said firmly. "Thin."

"I don't see that," Desdemona told him.

"No," said Othello, meeting her eye. "You like him."

"Yes, Desdemona likes him," said Iago meaningfully.

"Othello and *Iago* are banding together against me?!?" Desdemona asks Cassio in the bar. "I don't believe it!"

"Believe it, babe," says Cassio, slightly slurring his words. Desdemona gives him a look.

"I'm not drunk," says Cassio sitting up straighter.

"Not yet," says Desdemona.

Cassio dumps the rest of his drink in the empty salsa bowl.

"Don't worry," he says. "I'm fine."

"Great," says Desdemona tentatively. In the past Cassio's drinking made him a helpless tool for Iago and ultimately cost her her life. She wishes he would stop.

* * *

Othello came into my office today around three. He had the new course booklet in his hand.

"You've got Roderigo teaching 'Shakespeare on Film'?" he asked.

"As you see," I said defensively. Othello was department chair before me and often questions my choices. I find it annoying.

"I'm not sure Roderigo knows how films are even made," groused Othello. "I think he thinks the action is really happening, and someone turns the cameras on." I should have just laughed, but instead I tensed up.

"At least this way he'll get some enrollment," I said.

"Isn't the point to keep his enrollment *down*?"

"What exactly do you want me to do?" I complained. Othello looked at me coolly.

"Do what you please," he said. "As always." This wasn't about the course booklet. Iago must have told him about seeing me with Roderigo at the movies.

"Don't believe everything that slime-bag tells you," I said in alarm.

"Are you telling me you *didn't* go to the movies with Roderigo last week?" snapped Othello.

"What's it to you?" I said, raising my voice. "So what if I did?" Othello actually considered this for a minute and seemed to wash his hands of the whole affair.

"You're right," he said. "It's none of my business." This didn't suit me, either.

"Othello," I pleaded, "I slept with him *once*." That had an immediate unexpected effect.

"You slept with him?" he said incredulously. "You actually slept with Roderigo?" He stepped toward me, and I felt afraid. Abruptly I backed up, knocking my rolling chair clear to the wall. I may have yelped. The door burst open, admitting Lodovico.

"For Christ's sake," he said. "Pipe down, the two of you. You can hear everything from the hall!" Othello looked at him in surprise, came to his senses, and rushed away.

"Don't tell me," said Lodovico when I opened my mouth. "I don't want to know a thing about it."

"Right," I said, humiliated. Lodovico left and I sat down.

"What just happened?" I thought. It seemed a crazy eruption of something long dead, like a smidgen of dinosaur DNA crashing around in a suddenly reconstituted jungle. Is Othello jealous again? Of what? Heaven help us if he is!

* * *

For the next few weeks Desdemona doesn't do much. She worries, feels guilty about her correspondence with Lesimba, and goes through the motions at work. One day she opens her e-mail to find a startling message.

"I need you to know I'm not black," Lesimba says flatly. He has recently had a job interview at another university, where they had been disappointed by his lack of color.

"It was awful," he says. "I don't want that ever to happen again." Desdemona is horrified, both at the behavior of her colleagues at the other university and at the bald fact of Lesimba's race. Moreover, if she tells her colleagues, she may never get to meet him. He's the first non-Shakespearean who's ever interested her. What should she do?

* * *

What she does is wrong.

"This is awful, Desdemona," says the Duke, standing up behind his desk. The Duke is now the dean; he is on the verge of firing Desdemona for lying about Lesimba's race in the department account of their candidates.

"But how did he know?" wondered Emilia when Desdemona told her what was up.

"He knew," said Desdemona grimly, "because Lesimba himself sent a copy of his e-mail to the Duke. 'To avoid further embarrassment,' he said."

"But but but..." protested Emilia, "he'd already told *you*."

"He didn't trust me to spare him the useless trip," said Desdemona tonelessly. She is humiliated, because of course he was right. She *did* conceal his race out of self-interest. But why did he lead her on for so long?

"What is he, a sadist?" said Emilia.

"Or some kind of anti-diversity nutcase!" said Desdemona. "Posing as black and then bailing! What the fuck!"

The Duke wants Desdemona to finish the search.

"If I do," she says, "if I find someone black..."

"And good!" says the Duke, all but shaking his finger at her.

"Someone black and *amazing*," spits Desdemona, "can I stay?"

"That's not up to me," says the Duke stiffly. "But of course it would help your case before the Committee."

"Right," says Desdemona furiously. She leaves without saying good-bye.

Brabantio is crushed by this turn of events. He cannot face the dishonor.

"Let's go home," he begs her. By "home" he means Venice, where he thinks they can both find jobs teaching English as a second language.

"Oh, for pity's sake!" shouts Desdemona. Whatever happens, that option's out.

* * *

Baffled, angry, and grieving for the loss of her imaginary romance, Desdemona pins her hopes on Barbara, who is now the front-runner. One night Othello rings her doorbell. When Desdemona answers, he stands in the hall in his windbreaker.

"First of all," he says, "I apologize for what I said about you and Roderigo. Whom you spend time with is none of my business."

"Oh," says Desdemona, taken aback. "That's all right." She cannot think what is going on.

"May I sit down?" says Othello once he's come in. Desdemona hurriedly clears her faded couch of books, papers, used tissues, and crumbs.

"Coffee?" she offers nervously.

"No, thanks," says Othello, "this isn't a social visit." At that he actually takes out a notebook and opens it up.

"When did you first hear from Lesimba?" he asks.

"Uh, I'm not sure," says Desdemona, sitting down opposite Othello. She is very puzzled.

"Do you have his original letter of application?" asks Othello. Desdemona answers his questions as well as she can, but they seem endless. When did she sign the affirmative action statement? Did anyone know what she'd done? Did she make any promises to Lesimba, either about the job or about seeing him later? Othello isn't exactly sympathetic, but there is something reassuring about his interest, and she tells him the truth. When he leaves, she lies awake until early morning, remembering Othello in the past.

We had stayed up late talking, she remembers. That was when he opened up about his travels. His stories may or may not have been accurate, but accuracy was not a priority in the Age of Exploration. The point was ethnographic titillation, and I was definitely titillated. The next morning some Venetian traders came to see my father. Suddenly one of them was in the breakfast room doorway, only it was Othello. His reappearance just a few hours after he had left, combined with the way he was looking at me, could only mean one thing.

"Oh," I said, standing up. He was tall and strong, and his skin looked smooth, as if he had managed to sleep eight hours in three. I couldn't understand why he didn't choke from the sheer unlikeliness of his own existence.

"Maybe you should put that down," he suggested, nodding toward my hands. I looked down, and saw I had picked up a pewter platter.

"Oranges," I said stupidly, putting down the plate. We embraced, a few oranges rolling near our feet.

Desdemona sighs, and returns to the present. Why did Othello ask all those questions? From her bed she watches the light from passing cars grow larger and smaller on the wall next to her bed. Venice, she thinks, is history: a slowly sinking city vacated by its citizens so as to leave room for tourists and palazzo-hungry foreigners.

"I'd have to live in Mestre, or something," she thinks toward dawn, "and commute." Her orange cat falls asleep at her side, and Desdemona is careful not to wake him. Toward dawn she falls asleep herself.

* * *

Barbara came and gave a great talk. At the Mexican restaurant we took her to for dinner, the margaritas came in ice-blue glasses with a thick, jagged layer of salt on their rims.

"They make them with Jose Cuervo and triple sec," said Lodovico earnestly. "That's why they're so good." The others agreed fervently and at length, although I don't know what they found to say. No one was paying any attention to Barbara, who first of all was our guest and secondly was exhausted from her arduous day as a job candidate. She looked awkward and alone, but I was clean out of small talk. Finally Emilia pitched in.

"I love what you said about the willow," she told Barbara. I couldn't remember what Barbara had said, but of course I remember the willow in *Othello*.

Sing willow, willow, willow, I sang in the play – the willow being the emblem of forsaken love. God knows by then I'd lost Othello's.

Suddenly my colleagues were falling all over themselves to say something about willows.

There is a willow grows aslant a brook, intoned Montano.

"Gertrude," said Lodovico. "On Ophelia's death by drowning." This led us to a consideration of Virginia Woolf's death by drowning and the question of how many stones in one's pockets it would take to sink. Bianca and Cassio looked up from some highly amusing private conversation to join in.

"It depends on the speed of the current," said Cassio.

"The weeping willow," said Bianca with her usual precision. "*Salix babylonica.* Native to extratropical Asia, first imported to England in 1748 by a Turkish merchant of Aleppo named Vernon. *Salix babylonica.*"

Othello, inexplicably, was talking about Leo Africanus.

"Once in Kenya he was bitten by a lion," said Othello, glancing at Iago. Bianca, who was laughing again with Cassio, looked up and said briefly, "He never went to Kenya." It now became apparent that Cassio was drunk on margaritas, and also that he was hitting on Bianca. For a moment I thought, "Well, so much for my theory about Cassio," but then I realized that he was hitting on Montano, too, who was sitting on his other side. Both Bianca and Montano seemed delighted, and neither seemed aware of Cassio's attention to the other.

"That's why they called him Leo," Othello insisted, still aiming at Iago. "Because he kept having these run-ins with lions." Iago lifted a forkful of chicken mole to his lips, smiling imperturbably. Bianca was annoyed.

"No, it isn't," she said. "He was called Leo after Pope Leo X, to whom he was delivered by the corsairs who captured him."

"Nice use of the objective case," I needled, at which Bianca threw up her hands. She got up to go to the bathroom, sharply scraping her chair on the terra-cotta floor. This left the field to Montano, who actually popped a tequila-soaked shrimp in Cassio's mouth. I looked at Barbara. She seemed tense and unhappy to be a guest at this dinner from hell. What do we usually talk to job candidates about at dinner? I asked myself. Housing? Schools?

"Do you have children?" I blurted, and then realized I didn't know if she was even married.

"No," she said. Finally Othello stopped spewing misinformation about Leo Africanus and helped me deal with our guest.

"Thank you," I breathed silently, whether to Othello or to the God of Awkward Dinner Parties I couldn't say. Barbara really warmed to Othello, and soon they were laughing together. I must say, she'd be perfect for the job. Her hair is cut around her face in a soft Afro, and she talks with a very slight stutter she completely ignores.

"What was that stuff about Leo?" I asked Emilia later in the vestibule. I spoke softly, under the restaurant din.

"He seemed to be gunning for Iago," said Emilia, equally puzzled.

"But how?" I asked. "What's Iago got to do with Leo?"

"Couldn't say," said Emilia, opening the door for me.

* * *

At seven thirty the next morning my phone rang. I knew it would be Cassio, covered with remorse.

"*Oh, thou invisible spirit of wine,*" he moaned, "*Let us call thee devil! To be now a sensible man, by and by a fool, and presently a beast!*" I didn't want to hear it all again.

"I didn't sleep well, Cassio," I said, partly into the pillow and partly into the phone. "Take it to a meeting."

"Sorry," he said, pulling himself together. "The point is Barbara's great, and last night sucked. Something has to be done, or she won't accept an offer."

"You know what?" I said, still partly to the pillow. "I don't exactly care anymore. I may not even be here by then." But Cassio kept at it, reminding me how hard we had worked and how great a teacher and colleague Barbara would be. Finally I was in a standing position by the bed, tying on a bathrobe.

"I'll call her at the hotel," I said, cradling the phone on my shoulder. "We'll take her to the airport to make up for last night." Cassio was at my apartment, shaved and sober, before I had fed the cat. Barbara was nervous.

"Good," I thought. It meant she still wanted the job.

"Delta or American?" I asked as we got to the airport. Suddenly Barbara was sneezing hard.

"Allergies," she gasped. "American."

"Here," said Cassio, handing her the Kleenex box I keep in the back.

"I'm okay," she said, pulling out a hanky. At that Cassio shouted, "Watch out!" and I swerved to avoid an SUV. The hanky Barbara was blowing her nose into had three red strawberries on it, and seeing it had freaked me out.

"Where did you get that hanky?" I demanded—as if I didn't know. Barbara looked at me, surprised.

"Othello gave it to me," she said. "Last night."

"Last night?" I said, my voice rising. "When last night?"

"At the hotel," said Barbara, becoming alarmed.

"Oh, right," I said with a sinking heart. After dinner Othello had taken Barbara back to her hotel; and what, I wondered, had happened there?

"American," said Cassio loudly. "Arrivals. Here." I said a strained farewell to Barbara and drove off.

"Why did you flee?" he asked when I came back for him. "What the hell?"

"They won't let you wait," I said, which wasn't strictly true. Cassio just nodded. He had something else on his mind.

"You've got to help me," he said as we drove toward the exit.

"With what?" I said.

"You know," said Cassio unhappily.

"Oh, Cassio," I sighed.

"I've got to detox, and I can't do it by myself," he said. "Can I stay at your place a few days?" He looked anxious and afraid. "I can't go on like this!" he cried.

That's all I need, I thought. Someone detoxing in my condo. I didn't say yes and I didn't say no; later I drove to the river to think. It was cloudy, with a few gleams of sun; some ducks were splashing and grooming near the shore. I walked and walked, thinking of Othello. Did he spend the night with Barbara? After all my flirting with Lesimba, was *he* the one to cross the line with a job candidate?

"No way!" I thought. But would he have given her the hanky otherwise? In fact, I was full of questions about Othello. Why had he come to my house that night? Why had he baited Iago with misinformation about Leo? Above all, what about me? Did I care about Othello, still? Or again? I had walked so far down the river that I could see the city on the other side, its tower windows a wild, brief pink. I stood there excited and anxious. Lesimba had been a fantasy; Othello was real. The shapes around me faded with the light. I thought of Cassio.

"If we knew it would work this time," I had told him severely, "I wouldn't mind a bit." In the gray light by the parking lot, with the ducks tucked up for the night, I came to my senses and fumbled for my cell phone.

"I'm sorry I was a jerk," I said. "Of course you can stay with me." Cassio's so good. Whatever possessed me to speak to him sharply?

* * *

In Shakespeare's play, Iago, for no particular reason, decides to torment Othello so relentlessly with insinuations about his wife's infidelity that he murders her. Me. Murders me. Whirling through the play like a mad musician, Iago both horrifies and entertains the audience, with Othello as his violin. Finally Othello breaks.

Put out the light, and then put out the light, Othello says before putting out my lights. At the end everyone and his brother shows up in my bedroom suite as I lie dead: Montano, Cassio, Lodovico, Gratiano, Emilia, "Officers," and "Others." There's some yelling back and forth between the bedroom and the anteroom as they try to lock Othello in; there's some scuffling over who has what sword, although Othello always seems able to produce another. He finally kills himself with an auxiliary weapon they didn't know he had. At no point is there a real confrontation with Iago, although before dying Othello says, *I look down toward his feet—but that's a fable.* Othello wants to see if Iago has cloven hoofs, since in his disinterested desire to harm others he seems like the devil himself.

There wasn't any real confrontation this time, either. Present were the Duke, Othello, Iago, and me. Exhibit A was a document in which Lesimba described a trip through the desert at night. His group encamped around 2 A.M., got drunk, ululated like women, and danced. Eventually the Bedouins came from the hills to join them.

"Forget the content," Othello told the Duke, who was frowning and reading the message. "Look at this." "This" was a faint line down the left side of the paper.

"So?" said the Duke.

"Now look at this," said Othello, giving him a handout for one of Iago's courses. That, too, had a faint line down the left side.

"So?" said the Duke again.

"Duke," cried Othello. "There *is* no Lesimba. The messages are from Iago!"

I wish I could say Iago leapt up, upended the Duke's Queen Anne sideboard, made a dash for the French windows, and was pursued by the campus police. Or that the office erupted in a melee of "Officers" and "Others." Certainly some kind of drama ought to have followed Othello's dramatic announcement, particularly since it turned out to be true.

"What?" I cried.

"What?" said the Duke, almost as startled as I.

"You're mad," said Iago calmly. But Othello had what he needed to make his point.

"There's a flaw on Iago's printer drum," he explained. "Iago's 'Lesimba,' Duke. I knew it."

"You mean..." I said, incredulously.

"Yes," said Othello, wheeling to face me. "Iago cooked up all that travel stuff you love precisely to entrap you. And he did." Othello had interrogated everyone remotely connected to the affair, and when he got to the Duke's secretary he scored. Someone had "anonymously" sent printouts of the Lesimba–Desdemona correspondence so the Duke could see what I was up to. Of course Anonymous was Iago.

"This is absurd!" said Iago. But the Duke was scowling at him and making a noise.

"It was a test," said Iago quickly.

"Of what?" barked the Duke.

"Desdemona's sincerity," Iago improvised. "About affirmative action."

"You piece of shit!" I shouted.

"Desdemona!" said the Duke, turning his scowl on me. And so it went. It was clear to Othello and me that Iago was motivated by the same pointless malice we had seen in the play; but soon Iago was threatening to go to the media with the story of my misdeeds, and that put the

kibosh on any punishment for him. The Duke looked stymied, thinking, no doubt, of the bad publicity, the lawyers' fees, the howls from the
alumni...

"It could cause a serious drop in applications for admission," he said
gravely.

"Right," said Othello. He looked frustrated and exhausted; and eventually I, too, had had enough.

"I tell you what," I said to Iago. "We'll forget this on one condition."

"What?" he said warily.

"You're not allowed to wear shoes to department meetings. That way
we can check from time to time to see if your feet are cleaving in twain."

Othello snorted. Iago looked angry and offended.

"Joke," I said. "Just a little joke. No one would want you ever to suffer any actual consequences for your repulsive behavior." That was the
extent of my revenge, and I'm sure I'll pay for it later. But that was the
end of that, at least for now.

In the hall I was high and merry from the outcome of the meeting.
Othello, on the other hand, was quiet, and as we went down in the eleva-
tor, I suddenly felt self-conscious.

"Did you do that for me?" I wanted to say, "or what?" I couldn't
ask that, or any of the larger questions behind it; so after a minute I just started babbling. We crossed the campus chatting nervously, with me taking two steps to Othello's every one. Eventually
I told him Barbara had accepted the job, and he threw off his pensiveness.

"Wonderful!" he said, putting an arm around my shoulders and hugging me to him. "Good job, Desdemona! Good for us! Congratulations!"

Othello's touch, the first since we got here, went through my body
like a current. Then I fell apart. Why was he so happy about Barbara?
Maybe I wasn't the point at all; maybe Othello was just still trying to get
back at Iago. Suddenly that seemed the likelier explanation, and I felt my
face clog up with tears.

"I'm all over the place," I thought helplessly. Out there on the path,
with students going back and forth and bicycles and well-groomed trees
benevolently putting up with us all, I wanted to say, "What exactly did
you mean by giving the hanky to Barbara? And by the way, did you have
sex with her last week?" – but that was a non-starter, so I made up some
excuse and ran off at a fork in the path. Othello's face looked...startled?

Hurt? Mad? I wanted to get somewhere private so I could cry, whether from relief, confusion, or simple overload. In the ladies' room of the library I ran into a student and fled; finally I broke down in a secluded area of the bound periodicals, hunching my shoulders and weeping freely opposite *The Journal of Anxiety Disorders, 1982–2004.*

* * *

I was dreaming about a lion and the IRS when someone knocked on my door. To my surprise, I was on my ratty couch, not in bed; but then I remembered why. Cassio had woken me at 4 A.M. with the heebie-jee-bies, and when I got him back to sleep I had just crashed on the couch.

"Who is it?" I yelled, tired and fed up.

"It's me," said Othello's voice. I pulled a sweater over my nightgown and opened the door. Othello looked sleepless, angry, and hurt. My heart leapt up, happy and scared.

"What's the story with you, Desdemona?" said Othello, coming in without preliminaries. "Sometimes we're friends—or more—and some-times you're just rude. I wasn't expecting gratitude particularly, that's not why I did it, but you might have said thanks, good job, I'm glad I don't have to go back to Venice or shit. You know what I mean? Instead you run away as if you're under attack. What's going on? I'm in the dark here, and I'm sick of it."

Cassio had vomited in the night, and it occurred to me that my night-gown smelled faintly of having cleaned him up.

"Can you wait a minute?" I asked. "I need to wash before we talk. Make yourself some coffee." I grabbed up yesterday's jeans and ran to the bathroom. In the mirror I looked pale with lots of black hair flying and a wild shine in my eyes. I blew myself a kiss as I left.

"I think this is it," I said excitedly. But just as Othello and I were sitting down to toast, Cassio appeared in pajama bottoms, tousled and appealing. He seemed quite sane but his hand was bleeding.

"Desdemona," he said, looking at his hand, "where do you keep the Band-Aids?"

Othello turned to me in astonishment.

"Othello's here," I told Cassio.

"Oh, hi, Othello," he said, relaxed. "What are you doing here?" Othello stood up, knocking his toast jam-side down on the rug.

"I don't believe this," he said. "I don't believe this." Then he said, "I don't believe this," again. I was paralyzed and couldn't speak.

"You had sex with Roderigo," Othello said to me. "Then you fell for some e-mail concoction of Iago's, and now you're having an affair with Cassio. Where does this end? What are you doing to me, Desdemona?" At that he seemed to lose his grip and started yelling. He said something from the play about finding or not finding *Cassio's kisses on [my] lips*, shouted at Cassio, "*I see that nose of yours, but not that dog I shall throw it to*," and slammed out the door. Then he reappeared, looking crazed. "*Noses, ears, and lips*," he shouted, completely out of his mind, "*is't possible?*" Then he left. Cassio was dumbfounded. He stood there bleeding on my rug for a second; then he ran after Othello. I was in shock. Cassio's bare feet were coming back up.

"Desdemona, you want him back, is that it?" he said forcefully.

"Yes," I said simply.

"Then run! I can't do it for you; I'm bleeding. He's on Locust, heading home. Run!"

"Wait!" I said as he physically pushed me toward the door. "Give me my nightie!"

"Your nightie?" said Cassio, incredulous; so I grabbed it myself and ran with it bunched in my hand. Sure enough, there was Othello on Locust. I was panting by the time I caught up.

"Smell this!" I told him urgently.

"Have you gone nuts?" he asked, grabbing my shoulders. We were in front of an insurance agency's picture window, and a couple of agents looked up.

"I wasn't sleeping with Cassio," I cried, "I was cleaning him up! He threw up, he's in withdrawal, he's stopping drinking again." Othello looked at me as this sank in.

"He's staying with you to detox?" he said slowly. Absentmindedly, he sniffed the nightie.

"*Yes*," I said, walking purposefully. "To detox!" We started walking again, partly to get away from the insurance agency and partly just from momentum.

"You're not having an affair with him?"

"*No*," I said. "I never was. Everyone knows that. Every audience, the whole university, the other characters...no one but you ever thinks I'm having an affair with him!"

We were now at Fourth and Cleveland; pedestrians were waiting near us for the light to change. Othello looked dazed.

"Hah," he said. "Hmm." Then his face cleared. "Oh, well, *good*. Okay. I'm sorry, then." The light changed, and the pedestrians crossed. It was a muggy morning, sticky, with the threat of heat to come. Something was building inside me.

"This is like a repeating nightmare," I told Othello angrily. "Life after life, your jealous rage!" That seemed to release a whole truckload of things I had to say, and I went on for quite some time. Basically it came down to, how could you *kill* me, you moron, over a handkerchief, how could you have allowed Iago to convince you I was a slut, why didn't you ask me, etcetera, etcetera, and so on. Pedestrians kept pooling and crossing at the intersection, casting curious glances in our direction. Othello stood there listening, nodding, once or twice gently moving me out of the sidewalk traffic. When I came to an end, he put his arms around me, and we stood there as people went to work. I breathed against Othello's dark green shirt, and the warmth of his body turned my breath to mist.

"It's going to be hot," I said, after a while.

"Yes," said Othello. At that I felt a sudden lightness. I became aware that I was holding on to Othello, and I tightened my grip. He tightened his.

"Cool," I said, and his large body relaxed.

"Well, okay," he said. "Okay, then." I laughed into his shirt, and he laughed and kissed my head. We didn't move. Then I thought of something disturbing.

"What about Barbara?" I said to his chest.

"What about her?" said Othello. "She accepted the job, right?"

"Did you have sex with her the other night?!" Othello held me away from his body to look at me in alarm.

"*What?*" he said.

"Did you have sex with Barbara when you took her back to the hotel!"

"What makes you think that?"

"You gave her the handkerchief," I said. "The stupid handkerchief your mother gave you. I saw her use it on the way to the airport."

"She was sneezing," said Othello. "Barbara's *married*. What do you take me for?"

"Oh, right," I said ironically. "*I'm* the one with jealous thoughts." Othello looked briefly embarrassed, then pulled me back to his chest.

"Okay, okay," he said. "No, I didn't sleep with her. Thank you for asking." I snorted briefly, then he did, and then we both laughed and laughed. We walked for a while, and then we got a turkey and cranberry wrap and ate it on a bench in an office park. Then we felt exhausted and just sat staring, so from the outside we looked like Dustin Hoffman and Katharine Ross on the bus at the end of *The Graduate*. But inside I felt great. All the pins of the combination lock inside me were falling into perfect alignment, one at a time, and the core cylinder was starting to move. I was with Othello again. I hadn't felt this way in years.

"I hope Cassio got some help with his hand," I said eventually. About forty sparrows were chirping and hopping in a nearby hedge. It turned out Montano had taken Cassio to the emergency room, but he hadn't needed stitches. There was still my rug, of course, full of blood and jam. Did I care? Not a bit. I was with Othello; all would be well.

Oh my soul's joy, said Othello softly—as he had said once before on reuniting with me—*if it were now to die, 'twere now to be most happy.* Oh my soul's joy! Oh, reader, oh hearer, oh listener—thank you for reading my story. May all your reincarnations have moments like this one in this life of mine.

* * *

CODA: BARBARA

Two years. That's what I told my husband. He loves this place, dream job, nice house, but I'm stuck in this loony tunes department where everyone's a character from *Othello*. And white, of course, except for Othello, who's so excited to be back with Desdemona he barely knows I'm here. I've never felt so black.

"Two years, baby," my husband said. "I promise. Then we'll go wherever you want." May it be so. Well, I'm here, so I'll make the best of it.

Meanwhile, I dream – or something – of Shakespeare. I don't know if this happens to all English teachers or just me.

"Just you," he told me the other night. But from what I know of Shakespeare, he wasn't Mr. One Hundred Percent Truthful where women were concerned. In any case, he wants to talk. In heaven these days black folks are all the rage.

"Ever heard of Langston Hughes?" I asked. "Zora Neale Hurston? Edward P. Jones? Get with people like that and you won't have to come talking to me at night."

"Okay," he said, writing down names. "But I want to see you anyway. I like you."

"Good," I said. It never hurts to be liked. But now he wants to base a comedy on me, and I wish he wouldn't.

"It's about a black woman who dresses up as a white man," he told me eagerly. "By the end of the play things are so confusing that black and white no longer mean much at all. Don't you think that's good?"

"No," I said. "I don't." So then he asked what kind of play I *would* like, and I said I didn't know; but now I do, and next time he shows up I'll tell him. Write a story, I'm going to say, about a black woman who works two short years in a mostly white English department and then is happily employed for the rest of her life in a historically black or integrated university in a seriously integrated city in these United States. What do you think, Mr. William Shakespeare? Is that something you can write? Come on, dude. Take a chance. Give it a try!

PLAYING HENRY

"Oh, no!" says Clare, on learning her company's spring schedule. "The women in those plays suck!" Her company will perform four related Shakespeare plays, the Second Henriad, as it's called. At this point in her career Clare doesn't want to stand on the sidelines, cheering or grieving over some man's fortunes. She doesn't want to be the left-behind wife in *Richard II*; or any of the unmemorable whores, wives, or girlfriends in *Henry IV Part One* and *Henry IV Part Two*; or the silly war-prize bride in *Henry V*. What Clare does not know is that Terri, the guest director for the season, has decided to cast the play without respect to gender.

"You mean I could be Richard?" she says, when she learns.

"If you want," says Iris. Clare is the acknowledged star of the company, and Iris assumes she'll have her choice of roles. Iris does not resent Clare's success. She herself spent years away from the theater and has only recently returned.

"But I don't know about your Terri," says Iris. "She has a reputation as a nut."

"She's not *my* Terri," says Clare. "I've never worked with her before in my life."

"I don't like her," declares Iris. "She's didactic and flamboyant." Once Terri came to work in a turban. Is the gender-bending thing a cheesy move or is there really something to it? In these days of all-male *Swan Lakes* and all-female *King Lears* nothing could be more routinely scandalous than gender-neutral casting; but given what's at stake for her, Clare is disposed to approve.

Clare and Iris are having lunch with Geoff.

"Why do you want to be Richard?" says Geoff, pushing aside the remains of his kebab. "He's a loser. *And* a drama queen." After being deposed by his cousin Henry, Richard carries on and on about his plight. He is not exactly gay, but as one of Shakespeare's early experiments in full-throated masculine emotion, he's gender-ambiguous.

"Don't be silly," says Clare. She is dying to get her hands on Richard's late, great, soaring speeches. Geoff has learned that he will play Isabella, Richard's wife.

"Are you okay with that?" asks Iris.

"Of course!" says Geoff. "She's the heart of the play!"

"Oh, please," says Clare unkindly. "She's a weepy drip."

Geoff opens his mouth and closes it again. Iris looks warningly at Clare.

"Shall I get these out of your way?" asks a waitress, clearing a few plates.

"Thanks," says Iris to the waitress. To her old friend Clare she says firmly, "Clare, shut up."

"Yeah," says Geoff, forking a tomato. "Shut up." Geoff is half a generation younger than Clare and Iris, but he is a talented actor, and the three are on equal terms.

Clare considers for a moment. "Okay," she says. "I will." Geoff shakes his head but lets it go. He wants to talk about Terri, with whom he has worked in the past.

"She talks all the time," he says. "Sometimes right over your lines." It's not that Terri wants the actors to stop; she's just exhorting them in real time, as if they were athletes instead of actors.

"She's manic," says Geoff. He waves his arms in imitation of Terri. "La, la, la, la, la, here's an idea and another and another."

"Give her a chance," says Clare irritably. "We all agreed to invite her." Terri is well known in theater circles as a pain in the neck, but she is currently red hot, and the whole company would get a boost if their season were one of her hits. Clare has to admit, however, that so far the guest director has been very sure of herself and none too tactful.

"Lose the shades," she snapped at Clare once when Clare forgot to take off her sunglasses before going on stage. Clare finds the memory unpalatable.

"Let's go now," she says after a pause.

"In a minute," says Geoff, chewing a last bite of meat.

"Now," says Clare, raising her voice. "I'm done." Terri does not seem aware of Clare's position in the company. She could give Richard to someone else.

* * *

Clare began acting accidentally, playing random parts in plays at school. But as time went on, people noticed that Clare was really acting, not hamming it up.

"She should go to drama camp," her teachers would say. Then at drama camp the counselors would notice her, too. No one imagined a real career for Clare, but at every stage she was passed on to the next. It wasn't until she chose her major in college that her father got alarmed.

"Drama!" her father exclaimed when he learned. "But you're not going to be an actor!"

"I'm not?" said Clare. Her father had other plans for his firstborn child, and there were some bitter fights before the issue got resolved. Now one of the stars of an excellent regional company, Clare is a hard-working, determined professional. She believes in her luck, and she imagines that her belief itself is lucky. This time, however, her luck has run out. She learns that the part of Richard has gone to a tall, lithe Bengali actor named Sangeet whom Terri has brought in for the season. Clare is very disappointed.

"She just wants to make a point," says Iris sympathetically.

"What, you don't think a South Asian King of England is a great idea?" jokes Geoff, trying to be supportive.

"Don't be stupid," says Clare, annoyed. If a woman can be King of England, why not a Bengali man? But when she learns what her own part will be, she is angry. She not only won't be Richard, she won't even be Henry's son Hal. That would have been a great part.

"And Clare will play Henry," says Terri, standing commandingly in front of the actors. She is wearing a heather-colored caftan and boots with a raised square heel. Her hair is the color of cherry cough syrup, with gray roots. She assigns the rest of the roles in an offhand voice, as if who would play whom were a matter of little importance, and goes on to other things.

Clare looks at her in disbelief. Terri's eyes have a slight, hard bulge, and Clare wonders if she has a thyroid condition.

"Thanks," says Clare, tight lipped, when Geoff offers condolences. She rushes past him out the door. These four plays are the heart of the season and will be noticed by critics in New York. Clare does not want to be Henry.

* * *

Is Clare just being fussy? In *Richard II* Henry beats out Richard for the crown, and the next two plays bear his name. How unimportant can he be? But Clare is right. As the up-and-comer in *Richard II*, Henry is never more than adequately persuasive, and after defeating Richard, he stays in the background while Richard sings one great aria after the next on his predicament. In *Henry IV Parts One* and *Two* the action centers on Hal, turning his father into an instant has-been. The whole point of these plays is to prepare Hal for the crown, taking him through a brilliant, witty, ungovernable adolescence to full and layered manhood. Henry's reign is a shaky intermission between his cousin and his son; a decent interval between regicide and nationalist triumphalism.

All the soil of the achievement, Henry tells Hal at an emotional moment, *goes with me into the earth.* Henry has blood on his hands, having taken care of Richard through intermediaries; but the special bond between father and son (*a.k.a.* primogeniture) will re-sacramentalize the kingship. It will be the balm that anoints the heir, even though the father was unanointed. Meanwhile, Shakespeare is taking no chances with Henry. All he is allowed to do is pine for his son, experience mild guilt, and reminisce about his glory days.

"But he's the top dog, no?" protests her boyfriend Gustavo.

"Nominally," says Clare. "But not dramatically." Gustavo is relatively new in Clare's life. She does not know if they will last, but with her children grown and gone, she is very glad of his companionship. He is a Peruvian engineer, tall and cheerful, with an indiscriminate interest in the arts and an unflagging curiosity about the process of a theatrical production.

Clare undertakes some research, hoping she will find something that will help her connect to her part.

Henry ruled from 1399 to 1413, she writes in a notebook. *It must have been the most undistinguished epoch in all of Western Civ.* She reads and reads, but nothing helps. "There were some inconsequential religious revivals," she writes. In a Pirandello play, she thinks, the characters would be sitting around commenting on their plight. "Too late for the Middle Ages and too soon for the Renaissance," they might complain. "What's a body to do?" The only thing that really interests Clare is a picture of a courtier's shoe with the *incredibly long points* that were apparently fashionable then, as they are now. The six-hundred-year-old shoe is soft and low heeled, but its point makes it twice as long as the foot it contained. She imagines the courtiers moving around the castle with infinite care, trying to keep their points from flopping under their feet. They must have kept their distance to avoid getting tangled in each other's shoes.

* * *

Iris and Clare became friends in graduate school when they were paired in a skit.

"Did you know each other before this class?" asked the improv teacher, impressed by their first attempt.

"No, why?" said Clare. Iris was lying on the floor, Clare having shot her with an imaginary arrow.

"Up, up," said Clare, reaching for Iris's arms.

"I'm a dead wolf," objected Iris. "You can't just pull on my forelegs and expect me to get up."

Now Iris will play Henry's father, John of Gaunt. Gaunt is a great role, but he dies near the beginning of *Richard II*.

"I don't care," says Iris. She is pleased to have been entrusted with the most famous speech in *Richard II*, Gaunt's patriotic deathbed rant.

"*This precious stone set in the silver sea*," she intones, "*This blessed plot, this earth, this realm, this England.*" To get in the spirit of her part she sometimes calls Clare "son."

"Please," says Clare. "Anyway, I'm your nephew." She and Iris are going through the plays together, just as they did at Yale. These plays are riddled with fathers and sons, mirroring and contrasting and bouncing off each other. False fathers, absent fathers, jealous fathers, father acts…the theme borders on the obsessive in the Henriad. Should a man team up with his dad or should he rebel? The plays cannot rest in either possibility.

In real life John of Gaunt was an aggressive, fabulously wealthy English magnate with an insatiable appetite for power. At one point he decided that in addition to everything else he wanted to be King of Spain, so for a few years he dragged his men through a peninsular war. In Shakespeare, however, Gaunt is brave and true, the one man who stands up to the terrible king.

Landlord of England art thou now, not king, he shouts at Richard from his deathbed, which is a good way of putting it. Richard looks at the entire nobility of England as his own personal profit center. When Gaunt dies, the possibility of passionate, disinterested patriotism dies with him, and all the players are more or less out for themselves.

* * *

Passionate, disinterested patriotism was what Clare's father most wanted to practice and pass on to her. He lost no opportunity to instruct her in this ideal.

"Clare! Come here!" he called one day in October of 1973. It was the year of the Watergate scandal, and Clare was fourteen years old.

"What?" said Clare, joining her father in front of the TV. Archibald Cox, the special prosecutor who precipitated Richard Nixon's demise, was at a desk, reading a principled statement challenging the president at the risk of his own job.

"Look at that," breathed Clare's father as Cox pulled off his glasses, giving the camera a look between a shrug and a dare.

"What the hell," Cox seemed to say, tossing his glasses on the desk. His intelligent, layered look had in it the full awareness of what might—and did—ensue.

Clare's father was no Boston Brahmin like Cox, but in Clare's mind he was equally heroic. It was not just Cox's courage that Clare associated with her father, but his subdued passion, his complete immersion in his public role, and his perfect grooming. Cox was clean shaven and bow-tied; there was something honorable about his very haircut, which was recent and skillful. Clare's father had Cox's eyes, dark and alive in the depths of his face. He took his feet down from the embossed brass tray table he had brought back from Turkey, and leaned toward the TV.

"Nice work," said Clare's father, his eyes on the screen. He was as gratified by the opportunity to share this with Clare as he was by Cox himself, and Clare was reassured by them both. There was a God, and men like her father and Cox worked "under" Him, as promised in the Pledge of Allegiance.

"Cool," she said, thrilled. But Clare was also restive. She had desires her father knew nothing of. Behind her satisfaction in Cox was the knowledge of looming problems at home.

"I can't be what he wants," she thought on the couch. It was a murky, self-erasing thought, part anger, part fear.

Now Clare is watching TV with Gustavo. On a community cable channel Noam Chomsky is giving a talk.

"He's always there," Clare says. "Ever since 9/11." Night after night, in speeches, interviews, and conversations, Chomsky reminds the world of terrible behavior on the part of imperial powers.

"There's never been anything remotely like it," says Chomsky impartially. Clare and Gustavo missed the beginning of the talk, so they aren't sure what he means by "it."

"The opium wars?" guesses Gustavo. They listen for a while; then Clare wants to tell Gustavo her day.

"We're supposed to write a backstory," she tells him, turning down the sound.

"What's a backstory?" asks Gustavo.

"What went on before the play," she explains. "Or underneath it."

"But how do you know?" asks Gustavo.

"You don't," says Clare. "You make it up." Gustavo nods, but doesn't understand.

"This is usual?" he asks. "To write a backstory?"

"No," says Clare. "It's Terri. She lectures us out of books on acting that we all read years ago. Then she cooks up these assignments." This week's lecture was from Uta Hagen's classic *Respect for Acting*. Standing in the center of the stage, her legs squarely spread, Terri kept everyone waiting while she looked for a passage.

"Here it is," said Terri calmly when she found it. She bent the book at the spine and read with emphasis. "To prepare for a role, says Uta Hagen, *I must know as much as possible about my character. I must even investigate 'my' subconscious needs and the things I don't want to face about* 'myself.' I must glean facts about parents, upbringing and education, health, friends, skills and interests."

"Do you understand?" said Terri, looking up at them significantly. "These will give me the faith," she exultantly read, "that 'I' am!"

"If there's anyone," whispered Clare to Iris, "who doesn't need more faith that she *is*, it's Terri." Iris made a brief snorting sound.

"But isn't she right?" asks Gustavo. "Doesn't the actor think like that?"

"Of course she's right!" expostulates Clare. "It's acting 101! We do that all the time!"

Clare is more and more uncomfortable with Terri. What does she want? Whatever it is, Clare does not seem to be able to provide it. Tomorrow they will be rehearsing a difficult scene, and Clare is unsure how to make it work. In the scene, Henry and a friend, Northumberland, are plotting against Richard when they run into Hotspur, Northumberland's son. Hotspur is full of exciting news but fails to greet Henry, who is not yet king but still a duke.

Where are your manners, boy? his father reprimands him. *Have you forgot the Duke of Hereford?*

No, says Hotspur stoutly, *for that is not forgot which ne'er I did remember. To my knowledge, I never in my life did look on him.*

Then learn to know him now, says Northumberland decidedly. *This is the duke.*

"The *father*," Terri intoned earlier today, her eyes boring into Clare, "introducing the *son* to the family business." There is something special she wants to happen here, but Clare can't think what.

"Well," says Gustavo, trying to help, "what happens next?"

"Almost nothing," says Clare. "Hotspur bows and calls me *gracious lord*, and I just sit there smirking."

"Sit?" asks Gustavo.

"I'm on horseback," explains Clare.

"Smirk?" asks Gustavo. Clare understands that this is a vocabulary question, not a theatrical one.

"To smirk," says Clare, sitting forward on the couch. "To simper, to snigger, to leer." She wiggles her body in her attempt to illustrate the word. Gustavo grabs her and laughs.

"Do that again," he says. "*Es muy seductivo!*" Almost inaudibly, Chomsky continues to offer his lucid teachings to whomever will listen.

* * *

When Henry and Richard were ten years old, Henry became a member of his cousin's household. The young boys alternately played and fought as children do, but as future king, Richard knew he could win any fight. Soon Henry knew it, too. Later that year Henry was the sword bearer at Richard's coronation, his eyes glued to the gold-embroidered cushion on which the ceremonial weapon lay. Five years into Richard's reign came the Peasant's Revolt, of which Henry's family was the principle target. Richard abandoned Henry in the Tower of London, leaving the drawbridge down. An angry mob poured over the bridge, and if a random soldier had not saved his life, Henry would have died at its hands.

All this goes into the backstory Clare is cooking up for Terri. In spite of herself, Clare has become engaged in her task.

Now Henry is in exile, she writes. *His first wife is dead, and Richard has recently forbidden his remarriage in France. His children are hostages to the king. How much worse can it get?*

It got worse. When John of Gaunt died, Richard confiscated Henry's inheritance, appropriating all Gaunt's castles, manors, forests, jewelery, tapestries, furniture, horses, and plates. Henry is being harbored in some luxurious French palace, consorting with nobles and eating great food, but this is too much.

Henry can't sleep, writes Clare. *In the morning he feels murderously angry. But Richard isn't there, so he jumps on his horse and randomly gallops away. Some esquires ride with him, trying to keep up. They come to a forest where Henry dismounts.*

Now Clare is gripped. Her Henry leaves his men and sits by himself near a stream, thinking things through.

A leaf floats down the stream, rhapsodizes Clare, *piloting its shadow beneath it. Henry looks at it blindly for a moment; but when it is joined by another, and then another, he feels he is being shown the way. The leaves represent the ships he will have sent to Boulogne to carry him home. While Richard is waging war on Ireland, funded by money raised from the sale of Gaunt's stuff, Henry will gather an army to fight.*

Now Henry hears the snorting of his horse, tied to a tree nearby. He thinks of his men, who will be hungry by now, as well as anxious for his well-being.

"They will come with me," he decides. And he gets to his feet.

* * *

Clare is pleased with her backstory, but it doesn't help, and the next rehearsal is nothing short of a disaster. Clare and Terri are onstage with Northumberland and Hotspur when Terri lashes out.

"The problem with this scene," she announces, "is Clare. She's the dead spot, sucking out its life."

Clare cannot believe her ears. Neither can her fellow actors, both onstage and watching from the wings. They all stare, holding their collective breath.

"What, what, what?!" shouts Terri when she sees she has offended everyone. "You're all gaping! What!" She walks around the stage gesticulating, her heels striking the bare boards. "Clare, you're not *giving* them anything. You're supposed to have *aura*, for Christ's sake! You're what this scene is about!" Her caftan bunches at the shoulders as she waves her arms.

"Aura?" says Clare, wondering in a panicky way if there is some meaning to the word she doesn't understand. "All I get to say is, thank you so much for your support, and I'll pay you back later! How do I have aura?"

"How?" says Terri. She adjusts her caftan, as if insulted. "You're an actor, right? If the scene calls for aura, who cares what you 'get to say'? They said you were so great, but let me tell you, you're not!"

Clare has never in her life walked off a set, but she feels like doing so now. She stares at Terri in confusion, tense and flushed. Her eyes look as hard as the director's.

"No one likes you," is all she can think of saying. What would be a forceful thing to do?

"If you don't need me anymore today," says Clare stiffly, "I'll see you tomorrow."

"Go, go, go!" cries Terri, stalking off the stage herself. "I've had enough of you all!"

* * *

For the rest of the day and into the next, Clare rails about the incident to Geoff, Iris, Gustavo, and whomever else will listen. No one wants to take action on her behalf.

"Drop it, Clare," Iris eventually tells her. "Otherwise *you're* the diva, not her." Clare nods unhappily.

"I know," she says. "I know." For a few days she is too angry to work. She sits in the balcony, sulking, while Terri rehearses the actor playing Richard.

"*Let us sit upon the ground,*" says Sangeet on stage, "*and tell sad stories of the death of kings.*" Richard has just returned from Ireland, where he has dallied too long. In his absence Henry has won the allegiance of the most important nobles in England, including, of course, Northumberland. Richard knows all is lost.

Let us sit upon the ground, he says, *and tell sad stories of the death of kings.* This is posturing and self-dramatizing of him but also—in its way—sublime.

"Now there's a speech," thinks Clare, still longing for the role. The speech builds and builds, reconfiguring Richard from the selfish jerk he was as king to Everyman in defeat.

I live with bread like you, Richard limpidly concludes; *feel want, taste grief, need friends—subjected thus, how can you say to me, I am a king?* Feel want, taste grief, need friends—what a description of the human situation! You don't need a backstory to bring off something like that. Henry, on the other hand, is little more than a well-spoken foil to Richard.

"I've never had so much trouble with a part in all my life," she thinks.

* * *

Uta Hagen says that once you have learned everything you can about a character's upbringing, education, and health, you must find a relationship or situation in your own life that is *psychologically identical* to the character you play. She calls these *inner treasures.* Clare can find nothing in her life that is psychologically identical to Henry; but eventually she comes upon an inner treasure of her own. For weeks now, she realizes, she has been unconsciously rehearsing the gestures Noam Chomsky makes with his hands as he speaks, shaping his thought as if it were a tangible substance. Could Henry make those gestures when he talks? Chomsky's gestures imply self-possession, constraint, and mastery; perhaps they would work for Henry. Meanwhile, Clare is getting to know Sangeet. She likes him, and she thinks he's doing well.

"I saw him once in person," she tells him as they walk toward the subway one day.

"Richard?" says Sangeet, startled, having lost his place in the conversation.

"No, not Richard," laughs Clare. "Chomsky." When Clare went to see him, he was standing at a brown wooden podium, rocking slightly on his heels. He had notes but kept them rolled up in his hand.

"Henry can't have notes," says Sangeet thoughtfully.

"No," says Clare. "But do you see what I mean?" She wants Sangeet to agree that Chomsky could be a kind of model for Henry, and he does.

"Uncharismatic but intense," says Sangeet. "Eyes on the prize." Sangeet, too, has seen and heard Chomsky speak.

"*Exactly*," says Clare with satisfaction. Can she imply that while Richard ostentatiously flaunts his emotions, Henry's are concealed within? The real Richard once spent a fortune on a gem-lined robe. As a garment it was idiotic, but the thought of it inspires Clare. Can she imply that Henry's merely adequate exterior conceals a shining wealth of inner life?

"It's worth a try," says Sangeet encouragingly.

* * *

Clare finds herself pondering the title of the book Terri keeps quoting, *Respect for Acting*. Ever since her adolescence, Clare has struggled inconclusively with the question it refers to. Why *should* acting be respected?

"Plays are entertainment," Clare's father insisted. "Like TV." The serious business of life was public affairs.

"No, no," Clare tried earnestly to explain. "I want other people to know who I am." That made no sense to her father.

"Do something real!" he urged. The fact was, Clare saw her father's point. In a couple of weeks she was to represent Ghana at the Model U.N., and she had many heartfelt points to make about U.S. policy in Africa. Was it self-indulgence to want to act instead?

One day Clare's father took her to the Senate chambers, where he had a full day's work to do. Gerald Ford was in the White House, having granted Nixon a "full, free and absolute pardon." Clare does not remember, if she ever knew, exactly what her father's business was that day. But she knows he was often involved in legislative issues, briefing, arguing, drafting, and testifying as a bill took shape.

"Congressmen come and go," her mother told her once, "but your father is forever." Now, Clare reflects, Congressmen and women don't seem to *go* anymore. Once in office they just redistrict until they've got the votes to stay. Clare reflects that contemporary society has something in common with the late medieval scene: a thin layer of stupendous wealth at the top, a modest class of comfortable burghers, and the vast majority of the population powerless as peasants, living in the mud.

Was it different in her youth? In the Capitol Clare's father shepherded her from office to conference room to rotunda, stopping to greet or converse or banter without losing track of his goals. Clare remembers hallways and doors and grownups, all well dressed, assured, and mutually respectful.

"There was this sense of mission," she remembers. It held all the players together and made things workable. Or did it? Was that really the way things were, or just how Clare's father saw it—and passed it on to her?

"See?" he seemed to be saying. "This is for the greater good." In one room TV lights had been set up, and the cameras were testing conditions.

"Shall I interview you for them on Ghana?" her father asked softly. Clare considered being mock-interviewed while the TV crew got the lighting right.

"No way!" she said. But she laughed as she said it, safely held in the family conspiracy. Unquestionably, she was impressed. But when she was acting, she felt fully herself; when she was arguing policy she didn't. At the end of the day, Take Your Daughter to Work Day didn't work.

Predictably, another source of conflict soon arose between Clare and her father: Clare's obsession with boys. Often these were fellow actors, sometimes sincere and sometimes merely vain. Clare, dazed by hormones, couldn't tell the difference, and her father soon abandoned his efforts to point it out. But he did permit himself many witty remarks about Clare's posters of young movie stars with their shirts off, pouting and glowering at the camera. One in particular had figured for months in her private thoughts. She imagined being on stage with him, rehearsing a scene with a kiss.

"No, no," the director would cry every night. "You have to *mean* it!" Gradually the actors would be forced to do what they wanted to anyway, and the two would become unmanageably aroused. Sometimes this was apparent to the onlookers, to Clare's intense pleasure and embarrassment; sometimes she and the actor would get through their scene before falling in each other's arms backstage. Sometimes Clare kissed his image before getting into bed; and if he had been replaced by boys with the advantage over him of being three-dimensional, that didn't make it okay to mock the love of her youth.

"He looks like he just dipped his lips in a jar of Vaseline," her father joked one night, pausing in the doorway. Clare slammed the door with a violence that surprised them both.

"Go to hell!" she said with muted vehemence; and on a wave of anger she ripped all the posters down from the walls.

"Clare, Clare!" called her father, unwilling to barge in.

"Just go away!" shouted Clare. Of course, her father was right about the idol with the bee-stung lips. So was he right about everything? To punish him Clare hung up instead a poster of the former president of Chile Salvador Allende. Allende, a democratically elected socialist, had died in a U.S.-sponsored coup in 1973, but her father wouldn't acknowledge his country's role.

"Oh, please, Clare," he said. But later a U.S. Congressman leaked some incriminating documents, and the government's guilt could not be denied. Then Clare's father had been depressed for weeks, looking old and tired every day.

* * *

One night Clare can't sleep. She switches on the TV, where someone on C-Span is holding forth in all seriousness about what the Founding Fathers would have thought of cell phones and gay marriage.

"What's the deal with the Founding Fathers?" wonders Clare, reaching for the switcher. They seem to be ubiquitous these days. On PBS John Adams was on a yearlong cold-call to Holland, trying to raise money for the American Revolution. This was explained by a deep-voiced narrator while John and Abigail themselves moved around in ruffled outfits. Adams, it seemed, had a temper and would sometimes leap on the table and throw his wig at an opponent. Clare switches channels until she finds Noam Chomsky speaking from a podium – still, or again. He is talking about U.S. support for tyrants and torturers, not excluding Saddam Hussein. It makes Clare laugh, whether at Chomsky or herself she couldn't say.

"The course of imperial ambition," says Chomsky, "has been accelerated by the strategy of global rule by force." This is true, but it seems unnecessary for him say so. Now that Clare has appropriated him for Art, it seems redundant for him to go on being Chomsky night after night. He seems part real and part invented, like historical drama.

Clare switches off the TV and picks up a magazine. Her attention is caught by a profile of Osama Bin Laden that includes an account of an Islamic study group he attended as a teenager. The Syrian teacher, who was supposed to be teaching the boys soccer, was a piece of work. He told the boys about a son who shot his father for interfering with the son's religious practices.

Lord be praised, he exulted. *Islam was released in that home.*

Clare puts down the magazine and stares out the window. The trees outside are visible, if shrouded in gray. Something about the story makes her very unhappy.

* * *

"Do you want a ride to school?" Clare's father asked one day.

"Thanks, no," said the seventeen-year-old Clare coolly. Her father stood in the doorway of her bedroom, dressed for work. Clare looked at his clean, slightly worn, beloved face. It was fresh for the morning, intelligent, alert. His gray suit hung loose on his body because he had recently lost weight.

"Okay," he said sadly, and Clare's heart sank. At one level she wanted nothing more than to get in the car with him and drive downtown. They would listen to the morning news, attentive and relaxed; then they would deeply discuss it, calm in the rush hour traffic. But Clare and her father were in a fight that spring over Clare's summer plans. She had landed a good role in a real, grown-up summer theater, but her father had found her an internship with a rising Democratic congresswoman.

"It's a new day for women," he told her, "and I want you to be part of it!" Why shouldn't the young congresswoman be president some day?

"And I could be secretary of state, I suppose," said Clare ironically. "At *least*." Clare wanted to be Stella in *A Streetcar Named Desire*, not an intern in some congresswoman's office. Ultimately her mother had intervened on Clare's behalf, and her father had backed off.

The summer Clare spent as Stella in *Streetcar* was a true rite of passage. Not only was she practicing her craft at an unprecedented level, but a fellow actor, a college student named Howard, took a shine to her and introduced her to real, grown-up sex. By opening night Clare felt she had arrived somewhere, and the celebrations seemed made for her. She was angry when her father said he couldn't come.

"Sweetheart, I would if I could," her father said. He had to attend a reception for some Nigerian dignitary.

"I don't believe you," said Clare flatly. Her disappointment did not affect her acting that night; but after the cast party she invited Howard home.

"That may not be the best place for us," Howard laughed when she proposed it. "Your parents might come in to your room."

"They're comatose by now," said Clare. "I promise you." That was how she came to be lying under her boyfriend when her father came downstairs at 2 A.M. Clare stopped what she was doing and looked her shocked parent in the eye.

"Yes," she told him silently, eyes blazing. "That's it. Nothing you can do about it." This, she now knew, was why they were here.

"You're not the boss of me," she used to tell her father when she was small, and tonight she wanted to make that stick. Clare's father was wearing dark peach-colored pajamas with burgundy piping. As he stood transfixed on the third step, Howard's oblivious leg knocked an African sculpture off the Turkish tray table. For the rest of the night it lay on the rug, grinning up at the ceiling.

"Poor guy," thinks Clare, when she remembers Howard. "I wonder what became of him." Clare and her father had barely heard the door slam behind him, so engrossed were they in their fight. Clare was yelling at her father with her arms behind her back, fingers searching for the hook of her bra.

Never again did Clare's father try to dissuade her from her purposes. From then on, he came to opening nights, paid for classes and coaches, cheered and applauded with apparent pleasure. But after that something was missing between them. Clare herself vacillated between a sense of joy and relief on the one hand, and a current of mourning on the other.

"I had no choice," she thinks whenever the sadness overtakes her. But the loss of the early alliance cut deep.

* * *

Today the actors are rehearsing a scene in which Henry's allies are plotting against Richard. Suddenly an image of Franklin Roosevelt appears, partly on the scrim and partly on Hotspur's face. The actor playing Hotspur stops abruptly, shielding his eyes.

"What the fuck?" he says in his normal voice. From the rear the projectionist calls, "Sorry, we're having trouble with the new machine." Clare, Geoff, and Iris, sitting in the audience, look at each other. What is Terri up to now?

"FDR?" whispers Geoff. "He's not even current."

"I don't know," shrugs Clare. Soon more images appear. Nixon, Clinton, Bush Sr., Bush Jr., Rudy Giuliani, and Arnold Schwarzenegger all show up, smiling broadly. Nixon wags his V sign overhead.

"Oh, I get it," whispers Iris. Hotspur has just referred to Henry as a *king of smiles*. "It's about politicians' smiles, the continuity of."

"Duh," says Geoff.

"*King of smiles*," thinks Clare. Is Henry a great politician? Certainly he is accused more than once of being a little too good at winning hearts and minds.

Off goes his bonnet to an oyster wench, Richard complains. He is disgusted to have a rival who will bend a *supple knee* to *slaves* and *draymen*.

Eventually the technical problems are solved, and the actors return to the scene. Hotspur rants and raves and his elders wait him out.

"Nice," says Terri, exhausted. Clare can't remember her saying something so simple before.

* * *

In act 4, scene 1 of *Richard II* Henry has won the battle for the throne, and Northumberland is trying to run the hand-off of power.

Tell the people what you've done, he orders Richard, so everyone knows you deserve your deposition. Richard is understandably reluctant to comply.

Fiend, he hisses when Northumberland insists, *thou torment'st me, ere I come to hell.*

Urge it no more, my Lord Northumberland, intervenes Henry firmly. Calm and unprepossessing in victory, Henry lets Richard orchestrate the scene.

Here, cousin, Richard tells him, *seize the crown.* Clare and Sangeet stand on stage holding the crown between them, Sangeet tall and graceful and Clare, if truth be told, on the dumpy side.

Now is this golden crown, proclaims Richard, *like a well [with] two buckets;* Henry's is *dancing in the air* while Richard's, *down, unseen,* is *full of tears.* Henry, as usual, can't compete with Richard's glorious improvisations.

I thought you had been willing to resign, he says flatly. How do you animate a line like that? For all her efforts, Clare is unable when her moment comes to do so.

"Cut!" calls Terri, clambering up on stage. But it isn't Clare she's after. This is one of the high points of the play, and she wants Sangeet to milk it for everything it's worth. As they run through it again, Terri calls out directions from the sidelines, moving and crouching like a basketball coach. Sometimes she says the lines along with Sangeet, like a conductor singing with the orchestra. Her caftan falls forward as she crouches, swinging from side to side.

"Great," she says at the end; and indeed, Sangeet has done well. Clare, too, has tried, but without success.

"It's not my fault," she reasons. The scene belongs to Richard. Now the rehearsal is breaking up.

"Clare, I want to talk to you," says Terri, throwing some switches on the light board.

"About what?" says Clare, alarmed.

"In fifteen minutes," says Terri, striding off. "In the basement. Room C." Sangeet, with whom Clare has arranged to have coffee, is on his way out.

"Another time," he says, touching her arm.

"Another time," says Clare, distracted.

Room C is furnished with a beat-up metal desk and matching chair. The chair has no friction left in its main joint, so it twirls at the slightest movement. Clare waits for Terri with a beating heart. On the desk is a tinny green ashtray, streaked with hairline scratches.

"But nobody smokes anymore," thinks Clare irrelevantly. She swings back and forth in the ancient chair, alternately facing opposite walls.

"I can't take any more shit from Terri," she thinks. Should she threaten to quit? Should she quit?

"No!" she answers herself. That would be unprofessional, for one thing; worse, she would lose Henry himself.

"Imagine that!" she marvels. While she wasn't watching, as it were, the character she plays has gone inside her.

"But what do I mean by 'Henry'?" she wonders. Shakespeare's version still seems sketchy and dim; and so does the historical figure. Clare's "Henry" is something else. Of what does he consist?

"We need to talk about Henry," announces Terri before she's well in the room. Clare listens tensely, but nothing Terri says pertains to Clare's performance.

"Henry is jealous of Northumberland," declares Terri, "because Northumberland has Hotspur, and Henry just has Hal."

"True," says Clare. Better, says Henry, if *some night-tripping fairy had exchanged in cradle-clothes our children where they lay.*

"*Part Two,*" continues Terri, "is a remake, see? Everything that happens in *One* happens again in *Two,* only now Hotspur's dead." Perhaps Terri just needs to talk out loud about the Henry plays, and Clare is a convenient audience.

"Does she even remember that I'm the dead spot in the production?" sulks Clare, watching Terri pace the basement room. Cautiously, Clare allows herself to feel relieved. A high, dirty window lets in some light.

"I'm washed up in *Two,*" says Clare, attempting to be conciliatory. "From here on it's all about Hal."

"Right," says Terri, smacking a rolled-up script on the palm of her hand. Apparently it was out of order for Clare to say anything of substance. "Good, we're on the same page." Terri stands near the door, surveying Clare. Then she shoots.

"I'm going to give you one more chance," she announces, "but that's it. I've already told Geoff I might have you switch roles."

"What?!?" cries Clare, blindsided.

"Have you got a Meisner?" Terri demands. Through her rising panic Clare understands that Terri is referring to another book she loves to quote, Sanford Meisner's *On Acting*.

"Uh...I guess so," fumbles Clare, now standing up. "Sure. I must." Like Uta Hagen, Meisner was part of her past.

"Then read it," says Terri bluntly. "It might help."

"Terri!" cries Clare. "For God's sake!"

"You've got two weeks," says Terri and leaves.

Clare sits in the old chair, stunned. Geoff as Henry? Never! In the next room two stagehands are building a set. One stops hammering to scold the other.

"Shit," he says. "You messed that up good." Clare would like to go home, but the thought of taking the subway to the parking garage, finding her car, and driving home from there is too exhausting. She sinks into the chair and stares at the desk.

It is raining when Clare leaves the theater. She has no umbrella, so as she walks, she turns up her collar. A red, white, and blue bumper sticker on a passing car proclaims "dissent is patriotic."

"Ah, patriotism," thinks Clare, through her distress. When did the flags over car dealerships and strip-mall stores quadruple in size? Shakespeare himself practically invented patriotism in *Richard II*, which he wrote in 1595. The English had recently defeated an attempted invasion by Spain, and a wave of national exuberance was sweeping the country. *This royal throne of kings*, Shakespeare wrote in *Richard II*, *this scepter'd isle...This other Eden, demi-paradise*, and so on. In the next two plays, however, patriotism, patriarchy, and everything sacred is hilariously mocked by Hal and his hard-drinking friends.

"And yet he comes through at the end," thinks Clare, dodging a puddle. At the ends of both *Henry IV Part One* and *Henry IV Part Two*, Hal comes through for his dad, and makes patriotism look good. So is Shakespeare patriotic or not? And what about Terri? Is she just nuts? By the time she hurries into the subway, Clare is thoroughly wet.

* * *

"I'm going to tell you something," says Sanford Meisner on page 136 of *On Acting*. "The text is your greatest enemy." For a fraction of a second this makes no sense; then Clare hits her head with her hand.

"Oh, *right*," she thinks. "How could I have forgotten to disregard the text?" Terri and her disrespectful ways are forgotten. Clare is thrilled to be restored to something she knows.

* * *

In a "repetition exercise" that Sanford Meisner invented in the nineteen-thirties, the students repeat each other's inconsequential assertions until the mere fact of interacting with another person gives rise to a real emotion, and everything follows from that. Instead of dredging up some feeling from the past, students become aware of what is going on right then, no matter what they have to say and do "in character." Reading Meisner, Clare remembers what a revelation it had been to learn that an actor's emotions could be fully independent of her lines.

"You're wearing a blue shirt," she had told Iris in an acting class long ago.

"I'm wearing a blue shirt," Iris had agreed.

"You're wearing a blue shirt," Clare had repeated; and so on. To their amazement, they were soon experiencing a medley of authentic emotions, from jealousy to compassion, from curiosity to dread. It was like a game of telephone in which the message changed each time it was whispered; only here the messengers were the same two people, reacting to each other's reactions to each other's reaction to each other.

"I want you to give me twenty dollars," said Iris.

"You want me to give you twenty dollars," said Clare, and they were off, surfing the wave of need and love and fear. It was exhilarating. If all emotions were equally valid, none had the upper hand, and it made the girls feel shameless and free. This was what Clare had had an inkling of in high school. It had given her the strength to defy her father.

"Shall I interview you on Ghana?" her father had whispered that day at the Capitol. As a "diplomat" at the Model U.N., Clare had had to hide everything about herself but a controlled indignation about her opponents' stupidity. If she felt anger or fear she went to the ladies' room so no one would see, and while she was there she checked her make-up in the mirror. She carried a briefcase and wore a knee length pencil skirt.

"God forbid!" shudders Clare. "God forbid!"

In Meisner technique the repetition exercise is just the beginning. Later, of course, the script comes back, and script analysis, preparation, particularization, etc., come into play. But the actors learn to negotiate among the possibilities implied by the script on the one hand and the ones they generate between themselves on the other. This hide-and-seek game with the naked, real-time self was never less than thrilling to Iris and Clare.

"No!" their old acting teacher would shout, when anyone pretended. "False! Don't do that!" At first Iris and Clare had no idea how he could distinguish the real from the false, but soon they could do so themselves.

"You feel so ashamed when you fake it," Clare had said, and Iris had agreed.

* * *

At this point Clare has given up. She will do her best, but she knows it might not be enough. If she suffers a humiliation, her career will either recover or it won't.

"What can I do," she fatalistically thinks. Meanwhile, she is on mysteriously good terms with Henry; Meisner is an inspiration; and the company is rehearsing the two middle plays, where at least she has lots of lines. *Henry IV Parts One* and *Two* show Henry in decline, and the diminishment of kings is a theme that can at least occasionally distract Shakespeare from Hal.

"It's the Wheel of Fortune theme," Clare tells Gustavo. "One *heav'd a-high to be hurl'd down below.*"

"What?" says Gustavo.

"As soon as his heroes reach the pinnacle of power," Clare explains, "Shakespeare starts preparing them for disempowerment and death."

At the beginning of *Henry IV Part One*, Henry is past his peak. In historical fact he was only thirty-three, but in Shakespeare he is old and gray. All he wants now is to go on crusade. Unfortunately, however, Northumberland and Hotspur, his allies in *Richard II*, have risen up against him, and he has to stay home and fight. The real Henry did go on crusade, not to Jerusalem but to Lithuania, accompanied by *eleven knights…twenty-seven esquires, and a number of servants, grooms and minstrels*. He joined the Teutonic Knights and had a wonderful time drinking and killing pagans. Shakespeare's Henry, however, thinks of a crusade as a way to make amends for regicide, not as a youthful diversion. In *Part Two* civil strife once again makes a crusade impossible; in both plays, however, the real disappointment is not the frustration of Henry's travel plans but his poor relationship with Hal. Hal is off drinking in taverns while his father grapples with affairs of state. Doesn't the boy understand it's all for him? Finally, Henry falls ill. He is sleeping in his sickbed when Hal shows up for a visit, unsure if Henry is dead or alive.

This is a sleep, he muses, watching over Henry's bed, *that from this golden rigol hath divorced so many English kings*. The *golden rigol*, or circle, is the crown. But Hal's sense of the inevitable sleep, death, and divorce from the crown that must overtake him as well as his father does not seem to make it any less tempting. Hal picks it up from the pillow next to Henry and puts it on his head.

This from thee will I to mine leave, as 'tis left to me, he ringingly declares; and leaves the room. Henry wakes up, surmises what has happened, and is appalled. *For this*, he asks, has he striven and suffered?

Canst thou not forbear me half an hour? he rages when Hal comes back. No? Then just go out and *dig my grave thyself!* Hal's answer is off. He says the crown has caused his father so many difficulties that he, Hal, dislikes it and only *put it on my head to try with it, as with an enemy, that had before my face murdered my father*. Who would buy such a stupid excuse? But Henry leaps at the chance of reconciliation. My darling son, he cries, and pats the bed to make him sit down. Thrilled to have Hal close, Henry pours out a string of confessions, prayers, and last-minute advice.

Get your opponents off on crusade, he urges Hal. That way they can't stir up dissent at home. Yes, *busy giddy minds with foreign quarrels*, says Shakespeare's Henry IV. Timeless advice! Hal, however, has other things on his mind, mostly his own claim to the succession.

My gracious liege, he says, referring to the crown, *you won it, wore it, kept it, gave it me. Then plain and right must my possession be.* And Shakespeare, having punished Henry IV with old age and a guilty conscience, moves on to the frenzy of patriotism that is (with just a few discordant notes) *Henry V.*

* * *

Henry Bolingbroke became king of England, as I've said, at the age of thirty-three. Handsome, athletic, and rich, he had been pampered at home and *magnificently entertained* abroad. Then things changed for the worse. From his coronation on, he was plagued with rebel uprisings, a fractious Parliament, and a shortage of funds that was both severe and chronic. Six years into his reign, while riding in Yorkshire, he fell ill so suddenly *that it seemed to him he had felt an actual blow.* His problem, whatever it was, was *accompanied by . . . an unpleasant skin disease on the face and a prolapse of the rectum which prevented him from sitting on a horse.* Illness and the sedentary life were very hard on this ex-athlete. He seems, moreover, to have felt that his illness was divine retribution for his sins, particularly the sin of usurpation. In his will he referred unhappily to *this life I have misspent.* In addition to everything else were his painful struggles with his son. The historical Prince of Wales sometimes made a power grab when his father was incapacitated, and when he got better Henry would have to reestablish control. In an elaborate apology for one such episode, Prince Hal showed up in *a gown of blue satin full of small eyelet holes, at every hole the needle hanging by a silk thread with which it was sewed.* So appareled, he implored the king to kill him on the spot rather than condemn him to *live one day with his displeasure.* Henry threw away his dagger, burst into tears and embraced his dubious son. Such scenes were nerve-wracking. *It is not surprising,* as one scholar says, *that he died an embittered man.*

"Plus," thinks Clare, "insomnia." Clare is an insomniac herself. She is awake right now, although Gustavo, beside her, is fast asleep.

"Are you asleep?" she whispers disingenuously. His dark hair sticks out against the pillow; he sighs and straightens a leg. Clare leans on her elbow, looking down.

O sleep, moans aging Henry, *gentle sleep…how have I frighted thee, that thou no more wilt…steep my senses in forgetfulness?* Clare finds some comfort in the thought that Henry, too, is awake in the night. He is not in a stuffy bedroom like Clare's but in the halls of his palace, where his courtiers soon find him in his gown. They have bad news for him about his struggle with the rebels, and Henry takes it hard.

The happiest youth, he says in despair, if shown his future life, *would shut the book and sit him down and die.* This is extreme, but the feeling it expresses is not outside Clare's experience. She too has drunk of what Henry, with sublime understatement, calls *the cup of alteration.* Her struggles over her children, the sense of loss she sometimes feels about her father, and finally her own divorce have on occasion been too much for her. After a wasted hour going over all the things that hurt her most, she throws the covers back decisively and gets up.

"Henry," she thinks to distract herself. "Boulogne." Some shipping vessels ride at anchor just off shore. Men are loading provisions and gear into skiffs to row out to the fleet.

Clare goes to her study with a cup of tea and opens her laptop.

"Tide coming in," she types. But she is muddled from sleeplessness, and the words evoke an unexpected scene. Instead of Boulogne in 1399, she finds herself in Provincetown, Massachusetts, in 1991; and there she remains for the rest of the night. There, too, the tide is coming in. All over the long, shallow beach, archipelagos of sand are being swallowed up by the racing sea. It is a summer day, and Clare stands shin-deep in water, talking to her father.

"What were we talking about?" wonders Clare. "The fall of the USSR?"

"Good morning!" a memorable headline in *Pravda* had announced one day that year. "There is no Soviet Union!"

"Now there's *alteration* for you," thinks Clare. Nearby Clare's children are playing in the water with their cousins. As the moving sheets of water dazzle in the sun, Clare and her father shift ground, moving sideways or shoreward to avoid being swamped. What strikes Clare, as she re-inhabits the scene, is the absence of the usual caution between them.

"We were taking a break," she guesses. "How nice." On each temporary island, the children hastily build castles and dig moats.

"Quick," they shout to each other, as if something were at stake. It is a scene out of time; or at least a moment when time itself is hurtless. The earth turns and the moon pulls the water smoothly up the beach. Six years later Clare's father is dead.

"Quick, quick," shout the children, thrilled by the oncoming water. The children's moats and channels fill, their castles fall, and they rush as a group to the next island. They have no problem letting go.

Toward dawn Clare looks up from her laptop. She'll never reread what she wrote, and neither will anyone else. Certainly it doesn't help with Henry. But Clare is content with how she spent the night. When Gustavo leaves for work, she'll try to get some sleep.

* * *

Shakespeare wrote thirty-seven plays, not all of them great. Some aren't even good, and some, like *Timon of Athens*, are awful. *Henry IV Part Two* isn't bad, but it's not great. Unlike *Part One*, where there is some real suspense over Hal's loyalty and values, in *Two* we know ahead of time how things will end. Hal will reform, just as he did in *One*. That's a bore, and we want something new. The people of England, on the other hand, wanted something old. Almost as soon as they made Henry king, they wanted Richard back.

An habitation giddy and unsure, says a character in *Part Two, hath he that buildeth on the vulgar heart.* When Henry turned out to be almost as expensive as his cousin, many *vulgar hearts* felt betrayed. Over a decade after Richard's death thousands contested Henry's claim to the throne, saying they had seen the former king alive. The myth was stubborn and pervasive, like Elvis sightings, and a Richard impersonator named Thomas Ward actually *managed to pass himself off as the real Richard in exile in Scotland.* Henry was forced constantly to move Richard's body around and put it on display. This cannot have been pleasant; but Henry needed to prove he was the only living king.

Toward the end of *Part Two* this king must die. Thomas, one of his sons, foretells Henry's death.

He cannot long hold out these pangs, says Thomas sadly. The timing of Henry's illness is a shame, since the rebels have finally been vanquished, and it ought to be a joyful time. Now the crown is safe, but Henry's *sight fails, and [his] brain is giddy.*

Will Fortune never come with both hands full? he asks despairingly.

"*Will Fortune never come with both hands full?*" laments Clare in a rehearsal onstage.

"Etcetera, etcetera, and so forth," calls Terri, waving a hand. By now the cast understands that "etcetera, etcetera, and so forth" means they can skip the rest of the scene and move on to the next. Clare remains onstage as she has a major role in what follows.

"McAlister!" calls Terri. "Where are you?" Pierre McAlister, who plays Prince Hal, hurries onstage.

"Sorry," he mumbles, pulling on a sweatshirt. They are rehearsing the scene where he steals Clare's crown as she sleeps. There is a naked mattress in a bedstead onstage, and Clare gets on it to sleep. When she wakes up her crown is gone, and so is Pierre.

Canst thou not forbear me half an hour? Clare rages at him when he comes back. The rest of the cast is watching from the house, and Clare can feel something special in their attention.

"Hey," she thinks. Is she finally in the zone? When Pierre responds, however, Clare can think of nothing but him. She feels she has been real with Pierre, but he is being bogus in return. He would have interrupted her sooner, he says, to tell her how much he loves her, if he hadn't been choked by tears at her pain. It is not the insincerity of his words that gets her but something both smug and insecure about his manner of saying them. She feels angry and ignored.

"Affected little twit," she thinks. In her anger she is the more powerful, and that, at least, feels good. Pierre is taken aback, and Clare is glad to see him stumble over some lines. His speech, however, goes on and on, and halfway through Clare lets up. Pierre is telling the old, stupid story of putting the crown on his head only *to try with it, as with an enemy, that had before my face murdered my father.* Instead of taking this pathetic twaddle personally, Clare feels embarrassed for Pierre that he has such stupid lines. He seems okay with them, though. Clare listens for a moment, reclining on her bed. Unexpectedly, she feels a shift.

"Amazing," she thinks. Right there on stage Clare is not amazed at Pierre but at Shakespeare himself. "What a way with words," she inadequately thinks.

Now Pierre is winding up. If he ever, ever, ever coveted the crown for the glory it would bring him, *Let God forever keep it from [his] head and make [him] as the poorest vassal is, that doth with awe and terror kneel to it!* This is his third such impassioned avowal, on the face of it no more convincing than the others; but this time it works. Now Clare wants nothing more than to be friends with her child.

O my son, she says with all her heart, *God put it in thy mind to take it hence, that thou might's win the more thy father's love, pleading so wisely in excuse of it!* Will he sit beside her on the bed? From there she will give him her blessing and some precious last words of advice.

"End scene!" cries Terri standing up. "Stay where you are." Clare is startled, having forgotten Terri altogether.

"Did you see that?" Terri demands of the others. "What did you see?" Unbelievably, Terri is using Clare's performance as an example to the rest of the cast.

"She was marvelous!" raves Bernard Spitz, who plays the Earl of Warwick. "So true!" In her didactic way, Terri drives home the point.

"We don't know what was going on inside her, and we don't need to know," lectures Terri. "But *plenty* was going on." Dimly Clare registers a dramatic realignment of her relations with Terri; but mostly she feels interrupted. She sits on her mattress, slightly dazed. Iris and Geoff exchange smiles.

"It's not about the words you have to say," Terri continues. "It's how real you are on stage." The cast has heard all this before, but they have gotten used to Terri and don't mind hearing it again.

"Surely it's about both," says Clare later to Iris as they step out of the theater into a late city twilight. Lavender-gray tints shine from the silent buildings.

"Of course," says Iris. "But remember the cat?"

"What cat?"

"The one on the chair."

Clare looks blankly at her friend. Then she remembers.

A cat *sitting quietly on a chair,* Terri read aloud one day, watching *a bit of blowing lint,* is almost always more interesting than an actor onstage. *The audience,* says Uta Hagen, *will be riveted* on the real life of the cat while the actors are *predictably busy* pretending.

"You were all there," says Iris. "And Terri thought so, too." At that she breaks off.

"Oh my God," she says. "Can you believe people wear things like that?"

In a store window are some high-heeled shoes with *incredibly long points*, just as in Henry's day.

"No," Clare agrees, but her thoughts are elsewhere.

"I was the cat!" she thinks, and starts to glow with pride. "She meant I was the cat!" That means her troubles with Terri are over.

"I was the cat!" she says out loud. Now she is really pleased. In the lavender twilight, she stands on the pavement and glows.

* * *

Soon it is opening night. In fact, it is the third of four opening nights, since *Richard II* and *Henry IV Part One* have already been performed. Clare will not act in *Henry V* because, of course, she will be dead. In fact, she is dying right now, even though it's just act 4. There had been a prophecy that Henry would die in Jerusalem a glorious crusader, but the prophecy turned out to have been ironic, "Jerusalem" in this case referring only to a chamber in Westminster Abbey.

"Of course," thinks Clare as she's ushered off stage. "That's Henry for you." But she no longer holds his disappointing life and death against him. Watching act 5 from the wings, sweating a little in green velvet robes, Clare returns in her thoughts to his return from France. Of course she no longer needs Henry's backstory, having found her way into his current existence; but the story unfolds on its own.

"I was seasick," she remembers, standing in the wings. Thomas Arundel suggested some fresh air, but Clare stayed below decks, throwing up.

"I don't want the men to see me like this," she told him, retching. When they got to England they sailed up and down the coast, unsure where to land. One of their ships landed at Pevensey, but Clare went on to Yorkshire, landing on the Humber estuary. Clare remembers those first uncertain days, staying at inns that were ill equipped to handle the royal guest they had under their roofs. Once, lying in a room that unceremoniously abutted the courtyard, she heard one ostler tell another that she was to be king of England.

"Right," laughed the Second Ostler. "And I'll be Jesus Christ." The Yorkshire landscape felt uncanny to her, the hills and fields and hedgerows clearly but indescribably different from the hills and fields of France.

"I had gotten used to France," Clare thinks. In mid-July Northumberland signed on, and Clare's people knew they would win. The nobles were jubilant, laughing and cracking jokes, but Clare did not share their mood. Various people would have to be disposed of, chief among them, of course, being Richard. Clare was not overly troubled by the prospect of doing so; but these were delicate matters, and she wouldn't be safe until she had dealt with them. As we have seen, she wasn't safe even then.

"So when *was* I happy?" Clare asks herself. "When *did* I enjoy my success?"—and like a piece of lint drifting through the sunlight, the beach at Boulogne comes to mind. The tide is coming in, just as it did in Provincetown. Once it turns, she and her men-at-arms will have exactly three hours during which to sail for England. Clare's plans have leaked out and the Duke of Burgundy's men are looking for her.

"Let them look," thinks Clare, fearless. "Now is my time." She watches the water move up the beach in little pulses, the twin of her own excitement. In the outer harbor, three shipping vessels ride at anchor, their masters rushing, shouting, and praying under their breath for favorable winds. In between issuing commands and holding shoreline conferences, Clare watches the waves, her anticipation building.

"Don't worry," she reassures her men with each delay. "Don't worry," she buoyantly tells Arundel. The water sweeps over the flats, covering the green-black sea grass. As one gleaming bit of sand after another winks and is swallowed up, Clare makes a pact with them all.

"Next time I see you, I'll be king," she exults. To give an outlet to her excitement, she bends where she has seen a big sea clam send a spurt of water through a hole. She digs it up, slits its shell, and scrapes the creature out with her knife.

"Here," she says, extending it on her knife to Arundel. "Eat this. It will give you strength for the journey." Torn between obedience and disgust, Arundel looks at Clare with a tortured face, and Clare bursts out laughing.

"Go ahead," she says cruelly, and laughs a loud, abandoned laugh. She can hardly contain her joy.

On stage Hal is winding up, swearing he'll be a great king. Clare comes back to the present, ready to be Clare again.

"Are you going out in that?" whispers a stage assistant who has come to supervise the curtain call.

"Yes, why not?" says Clare, adjusting her green robe. Terri appears in a black caftan.

"Where's your crown?" she hisses. "I want you in your crown." She tells Clare to stand in the center tonight, the place of honor.

"Oh, really?" says Clare, looking significantly at Terri. Terri's bug eyes flick over Clare without conceding anything, and she pushes Clare on stage. When Clare takes her place the audience seems to clap harder.

"Thank you," Clare smiles at them. She bows, feeling fine; but then a painful feeling overtakes her.

"Dad," she sadly thinks. *Will fortune never come with both hands full?* All the old conflicts flare up; all the old anger and need. On the one hand, she has been proven right by her success; on the other hand, (a) he isn't there, and (b) she hasn't helped a deeply troubled world. Would he be proud or not?

"What's the use?" she dully thinks. Then she sees Gustavo sitting between her children and Iris, who isn't in *Part Two*. They stand, and the whole theater stands with them.

"Bravo!" shouts Gustavo, taller than the rest. Half-blinded by the footlights, Clare smiles again, aiming for her own people first. Someone throws a flower on the stage, and her smile broadens to a grin. To the shadow of her father she gestures with a wave. If he doesn't get it yet, he will.

"Sorry, Dad," she tells him, bowing. "This is what I do." She's said it before, and she'll say it again. Clare walks off the stage with the others, prepared to be Henry as long as necessary. Then she'll be someone else.

TIME TO TEACH *JANE EYRE* AGAIN

Not *Jane Eyre* again. Other people are moving on in life or going around in circles or failing utterly, but I'm still doing business at the same old stand. Every year a new load of students is dumped like laundry in front of me, needing to know *Jane Eyre*. Sometimes I take comfort in the thought that it's not just me. All over the country, in Cleveland and Galveston and Tacoma as well as better-known places like Miami, in major universities and state teachers colleges, everyone does his or her share. The new cohort group is divided into thousands of groups like the one I have to face at eleven thirty, and everyone takes a whack. It's a community effort, like doing the wash in an Indian village. Everyone down to the river! Sometimes I can almost hear a cheerful hum, all of us preparing together. There should be preparing-*Jane-Eyre* songs, and they should be played in supermarkets like Christmas music at the season of the year when *Jane Eyre* is normally taught. It would lessen the sense of shame. Now it is November again, the season in which I normally teach *Jane Eyre*. The oak tree outside my study window is full of dead leaves. That's the way oak trees are, they hang on and hang on, sometimes right through the winter. Some years we don't get rid of the old oak leaves until the new ones come out in May.

But if you want a description of November, don't turn to me. Open your books to page one of *Jane Eyre*. Ready? Heeeeeeeeere's Charlotte!

Folds of scarlet drapery shut in my view to the right hand; to the left were the clear panes of glass, protecting, but not separating me from the drear November day. At intervals, while turning over the leaves of my book, I studied the aspect of that winter afternoon. Afar, it offered a pale blank of mist and cloud; near, a scene of wet lawn and storm-beat shrub, with ceaseless rain sweeping away wildly before a long and lamentable blast.

That's great, isn't it? I think that's great. The problem is, what can you say about it? Mark always says, "Just say what you said last year. It's all in your notes, isn't it?" It is in my notes, but it's not that simple. Part of the problem is my notes. Sometimes they look like this:

> 328 St. John at Rosamund's feet
> 261 Jane flooded by love
> Class feeling
> Feminism–longing for action
> 279 "I care for myself"

I suppose that meant something once, but what? And even when my notes are good it doesn't help. Sometimes I come across whole eloquent paragraphs that work themselves up to a point, and I think, Lady, what are you hollering? It's like watching someone on TV with the sound turned off. There's someone at the podium waving her arms and rolling her eyes, but that's all you know.

Mark, listen. You have to bring it up in the system. All the way up. It has to come out of core memory all the way to the skin, where it becomes hot and damp and raises the temperature of the surrounding air. This computer metaphor isn't working out, so I'll get to the point. Teaching is an act of assertion. You can't just spread your legs.

And now for a little self-stimulation. I have to leave the house at eleven, I'm still in my bathrobe, it's ten fifteen, and I have to feed the dog. That leaves about fifty minutes to prepare if I get started this minute, but really I'd rather be dead. Everything I know about the book swims in a stew–nothing is worth separating off from everything else and actually saying. The passages I marked in previous years are all equally important; there are too many of them and they all illustrate the same large, obvious point. I sit here feeding myself *Jane Eyre* like a mother whose child won't eat. For every teaspoonful that goes in the mouth, three land on the cheek, are dropped on the tray, get caught in the hair, or go into the bib. Some that go in come out again. Is anything worse than this? "Structure of the book is episodic rather than architectural," I read in my notes. Later I read exactly the same sentence. Still later I read, "The plot bumps along. Not patterned, as in *Pride and Prejudice.*" Okay, okay, I'll definitely make the point about the plot. That'll take forty seconds. What next?

Charlotte Brontë herself had problems as a teacher. She wrote about them in her diary like this:

> Friday August 11th…I had been toiling for nearly an hour with Miss Lister, Miss Marriott, & Ellen Cook striving to teach them the distinction between an article and a substantive. The parsing lesson was completed, a dead silence had succeeded it in the school-room & I sat sinking from irritation & weariness into a kind of lethargy. The thought came over me: am I to spend all the best part of my life in this wretched bondage, forcibly suppressing my rage at the idleness, the apathy, and the hyperbolical & most asinine stupidity of those fat-headed oafs, and on compulsion assuming an air of kindness, patience, & assiduity?

I know what she means. But really, my problem is different. I don't teach articles and substantives, I teach *Jane Eyre*. Moreover, in any given class, 25 percent of the students are brilliant. The fatheaded oafs don't have a chance. After the parsing lesson Charlotte had to take her students for a walk. Then Lister, Marriott, and company pestered her with "vulgar familiar trash" at tea. Finally at dusk she

> crept into the bedroom to be alone for the first time that day. Delicious was the separation I experienced as I laid down on the spare bed & resigned myself to the luxury of twilight & solitude. The stream of Thought, checked all day came flowing free & calm along its channel.

Ah, Thought. How wonderful it is to Think. Right now, however, the effort to think about *Jane Eyre* has dried up Thought at the source. What about Jane as a governess? Is Adele a fatheaded oaf? Also I remember there's a very important scene in the silk factory where Mr. Rochester tries to dress Jane like a tart. Maybe if I start writing about it something will come to me. What I'd really like to do, though, is go to sleep. I know I just got up, but maybe a twenty-minute nap would clear my head. The thought is irresistible. I see an image of my bed in the next room, unmade, accessible, warm with memories. But this is instantly succeeded by an image of myself washed and dressed and standing, an hour and forty minutes from now, in front of fifty young adults. I will be wearing a wool jacket and good boots, not this smelly nightie. There will be nothing but the force of my will to hold the group together; the edges of the classroom will be restless, like the outlying provinces of empire. If they go, the whole class could follow. These are beautifully brought up students, they never pick on me or complain, but if they lose interest I'm dead. Other teachers I know just keep talking. Some students listen, some dream; later in the hour some who were napping perk up. I think that's fine; I just can't do it. It's something chromosomal. The lecture gene was left out. If the class doesn't quiver like a dog about to be fed, the heart goes out of me completely. I become dry, desperate, controlling. The subject shrivels up like plastic wrap near a hot plate. Minute by minute I long to go home.

Bed's out; but I still can't face *Jane Eyre*. I wash the oatmeal pot and check the answering machine for messages. Mark's mother, my yoga teacher, and someone from the Green Machine sound as if they were calling from Albania. It's only the cassette, but I don't know where to get a new one. The Green Machine thinks we owe them $59.45 and has thought so for several years. The day I came home to find Leslie Middleman's earrings on the table next to my bed there was a notice on the door framed by big yellow daisies. "The Green Machine wants to kill your weeds!" it said. A friendly greenie was choking some bad crabgrass by the throat.

What would Jane Eyre have done if she had come home to Thornfield one day and found Leslie Middleman in bed with Mr. Rochester? I say "in bed with Mr. Rochester" because that makes it more dramatic. I don't think it would be worth fictionalizing the period between my finding Leslie's earrings and Mark's admitting they were having an affair. Now that I think about it, it seems incredible that I didn't actually *know* what was going on until Mark admitted it. Jane wouldn't have taken five minutes to understand the whole thing. One look at the earrings and she would have heard a voice saying, "leave Thornfield at once." Eighteen pages later she would have been gone. She wouldn't have hung out with Mr. Rochester for three days, threatening, crying, sulking, and fucking. That wasn't her way. She would have stayed just long enough to hear the story of his life, and then she'd be out of the house. "I do love you," she would have said before leaving, "but I must not show or indulge the feeling: and this is the last time I must express it."

What integrity. Remember, Jane was besotted with Rochester. She had had a horrible, deprived life, burnt porridge, no love, dresses made of crummy material, and here she was on the verge of wealth, sex, love, everything. Inside her was this chaos of desire. She heard it like "a flood loosened in remote mountains." Then she found out about Bertha, Rochester's wife.

> The whole consciousness of my life lorn, my love lost, my hope quenched, my faith death-struck, swayed full and mighty above me in one sullen mass.

"It came," she says. Jane lies faint, sinks in deep waters, feels no standing. As far as I can make out, Jane has an orgasm of grief. Can I tell them that? Maybe. It depends on the atmosphere. Sometimes eroticizing the text makes me feel overwrought, like a jumped-up TV producer trying to get people INTO the story. The class withdraws, insulted. Mild as cow's breath on a cold day, a mist of contempt settles over the room. But sometimes the right sexual reference skewers the book. The connection is made, the light dawns, the passage is marked in deep transparent yellow. And who's to say that years later, when a student in that class thinks of *Jane Eyre*, her thoughts don't beat to the faint remembered pulse on page 261, where Jane is ravished by grief?

I take a few notes on my notes. The point about the episodic structure of the book makes sense again, so I jot it down. The point is that Charlotte herself led a life of never enough. In each episode there is a scarcity of material, a terrible danger of running out. I can relate to that. It was heroic of her to keep writing when things kept threatening to stop.

If I don't stop now I'll be late. It is suddenly hard to stop; with a margin of minutes I suddenly have a good idea for the class. I churn the pages of the book, focused, awake. If I don't find the page references, how will I make my point? When the phone rings, I ignore it, but when it rings again I know it's Mark and pick it up.

"Mark, later, please, I've got to go…No, I really have to…Don't be mad at me, Mark. Are you mad?…Shit. Now you've made *me* mad…For

God's sake, I've got a class in thirty-five minutes and I'm not even dressed yet…So what?…You are?…Oh, no…That's awful, Mark, I'm really sorry…Oh, dear. Listen, I really have to go. I'll call you later…Take it easy…Yes, of course…No, I'm not mad…You too."

This is crazy. I wash and dress in record time and tear down the highway at speed. Out of habit I flick on the radio. A female voice sings, "We're living in a material world, and I'm a material girl." It's Madonna, whom Amy has just discovered. Amy is twelve; she dances around her room singing this stupid song watching me to check the effect. Is "Material Girl" better or worse than "Bills, Bills, Bills"? The idea that it's empowering to get very assertive about how men should pay your bills drives me nuts. I tried to discuss these issues with Amy recently, but she didn't want to hear about it. To show her displeasure she turned her mouth down into the scornful/vulnerable expression that has been a reliable early-warning sign since the day she was born. I let it go. But why am I teaching other people's children *Jane Eyre* while my own child watches MTV? I think again of Jane Eyre and Mr. Rochester in the silk warehouse. "The more he bought me," she said, "the more my cheek burned with a sense of annoyance and degradation." In my mind's eye is a video of Madonna whirling around the silk warehouse with a male chorus buying and draping and ogling.

"But it's parodic," my friend Jeremy has told me. "Lighten up. It's just a joke."

To focus my mind I think, "*Jane Eyre. Jane Eyre. Jane Eyre,*" but that's as far as I get. Part of my attention is absorbed by the speed with which I am driving. Any cops? No cops. When I drive past the wetlands a cloud of milkweed fluff hits the windshield at eighty. Never mind cops, what if I kill myself? Is it worth taking chances with my life just to be on time for class?

Yes. It is. This is a matter of life and death.

Outside the classroom, however, things are relaxed. Seeing me, people break off their conversations and saunter in. Annie Suyemoto, wearing ripped blue jeans and a thin white camisole top, is in line at the express money machine.

"I'll be right there," she calls.

"Okay," I call, walking fast. A student with a face like a potato stops me outside the door.

"One thing I don't understand," he says. "Are we supposed to like St. John or not? He's very Christian but I think he's a jerk." I look at the potato-faced student as if I were seeing him for the first time. Blessings on your head, whoever you are! I say, Yes, he's a jerk, or No, he isn't a jerk, or Interesting question, why don't you bring it up in class. And now there will be a class. We have a student, he asked the question; we have a teacher, she gave the answer. These are the necessary preconditions for a class. Having answered this student, I suddenly feel capable of answering any number of students. I have answers to all questions any student anywhere could ask about *Jane Eyre*. To understand how Brontë feels about St. John we should compare him to Helen Burns, the other figure of Christian goodness. Then there's the question of passion. Is St. John's passion perverse? Topics develop and divide like microscopic life. I am ready for class to begin. At my desk a student in chains and tight black pants asks for an extension on her paper. She seems upset, and I wonder, could this be Lucy X? I glance at her stomach but it's perfectly flat. I know about Lucy X from Marjorie Marlinsky, who works at a women's counseling center. Lucy's a computer science major and doesn't even need this class for distribution, but Marjorie couldn't convince her to drop it.

"She can't make any decisions," Marjorie told me. "It's terrible, the pressure she's under."

"No problem," I tell the student warmly. "Just let me know when you can have it in." It wouldn't help to ask her name. Marjorie said they use pseudonyms.

Annie Suyemoto sits down in front, puts one leg up on a post. Today it's basketball sneakers, other days it might be penny loafers or flats with sexy little socks. I really like her.

"Okay, listen to this," I say when things are quiet. I read:

Folds of scarlet drapery shut in my view to the right hand; to the left were the clear panes of glass, protecting, but not separating me from the drear November day. At intervals, while turning over the leaves of my book, I studied the aspect of that winter afternoon. Afar, it offered a pale blank of mist and cloud; near, a scene of wet lawn and storm-beat shrub, with ceaseless rain sweeping away wildly before a long and lamentable blast.

When I finish there is a silence. Friendly or dead? Am I the teacher, the Voice, or am I a very foolish woman? I don't know what made me start with that passage; I am stalled after take off, engines cut and the sea shining hideously beneath me. I remember reading that the scarlet drapery shutting Jane into her window seat represents the womb or menstruation or something, but I make it a policy never to start a class discussing wombs and menstruation. Rain is a good topic to start off with, if only I could think of something to say about it. Idiotically, I look out the window as if I expected a deluge. A traffic light, pale in the midday sunshine, changes from red to green. A line of cars starts up. I wish I were in one of them, driving away. I am losing my sense of how long this has been going on.

Into the silence, Annie speaks.

"It makes you want to be there," says Annie. "Even though the weather is bad."

"Exactly!" I say. Is Annie brilliant or is she brilliant? Anyway, she makes me feel brilliant. Her true blue response shoots through my system, realigning all the synapses and exciting within me a powerful desire to speak. A door flies open and language pours into the anteroom, ready to come out. Grammatical structures rush forward, bewigged and perfumed, to keep order. Stalling for time, I take a few more comments, and then I go for it. Words come from nowhere in beautiful shapes. Sentences fly out whole, leaping subordinate clauses and arriving flushed but unwinded at the end. I am surfing the long, ever-breaking wave of Thought, and there's nothing like it.

Do you want to know what I said? Would you like to judge for yourself whether or not it was brilliant? No problem. I talked about desire in *Jane Eyre*, how desire is by definition a matter of lack, how Jane wants what she has not got, Rochester, love, and we want it with and for her; but how secretly the book makes us desire the realities of Jane's life even more than the things she hasn't got. Jane is restless, inflamed by scarlet desires; but she is also a clear pane of glass through which we see the world as it is. Through her we can savor the bad weather, the scarce pleasures, the "one delicious but thin piece of toast," the time Bessie let her eat off a special plate, the "clean and quiet street" where a post office has a single letter for Jane Eyre.

Look, for instance, at the famous opening passage of chapter twelve.

First Jane stands on the battlements of Thornfield and longs for something beyond her quiet, governess life. She tells herself stories full of "all the incident, life, fire, feeling that I desired but had not in my actual existence." She yearns toward "the busy world, towns, regions full of life I had heard of but never seen." Three pages later she meets Mr. Rochester, whose sexual privilege it is to incarnate the busy world itself. The desire calls up its object, and the rest of the book is spent pursuing and evading it. But where does Jane meet Rochester? On a walk. On one of those walks women in Jane Austen and Charlotte Brontë are always taking. They take walks because they haven't got a damn thing else in the world to do. Often they go to the post office. "One must walk somewhere," said Jane Austen in a letter, "and the post office gives one an object." So Jane Eyre puts on her bonnet and cloak and walks two miles to town. Here is how it went:

> The ground was hard, the air was still, my road was lonely;…the charm of the hour lay in its approaching dimness, in the low-gliding and pale beaming sun. I was a mile from Thornfield, in a lane noted for wild roses in summer, for nuts and blackberries in autumn, and even now possessing a few coral treasures in hips and haws, but whose best winter delight lay in its utter solitude and leafless repose. If a breath of air stirred, it made no sound here; for there was not a holly, not an evergreen to rustle, and the stripped hawthorn and hazel bushes were as still as the white, worn stones which causewayed the middle of the path.

Do you see what I mean? Winter. Utter solitude and leafless repose. A few coral treasures in hips and haws. Sandwiched in between the passionate moments on the battlements and the appearance of Mr. Rochester is a walk. Wouldn't you like to be on that walk? In the next paragraph is a sheet of ice covering a brook; do you see how the book is a pattern of fire and ice, scarlet and white?

Sitting in their blue plastic chairs, my students listen up. The chairs have one wide, flat arm for taking notes; many of the students are filling up their notebooks with what I say. Peter Greenberg and Julie Sobel, however, take no notes. Peter and Julie can't take notes because they need to stare at me while I talk, or else they won't understand a thing. There are a few students like Peter and Julie in every class. Their eyes have to be turned, like satellite dishes, toward the source of information, which I have the honor of being. Peter looks like the astonished fetus at the end of *2001: A Space Odyssey*. Julie looks more like a whale. Her intake valve is open, she'll strain for plankton later. This makes it sound as if Julie isn't smart, which is incorrect. She's pleasant enough to look at, too, with light springy hair, a round face, dark blue eyes. But her preliminary processing mechanism, like mine, is stupid. It has one switch, on or off. When the interest level in the classroom rises to a certain level the switch flips to "on," and there she is. I say "there she is" because when she's not interested I don't see her. Only when things get cooking does she burn in.

Other students in this class are: Haskell Springer, who almost qualified on the U.S. equestrian team during the last Olympics; Barbara Guetti, whose father is so tyrannical and whose mother so deeply depressed that Barbara has to wear a different tie every day; Greg Urtiaga, who worked in a Kentucky Fried Chicken store and participated in chicken fights last summer; and Ursula Lang, who was a student of mine in Freshman Composition, where I didn't much like her. Somewhere in the class is Lucy X, pregnant and miserable. There is a woman from computer services who comes on her lunch break and a senior who comes in his ROTC uniform. These people discuss the imagery of fire and ice in *Jane Eyre* in a loose, associative way, the way Phil Donahue's guests discuss their sex lives. I let them talk, responding when moved to do so and not when not. Haskell Springer points out that Mr. Rochester's horse slips on the ice when Rochester and Jane first meet, but everyone agrees this has no symbolic value whatsoever. I wonder if the other students think it's as funny as I do that Haskell never fails to bring up a scene with a horse in it. As the discussion goes on I jot down notes, intending to set things straight at the end of the hour. In addition to qualifications and corrections of what the students are saying, I have in mind a large general point, something that will sum things up and show us where we have been going. Then it seems the point has been made. I couldn't say when or by whom, but when I look at my notes they don't refer to anything that hasn't already happened. I crumple up the notes and throw them away.

The hour has gone by quickly. I keep them five minutes over to explain the upcoming assignment, after which I listen to individual bulletins of illness, emotional distress, overwork, and death in the family. I let everyone who needs one have an extension on his or her paper, and then I'm alone. Styrofoam coffee cups and cans of Sprite are scattered around the classroom, sitting on the arms of the molded blue chairs. My shirt is rather wet. The class is over.

Do I feel a sense of anticlimax or exhilaration? I do not. When I first started teaching it used to take hours to get over it, but now decompression is instant. As soon as the last student finishes her tale of woe, I shove my books and papers into my briefcase, and a happy thought fills my mind. Lunch!

On Wednesdays I generally have lunch with Jeremy and Sophie, sometimes in the faculty dining room but usually in the student cafeteria. Jeremy teaches postcolonial literature and is always going to South Africa these days; Sophie works one-on-one with foreign graduate students.

"Doritos chips," says Jeremy when he sees my tray. "Nacho cheese or BBQ?" The joke is that I eat too much junk food and Jeremy is too fastidious and upscale in his food tastes. It wasn't much of a joke to begin with, and with repetition it has become a real force for entropy. The world around me dims with boredom; then I recover and sit down.

"I don't know," says Sophie. "Sometimes I have a longish conversation on my cell, but mostly I just call the kids or something to find out where they are."

"Then get by-the-second billing," says Jeremy. "I'm telling you, it really makes a difference." Topics we have covered at past lunches include whether Sophie wants a flip-cover, bar, or slider phone; whether she's going to use it a lot for text messaging; and whether she's going to need infrared connectivity. I comfort myself with an egg salad sandwich while they talk.

"Did you see Doonesbury this morning?" Sophie finally asks me. I did not. Then Sophie tells a funny story about a Cambodian student of hers, and Jeremy says he will be spending Christmas break in New York.

"I haven't been to New York in months," I say. I think about New York for a while, trying to work out where we would stay if we went, and then I tell Sophie and Jeremy something that happened in New York last winter.

"I was walking through the lobby of an apartment building on Central

Park West," I tell them. "Not super-fancy, but near Lincoln Center, with art deco doors. I was wearing an old coat over blue jeans and thinking, Really I should do a little better than this when I come to New York. Just then two women went by looking great.

"'That's the look,' I thought, studying them. Their clothes were witty and post-modern and mismatched, one colorful, the other black-and-white. As I turned to take another look, the colorful one detached herself from the other and hurried back. Before I knew it she was standing in front of me in her magenta cashmere scarf, talking eagerly.

"'You're Caroline Jacobs,' she said. 'Do you remember me? You were my teacher. I had you in three classes, including Freshman English. I saw you just now and I had to come tell you. Everyone has someone who really makes a difference, and for me it was you.'"

"You're kidding!" exclaims Sophie, delighted.

"What happened next?" asks Jeremy, curious. "I don't remember," I say. "I was flabbergasted."

"Did you recognize her?" asks Sophie.

"Not at all," I say. The three of us start adding up how many students we teach per year and multiplying by how many years we have been teaching. In my case it was seventy students per semester, of which about twenty are repeaters. Times two minus twenty is 120 per year. Times ten is 1,200 students. Everyone agrees that I am not at fault for not recognizing the student in New York.

"Of course, it's different for me," says Sophie. "Because I work with students individually." Sophie has actually visited ex-students of hers in Brazil and India.

"Yes," I say. "That's an advantage."

"Sometimes," says Sophie.

When lunch is over I walk Sophie and Jeremy back to the main campus and head for the library. The weather has degenerated, and it looks like rain. I am still thinking about the woman in New York.

"Oh, thank you!" I remember saying, but after that it was as if I had forgotten my lines. We stood like two animals who had heretofore only observed each other from the safety of our cages. Suddenly we were out on the paths with the people. She was doing something in theater and would be going to the Yale School of Drama soon. Well, good luck to her. I wish I had talked to her more. I never saw her again.

It is rainy and dark by the time I drive home. We are only a month from the shortest day of the year, and the darkness is becoming oppressive. Worse than the darkness, however, is the immediate danger of a quarrel with Mark. I have agreed over and over that the Leslie Middleman episode is in the past, but whenever something reminds me of it every gesture of Mark's makes me mad. I decide to pay the Green Machine and be done with it. They're wrong about the bill, but it's worth $59.45 to be done with their reminders. You can't hold the line every time.

Mark finds the envelope on the table in the hall after dinner. "I thought you said we weren't going to pay them," he says. I am in my study reading Elizabeth Gaskell's *Life of Charlotte Brontë*; Mark is in the doorway wearing the kimono his parents brought him from Japan.

"I changed my mind," I say. I am reading the description of Brontë's funeral; rather than think about the Green Machine, I ask Mark if he wants to hear it.

"Few beyond that circle of hills," I read aloud, "knew that she, whom the nations praised far off, lay dead that Easter morning." Her father and her husband, "stunned with their great grief, desired not the sympathy of strangers." Only one member from each family in the parish was allowed to come to the funeral, and "it became an act of self-denial in many a poor household to give up to another the privilege of paying their last homage to her."

"Her husband?" asks Mark. "I thought she was a spinster." Of course, I think, annoyed. That's the whole point about the Brontës, isn't it? If you know one thing about them it's that they were lonely, frustrated spinsters.

"Well, weren't they?" insists Mark.

"Yes," I say. "They were. But in the end Charlotte married her father's curate. She was thirty-eight."

"That's nice," says Mark, trying to stay out of trouble. I don't know whether it was nice or it wasn't nice. Mrs. Gaskell claims that Charlotte liked the man perfectly well after marrying him; but Mrs. Gaskell isn't to be trusted. In any case the marriage didn't last. Charlotte died the next year of pregnancy toxemia. When Amy goes to sleep I take a walk. Mark and I didn't fight, but we didn't really relax either. What was the point of today? I ask myself. I don't know any more about art or life or *Jane Eyre* than I did this morning. I haven't made any money.

I haven't written anything or had any fun. Why did I bother to get out of bed? It is mild and drizzly; my discontent envelops me in the dark like a vaporous exhalation. I'm passing, of all things, the post office. Now a man on a horse should appear in the mist and eroticize the text. But instead of love, I find myself thinking of death. What will remain of me when I'm gone? Amy, of course, thank God; but what will remain in the world of my efforts?

"Nothing," I think, plodding along the sidewalk. Intellectuals are not supposed to care about leaving a physical memorial to their time on earth, but they do. George Orwell, for instance, worried about the physical space his books would take up by the end of his life. A couple of shelves, he thought; whereas a coal miner could fill whole houses with the product of his labor. I think Orwell was too hard on himself. What if you counted every printed copy of Orwell's books, instead of only one of each? I myself, I suddenly think, passing under a streetlight, would be proud to undergo the trial by bulk. Let everyone I've ever taught come to my funeral, and I'll match my output against any coalminer or long-shoreman in America. If I teach another twenty years, that's nearly four thousand people. You'd have to hire a football stadium to get them all in! Let Amy, now in her fifties, gather my students from all nations and states! All age groups will be represented and all cultural persuasions. Lucy X's baby will be in the prime of her life. She was never officially enrolled in the British novel course, but the rights of the fetus will by now be so well established that merely having been present in the class-room, even in an embryonic form, will be enough. It occurs to me with the force of a conviction that Lucy X is the girl with the long, punk wing of reddish hair sticking out of her head. What shall I do about that?

I'm walking faster now, warm and loose. Did you know that walking for ten minutes has a more measurable calming effect than a Valium? It has stopped raining, but there's a nice soft mist.

I think I'll take the long walk tonight, up the hill to the observatory. There won't be any stars, of course, but perhaps I don't need them. I am expanding into the atmosphere anyway, into the houses and yards of my neighbors, into the air, into the bare, wet trees of this suburban town-ship, muffled and blurred by the mist.

It is time to take the photo at my funeral. From a point at the top of the stadium, the photographer plans his shot. He wants the photograph to resemble an American Airlines ad, with hundreds of airline employees smiling and looking up. What strikes me, as the students pour onto the field, is again this question of age. When I was teaching them, these people were always between eighteen and twenty-two years old, and I alone was an exile from youth. Only for me did the seasons pass; for the students it was always spring. But now I see that I was mistaken. There are people of all ages here, fading and blossoming and falling to earth. Together these people represent the march of time, the staircase of generations. The photographer, however, does not want them lined up according to age. The point of his photo is the Democracy of Literature, so he wants a pluralistic look. When everything is right, the photographer will send word to a stadium technician, who will light up the scoreboard as if for a touchdown. Haskell Springer, also recently dead, watches with me as the moment approaches.

"What you said about the students staying young," he says. "Sportswriters have the same problem. The athletes stay young, too."

"Hah," I say. "I never thought of that."

"Sure," says Haskell. He died from an equestrian accident, but before that he was a sportswriter for *The Washington Post*. It was Haskell's idea to signal the students by lighting the scoreboard, which will happen any minute now. The photographer is nervous and excited.

"NOW!" he shouts into his headset. Floodlights go on all over the field. Across the field is a familiar face.

"Amy!" I cry. "I think that's Amy!" "Where?" asks Haskell, just to be nice.

"There!" I point. "In the press box." I see Amy as Haskell must see her, a pleasant-looking, completely undistinguished middle-aged lady. But at that moment somebody distracts her, just when she wanted to face forward for the picture; and when her face turns back my way it has a downturned mouth, vulnerable/scornful, just as it did when she was five.

"Amy!" I cry, waving wildly. I am very glad to see her. A band, stationed in the bleachers, plays a military march. People are crying as at a parade. Everyone lifts a copy of *Jane Eyre* and cheers.

IN THE FOREST

In the forest, Orlando and Adam are starving, particularly Adam.

"That's okay," says Adam, Orlando's old servant. "I'll just die." Orlando doesn't agree with this. He finds a soft, mossy mound under a tree and lays Adam's old body where it will be least uncomfortable.

"You stay here, old man," says Orlando. "I'll come back with food, call me a monkey's uncle if I don't." Adam smiles faintly.

"I won't be calling you much of anything if we don't eat something soon," he says. "And I mean soon." Orlando builds a pillow of fallen leaves under Adam's aged head.

"Very nice," sighs Adam as Orlando leaves. "Thank you, my boy."

Soon Orlando comes upon a picnic in a grove. Some men have spread food on a rough table; others are sitting on the fragrant ground, laughing and joking. Above their heads, the tops of the pines touch each other lightly in the breeze. Orlando draws his sword.

"Hold!" he shouts. "No one eats! Give me your food!" The men are startled. It is noon on a sunny day, although because of the pines they themselves are in shade. Now there has been a crashing of twigs and bushes followed by the eruption of this tense sword-waving man. They are all skilled swordsmen themselves, but their swords aren't handy just now. More to the point, fighting back would violate the spirit of the moment, which is mellow.

"Chill," murmurs one of the men uneasily, and another half-stands. Their leader, the Duke, is unalarmed. Nothing in the forest seems to catch him off guard.

"Welcome!" he says to Orlando, not to disarm him but because he feels genuinely welcoming. "What's ours is yours!" In response to Orlando's shouted explanations, he takes a game bag from Amiens and stuffs it with food. "Take this," he says kindly. "Your old friend must eat his fill." This is before he has any idea that Orlando is the son of *his* old friend Sir Rowland de Boys.

Orlando stops short, stumbling on uneven ground.

"Eat his...?" he repeats, confused. Filtered rays of light drift through the branches, and Orlando notices some musical instruments propped against the tree trunks. Now the men are concealing smiles. Orlando is embarrassed to have misconstrued the situation, but he knows, too, that in this play he is responsible for gestures of masculine assertiveness, and he cannot fault himself for having made one.

"Please excuse me," he says when he recovers. "I *thought that all things had been savage here, And therefore put I on the countenance of stern commandment.*" The Duke is pleased with the way Orlando expresses himself. He himself has had plenty of experience, while in power, of putting on some countenance or another to suit the occasion, and *stern commandment* was certainly one of them.

"Like my puff-sleeved royal blue shirt," he thinks. "It was something I put on before going to work." Would he wear that shirt in the forest? Absurd! The very thought makes him laugh.

"Off you go," says the Duke, laughing at his private joke. "Bring your friend. The two of you will stay with us."

"Yes, thank you," says Orlando, but he is light-headed from hunger and scarcely knows what he's agreeing to. He is extremely concerned about getting some food into Adam before it's too late.

"I'll be right back," he promises, trying to smile. As soon as he is out of sight he starts to run.

* * *

Q. Compare Orlando to, for instance, Macbeth.

A. When Macbeth takes out his sword, his *brandished steel* smokes *bloody execution*, and he doesn't apologize later. In tragedy and history someone has to get hurt, either oneself or the other guy.

Q. But this is a comedy.

A. Right.

Q. Does Orlando ever hurt anyone?

A. Yes.

Q. That's correct. How many times?
A. Uh…
Q. More than once?
A. Uh…
Q. Never mind, we'll discuss this later.

SOLILOQUY: DUKE SENIOR

Who exiled me to the forest? My younger brother, Frederick, when he usurped my dukedom. I know it's customary to make excuses when this happens, but I have none. My brother usurped my dukedom not because I was negligent of my duties or because I planned to come back in disguise and test his reign, but "just because," as children say. One minute the shiny thing was mine, and the next it was his. Poof, gone, and I was in the forest, serenading stones.

Some lords have come with me, Amiens and some others. We do what we please. At court I couldn't tell if these people really liked me, but now it seems they do. I like them, too! I only wish old Rowland were with us, Sir Rowland de Boys. He'd love it here, poor guy. Well, we all have to die, I suppose. If I die in the forest and never go home? What a question! I feel quite cheerful, and that's it. When we need something to eat, we kill a deer.

That young man who was just here? He looked like someone I know, but I can't think who. Truly, I'm losing my mind! Well, I'm better off without it, don't you think? *Come, shall we go kill us some venison?* It's time to eat.

COMMENTARY

Come, shall we go kill us some venison? writes Shakespeare—but the mention of killing for food casts a shadow on his sunny scene.

Keep moving, he tells himself. That was his MO as a writer, and it served him well. The Duke can have second thoughts, perhaps.

And yet it irks me, says the Duke, that the deer should be *gored* on their home ground.

No, that won't do. Shakespeare doesn't want a Duke who explores his conflicts, over this or anything else. Enter Jacques, invented on the spot.

Jacques will comment, or *moralize,* on the issue of deer-slaying, but he is not One of Us, and we won't need to take him totally seriously.

"Let's find Jacques and discuss it," says the Duke eagerly. "I love him in his *sullen fits."* If it is Jacques who voices our guilt and remorse, we can be amused, not ashamed.

* * *

A fallen stag lies by a brook.

"*Sweep on, you fat and greasy citizens,*" calls Jacques as a *careless herd* sweeps by. "Don't anyone stop to help!" Entertaining way of putting it! Note, too, that the emphasis on the heartless herd deflects our attention from the human hunters. Abandoned not only by the herd but by his *velvet friend,* as Jacques memorably calls his mate, the wounded stag weeps into the stream.

"Just what *worldlings* do," improvises Jacques—"give *more to that which [has] too much.*" The stag is briefly confused, but then he understands. The brook is already full to overflowing, so his "gift" of tears is like the "gifts" people pay the rich as bribes.

"Yes," agrees the stag silently. "That's right." He is not bothered by Jacques and his similes. He can sense he does not have long to live, and Jacques can see him out. It would have been better, of course, if his *velvet friend* had stuck around for the farewells, but as she hasn't, Jacques will do. What the stag minds is the noise of the brook, which seems to be getting louder all the time. He wonders if his eardrums will burst, and he will die in silence, deaf.

"I'd be fine," he thinks, "except for this awful noise." The brook isn't really getting louder, but as the deer's condition worsens, he is less and less able to cope. He tries to think of gentle sounds as an antidote.

"A tree in a slight wind," he tells himself. "A thoughtful bird." Jacques thinks of more amazing things to say about him, all with a satirical bite.

"A twig snapping underfoot," thinks the deer, and dies.

* * *

Celia, Rosalind, and Touchstone are exhausted, and Celia is faint from hunger. Rosalind, for one, feels like crying; but as a man, she declares, she shouldn't cry but comfort women.

"*Well, this is the Forest of Arden,*" she says, partly for lack of anything better to say and partly to impress upon her own mind the fact that they are now in a different world from the one they are used to. They're in the country now. Perhaps there is some special way of getting food and shelter here—*entertainment,* as she calls it—that she doesn't know about. In the city they seem just to be there without one's having to procure them. They are not really in a woods but in a high pasture. The hill on which they stand is covered with low, uneven grass, as if bitten by determined sheep. In the valley are a stone house and perhaps a river.

Rosalind knows she isn't really a man. She has just dressed up as one because she and Celia thought they'd be safer in the forest if she did. Now that she is dressed as a man, however, she feels a masculine responsibility for her companions, and it is making her irritable that she can't fulfill it.

"This must be how men feel all the time," she thinks. It accounts for the general irritability of men. Celia can see that Rosalind feels in charge.

"Look at that," she thinks. "All it takes is the doublet and hose, and a perfectly nice woman suddenly turns into a man with issues." She and Rosalind are cousins and very close.

"*We still have slept together, rose at an instant, learned, played, eat together,*" she begged her father when he came to banish Ros. Celia went so far as to compare their relationship to that of *Juno's swans…coupled and inseparable.*

"Yes," Duke Frederick said. "We kept her around for your sake, since you liked her so much. But she's her father's daughter, and now I want her gone." Duke Frederick had recently usurped the dukedom from Duke Senior, the one we have already met.

"If you had any sense," Duke Frederick went on, "you'd want to get rid of her, too."

"Well, I don't," said Celia disrespectfully.

"People are taking her side," her father argued. "Can't you see she's stealing your limelight?"

"That's ridiculous," Celia told him sharply. "Ros doesn't have a political bone in her body!"

"*Thou art a fool,*" her father said, and left the room. So Celia went into exile with Rosalind, as she had threatened she would do. Now her grand gesture of solidarity is being undermined by hunger, exhaustion, and annoyance. It crosses Celia's mind that if it weren't for Ros, she would be having a tasty bun about now with a cup of tea. It cannot be denied, however, that the evening clouds are lovely, fiery red at the rims, soft and gray in the belly. If only she weren't hungry, she could enjoy this gorgeous view.

Just then an older man and a younger one approach on the path.

"Pull yourself together!" says the older man. "Get a grip!"

"*Phebe, Phebe, Phebe!*" moans Silvius.

"It never works to fling yourself at women," Corin scolds. "Remember who you are!"

"You don't know anything about it," groans Silvius.

"Right," says Corin tartly. "I've never been in love."

"Not like this! Not like this!" and Silvius comically tears down the path as if he is too agitated even to go on talking. Corin shakes his head. He hasn't yet noticed the others, who are above him on the hill.

Rosalind is eavesdropping intently. She has recently fallen in love herself, so she identifies with Silvius.

"*Alas, poor shepherd!*" she says. The man she loves is Orlando, whom she met before they all left town. Touchstone falls into a not-very-amusing parody of Silvius.

"Please!" says Celia. She is out of patience with them both. For one thing, she has seen that Orlando was as taken with Ros as Ros was with him, so this sighing of Ros's about her *wound* and this comparing herself to some lovelorn country schnook is disingenuous. In fact it is hard for Celia to think of anyone who *wouldn't* want Rosalind. She is spontaneous, delightful, and endlessly fun. Celia likes Orlando fine, but this is not the moment to be thinking about Orlando. If they don't get hold of this Corin fellow, they might spend the night in a ditch.

"Look," says Celia. "One of you go ask that man where we can eat. And sleep! We need a place to spend the night!"

Corin stands lost in thought, watching Silvius run downhill. As the older shepherd he should be past the torments of love and glad of it; but what he actually feels is a sharp pang of regret for a woman he once loved who only liked him as a friend. She married a goatherd and was subsequently known for her excellent cheeses. Corin also misses his wife, who died some years back, leaving him to fend for himself. Suddenly two young women and a man are standing before him on the path, asking for help. One of the women is wearing some ill-fitting men's clothing, and the man is in a clown suit. Motley, they call it.

"Who are you?" he asks.

"*Your betters, sir,*" the man says rudely.

"*Else you were very wretched,*" says Corin politely. But he thinks to himself, "Well, I knew *that!* Only well-born people would go out in public playing dress-up!" Now the cross-dressed woman reprimands the man and appeals to Corin for help.

"I'd help you if I could," says Corin. "But *I am shepherd to another man and do not shear the fleeces that I graze.*"

"Huh?" says Touchstone.

"He means he's a hired hand," guesses Celia. Corin nods.

"I don't own my own sheep," he says. "I don't even have my own place."

"You don't live there?" asks Ros, pointing to the house in the valley.

"Oh, no," says Corin. "That's my master's house. But (a) he's not very nice, and (b) the house is up for sale."

"What if we bought it?" says Rosalind quickly. Corin considers. Silvius had planned to buy the house, but now he has other concerns.

"I like it here," says Celia. "Let's do it."

"I'll *buy it with your gold,*" Corin agrees. Why not? These people can't be any worse to work for than his master, and they might be better. By nightfall the new people are installed and a meal has been scrounged from leftover food in the pantry.

"We'll see," Corin thinks, clearing the table. "We'll see." He scrapes the remains of an onion pie into the sink.

* * *

A. Gold? In the forest? Where are we, anyway? One minute we're in a woods somewhere, but now there seem to be sheep.

Q. We're in some grab bag of a non-urban setting. Later we'll run into a lion and, I think, a palm tree. But this is a form of pastoral, so whatever the setting, there are always shepherds and sheep.

A. What is pastoral?

Q. (*waving a hand*) I can't go into that. Books have been written on the subject, one of them called, *What Is Pastoral?*

A. Come on.

Q. (*sighs*) Peacefulness, piping contests, rural contentment.

A. Yeah?

Q. Being okay with having no money or status.

A. And yet these people have money!

Q. *Let's get our wealth together,* Celia told Ros before leaving for the woods. But in pastoral literature a focus on who exactly owns the sheep, etc., is rare.

A. It's unique in its focus on the material conditions of the shepherd's life?

Q. I don't know about unique. I said rare.

A. Okay, rare. Do you like this scene?

Q. Yes, I do. A little grittiness in with the *bergerie.*

A. (*snorts*) *Bergerie.* Great word. (*Q and A exchange a smile.*)

* * *

In the forest, Orlando has lost his way.

"If Adam dies," he thinks, running down an unfamiliar path, "I'll never forgive myself." He sits on a rock and tries to calm down. He is too tense to eat, although he is spacey from hunger.

"What shall I do?" he cries. He remembers telling Adam as he left, "*If I bring thee not something to eat, I will give thee leave to die, but if thou diest before I come, thou art a mocker of my labor.*"

"I take it back," cries Orlando out loud. "You don't have leave to die under *any* circumstances." It amazes him to think of the playful mood he was in just a few hours ago. For a moment his distracted brain dissects his own great prose.

"The symmetries and antitheses," he thinks wonderingly. The progression of the vowels through *eat, die, come,* and *labor.* Eee, eye, uh, ay, thinks Orlando. The spot he is sitting in is landlocked, one tree like the next. Unable to find peace or guidance, Orlando springs from his rock and runs off. Adam, meanwhile, lies where Orlando left him, smiling when he, too, remembers Orlando's playful words.

"I don't want to disappoint him," thinks Adam affectionately. His job is to concentrate on a little piece of sky he can see between the leaves overhead. As long as it's there he's okay, but if the leaves or a cloud obscure it, he starts to go under. What makes that bad is not the immediate nausea but the vision that goes with it. When Adam can't see blue sky, the air above him thickens, and a certain awful scene runs through it like an endless tape. On the tape Orlando and Oliver have their hands on each other's throats.

"Sweet masters, be patient," Adam hears himself crying helplessly. *"For your father's remembrance, be at accord."* Adam went to work for the de Boys family when he was practically a boy himself. He was paid reasonable wages and reasonably well treated, but that didn't account for something extraordinary that happened as time went on. Without ever having been particularly devout—without having had, in fact, any spiritual aspirations whatsoever—at a certain point Adam realized that he was not working for money anymore but out of perfect love. It was a true transformation, and once in his life he had to tell about it.

"It wasn't them in particular," he explained to his favorite sister. "I would have loved anyone after that. But it was the de Boys boys who were there, as they had been all along. Young and old, I loved them all."

"But Oliver's so awful," said his sister.

"Only since Sir Rowland died," he said—not that Oliver's awfulness affected Adam's feelings for him in the slightest. "I don't know what's gotten into him." Oliver had refused to give Orlando his share of the inheritance, insulted and abused Adam, and finally tried to have Orlando killed.

"What, boy!" shouted Oliver when Orlando finally demanded his due—and hit him as hard as he could. Adam could not fault Orlando for grabbing Oliver in a choking hold at this point, but it was horrible to see the two men he loved at each other's throats. Soon he learned that Oliver was planning to burn down Orlando's house with Orlando in it.

"We've got to leave town," he told Orlando forcefully. "Here's five hundred crowns to fund our escape." Orlando knew they were his life savings.

"No!" he said; but Adam wore him down.

"Here is the gold," he insisted. Orlando shook his head.

"They don't make them like you anymore," he told his servant.

Lying on the ground, Adam relaxes a little. A bird is singing nearby. It is a white-throated sparrow, trying to sing, as all white-throated sparrows do, "Poor John, Peabody Peabody Peabody." But this one is stuck.

"Poor John," he sings, a high note followed by a low one, and pauses. Adam passes out.

"How long was I out?" he thinks when he comes to. Has something befallen Orlando? Adam is upset, but at the same time relieved.

"I can go ahead and die now," he thinks. Then he hears, "Poor John," without the "Peabody, Peabody, Peabody," so he knows he wasn't gone for long.

"Peabody, Peabody, Peabody," Adam sings back from his reclining position. He hits the right note, shaky but on key. Adam sighs, and resumes his concentration on the leaf canopy, looking for a patch of blue. The trees are oak and beech, with a few white birches. One of the beech trees is elephant-footed, huge, and comforting. It does not want Adam to die.

COMMENTARY

There was always a past, it seems, when things were better. In *the antique world,* as Orlando calls it, people just did the right thing, like Adam; nowadays *none do sweat but for promotion.* This is true no matter when you live. The fantasy of a great, lost past first found written expression in the eighth century B.C.E. when Hesiod wrote his *Works and Days.* Once upon a time, he says, there was a Golden Age when no one had to work, and everything was owned in common. People lived *like gods without sorrow of heart, and the earth unforced bare them fruit without stint.* The Golden Age bears some resemblance to the world of pastoral—which is not surprising, perhaps, since Hesiod himself was a shepherd. He only became a poet, he says, when he met the Muses in a field one day, and they dictated some verses for him to write down.

Adam offers gold and reminds us of the Golden past. He also has a way with words. The five hundred crowns he gives Orlando, his life savings, were intended, he says, as his *foster-nurse* in retirement. Without money *unregarded age* is thrown *in corners.* Money as a *foster-nurse!* *Age in corners thrown!* Adam may be a low-status character, but he's not a clown. In terms of self-expression, he can compete with the highest of the highest born.

FLASHBACK: SILVIUS AND PHEBE

Sitting all day with their sheep, many shepherds find their way into a special silence. Their minds expand, and their thoughts arise and pass like clouds. Silvius, however, tends toward practicalities, which is how he has accumulated the funds with which to buy a house. Then he ran into Phebe in the forest and for no reason fell in love. After that he was excited about nothing but her. It was the first profound thing in his life, and he was completely unprepared.

Phebe was carrying a basket of eggs the day he met her. They were in a shady part of the woods, so it was muddy underfoot.

"Where are you taking those eggs?" asked Silvius, just to be friendly. Phebe put the basket on a tree stump and wiped her hands on her apron.

"Oh, you know," she said vaguely. "Same old thing." Silvius's heart rate picked up. It wasn't what she said, of course, since she had scarcely said anything. It was her hands. Phebe's hands looked both capable and vulnerable, with a slight chubbiness to them. They seemed utterly particular, and Silvius felt a shock of intimacy, as if he had seen her naked. Then he was pierced with the strangest thought.

"I could see myself in Phebe's hands," he thought. It wasn't exactly a sexual thought, but it wasn't *not* sexual, either. It was as if the metaphor and the literal meaning of being in someone's hands suddenly fused, so there was no difference between the thought of having her actual hands on his body on the one hand and depending on her on the other. The sudden feeling of surrender, need, and freedom was overpowering.

"In her hands?" asked a friend later. "You mean, her hands on your dick?" Silvius winced.

"That's too specific," he said, although by this time he had imagined many specificities.

His friend snorted. "You've got some other way to get things done?" he asked. It was this kind of comment from friends his own age that had made Silvius seek out Corin. Corin was older and understood.

"I'm in free fall," cried poor Silvius.

"What's she like?" asked patient Corin.

"Brown curls," he said dreamily. "A little bedraggled." Corin had heard this a dozen times.

"I meant as a person," he said.

"A blue apron on a white dress," breathed Silvius. "The dress was long, and muddy at the hem."

"Your shoes are muddy," Silvius told Phebe at the time. "Shall I clean them for you?"

"What?" said Phebe, surprised.

"It won't take a minute," Silvius persisted.

"Oh, I guess not," said Phebe, picking up her basket. "I'd better be going now." Silvius cast about for something to say.

"Did you ever find that lost sheep?" he says quickly.

"Lost sheep?" she said, looking straight at him. "What are you talking about? I haven't lost any sheep." Silvius remembered too late that it was some other shepherdess who had lost a sheep.

"Oh, nothing," he said, flushing. Then she was gone.

"I'm not a virgin," he tells Corin, "far from it; but it's all been pretty quick and done when it's done. I just assumed that one of the girls would get pregnant, I guess, or make a fuss, and at some point I'd be hauled before a priest. I never thought of this! What shall I do?"

Corin listens to Silvius, thinking meanwhile some thoughts about love. Like a river, he thinks, it rises out of nowhere, and once it starts it can't be stopped. From a pinpoint of earth scarcely damper than what surrounds it comes the River of Love, flowing with a power that's beyond us. Too broad to ford, too strong to swim. How do these things start?

COMMENTARY

"See that?" says the Duke when Orlando leaves the grove.

"See what?" says Amiens.

"*We are not all alone unhappy,*" the Duke grandly says.

"What?" says Amiens.

"Orlando," smiles the Duke. "We've got our troubles; he's got his." The Duke's troubles, of course, are exile and disempowerment.

"Roger that," murmurs Amiens. But the understanding that *we are not all alone unhappy* is key to Shakespearean comedy – and is indeed in all times and places a key to mental health. To have a sense of other people's suffering is to take one's own less hard. What if Lear could have spoken openly with Gloucester about their respective problems with their children? What if they had agreed that *everyone* has problems with their children? Tragedy, of course, depends on the idea that an individual's sufferings *are* personal; but this is comedy, which asks us to lighten up.

The Duke, as I hope I've made clear, is a poster boy for mental health. This world, he is aware, *presents more woeful pageants than the scene wherein we play*. So let's get over it! From the idea of our lives as pageants or scenes, it is a short leap to the most famous speech in the play, Jacques's extravagant riff beginning *All the world's a stage*. Certainly the idea of adopting changing roles is more encouragement to lightness. First we play babies, says Jacques; then schoolchildren; then adults. Then, one and all, we end up old: *sans teeth, sans eyes, sans taste, sans everything*. No sooner has Jacques come to this comic/doleful conclusion than Orlando returns with Adam, sans strength.

"So this is Adam," says the Duke warmly.

"What's left of him," says Adam, smiling weakly from Orlando's arms. He knows Orlando wants him to recover, and he will if he can.

"But I don't know," he thinks to himself. He doesn't feel all that robust.

SOLILOQUY: DUKE SENIOR

I've got it! Orlando is the youngest son of my old friend Rowland de Boys! Imagine finding him here. We're going to my cave now so he can tell me his story. You never know what'll happen next! Life's full of such surprises. Come, come!

* * *

Rosalind and Celia settle into the stone house, where they are happy. The house lacks many of the amenities they were used to at court, but it has blue and red anemones in a jar on the kitchen table, and this makes up for a lot. The table is plain scrubbed wood. The girls don't actually do any chores, but they experience rural simplicity anyway. In the afternoons they sit in the dooryard, framed by rose hollyhocks so tall they bend at their tops.

"You'll never guess who I saw in the woods today," Celia says to Ros one afternoon. They have been laughing at some verses they keep finding pinned to trees. *Let no face be kept in mind but the fair of Rosalind,* declares the besotted scribbler. Now it seems that the person Celia saw in the woods was Orlando, and that none other than he is the author of the verses. Rosalind suddenly sits up straight.

"Wait!" she says. "*What did he when thou saw'st him? What said he? How looked he? What makes he here? Did he ask for me?*" and so on. Celia is highly amused.

"*I found him under a tree,*" she says, "*like a dropped acorn.*"

"*It may well be called Jove's tree when it drops forth such fruit,*" says Ros solemnly. If a tree is dropping acorns, of course, it's an oak, and the oak is sacred to Jove.

"I just thought he was cute," laughs Celia. Rosalind may simply have Jove on the brain, since her name as a male impersonator is Ganymede, and Ganymede was *Jove's own page.* He was also gay. Perhaps Rosalind thought he would be easier to emulate than someone more macho. But at the moment she is distressed to be got up as any sort of man, gay or straight, because if Orlando is around she'd like him to know she's a woman, not a man.

"Oh, *what shall I do with my doublet and hose?*" she moans.

"You'll think of something," says Celia, and indeed, Ros does. She decides she'll find Orlando and tease him about his lovesickness.

"I mean, he's got to stop hurting these trees!" she jokes, for Orlando has gone so far as to carve his smitten doggerel in tree bark. As Ganymede, Ros decides, she will pretend to be Rosalind and demand that Orlando woo her as part of his cure. Soon she has found him and pitched her idea.

"*I would not be cured, youth,*" says Orlando stoutly. But he goes along with it anyway, and soon "Ganymede" (pretending, remember, to be Rosalind) is regularly instructing Orlando in love's impermanence.

"*Men are April when they woo, December when they wed,*" she sagely says. "*Maids are May when they are maids, but the sky changes when they are wives.*" Again and again they meet; again and again Ros balances on the high wire of her own emotions while playing the violin of worldly wisdom. Orlando is dazzled. S/he (Rosalind/Ganymede) even gets him (Orlando) to kiss her/him as part of the game.

"Whoa," thinks Orlando, his head in a whirl. "This is something! I'm not sure exactly what." This event has been a bonanza for contemporary critics, who love to find queer corners in the literary canon. In this case they are clearly right.

COMMENTARY

Shakespeare was in the entertainment business. He needed material, and he wasn't particular about where he got it. The idea of copyright protection came over a century later, along with Romantic-era enthusiasm for originality; in Shakespeare's day a writer felt as little guilt for "plagiarizing" as a Hollywood studio does for churning out a remake. In fact, students at that time were taught *imitatio,* an ancient Roman method of using the art of the past. Their teachers asked them to copy the form of a text while providing new content – or to provide a new form for the existing content. If new art arose from the process, so much the better; but the real point was to get the student thoroughly soaked in the past.

Obviously I have an interest in these matters since I myself am practicing *imitatio,* taking what I like from *As You Like It.* So it is worth noting that *As You Like It* was itself a remake – of Thomas Lodge's earlier prose work, *Rosalynd.* In fact the quirkiest, most "original" thing about the play, Orlando's wooing of a man playing a woman who is actually a woman playing a man, is lifted straight from Lodge. As always, it's the execution, not the material, that counts. These days, no one reads *Rosalynd,* while *As You Like It* is immortal.

* * *

Corin is talking with Damon as they bring home their sheep.

"She's in love with him, you say," says Damon. "And he loves her."

"Yes," says Corin.

"Yet she tries to persuade him that love is momentary, lovers unfaithful, the whole thing a delusion, and so on."

"Yes," says Corin.

"That's twisted," says Damon, shaking his head. "City people!" Corin likes his new friends, but he does have some reservations about them.

"It's not that they play while we work," he muses out loud. "That's fine. It's that they like me to represent rural simplicity, and I don't always feel like doing it."

"What's 'rural simplicity'?" says Damon, making a face as if he'd bitten into something sour.

"*This*," says Corin, spreading his arms to include the fields, the hills, the single hilltop tree. "They need to look up from their games and see the shepherd in the distance with his sheep. On Sundays they like to pass him in the lane with a woman and know there's a structure of work and rest from which they themselves are free."

"I see," says his friend.

"If there's no one here poorer and more traditional than they are," says Corin, "why not stay home?"

"A structure of work and rest from which they themselves are free," Damon repeats to himself. Does Corin lie awake at night thinking of things like that to say?

Now Corin is telling him about a new development. Rosalind, it seems, or rather "Ganymede," has taken Silvius's part and is attacking Phebe on his behalf.

"It's supposed to be amusing," Corin tells Damon, "but I think she goes too far."

"Yeah?"

"She says things like, 'Babe, you're not getting any younger. *Sell when you can, you are not for all markets.*'"

Damon laughs, although he knows there's nothing wrong with Phebe's looks. The younger shepherds can hardly keep their hands off her. But Damon himself has suffered from Phebe's refusals, and he doesn't mind hearing her maligned.

"But it's hopeless," says Damon. "She just doesn't like him."

"No. You know who Phebe likes?"

"Who?"

"Ganymede. She's fallen for the male impersonation."

"No kidding," says Damon, impressed. Just then Corin's attention is drawn to something dodging around behind a tree. It is Silvius, wearing a floppy-brimmed green hat.

"Hey, Silvius," calls Corin. "Come here." Silvius pretends to be surprised. He picks his way through to the herd to say hello.

"That's some hat," says Damon when Silvius gets close.

"Thank you," says Silvius, avoiding Corin's eyes. Corin knows what he's up to.

"Another mail delivery?" asks Corin pointedly. Silvius has been carrying messages from lovesick Phebe to "Ganymede," although Corin has told him not to.

"You think you can win her favor doing that?" he says. But Silvius can't help himself.

"That's twisted!" says Damon after Silvius leaves. Truly, Corin reflects, Damon does not have a wide range of expressions available to him.

"Yes, it is," says Corin. "And you know something else? I think Phebe is in love with 'Ganymede' *because* he's so mean to her, not in spite of it."

The two men are silent for a moment.

"That's not the first time something like that has happened," says Damon quietly.

"No," says Corin. Damon may not have much of a vocabulary, but he's more thoughtful than he looks. For a moment both men contemplate their own perversities in matters of the heart and how their lives have been shaped by them.

"Silvius is a fool," says Damon at length. Now they are climbing the last hill home. There are no trees on this slope, but the sun is so low that stones and clumps of grass cast shadows of their own. At the top of the hill they rest. They are looking forward to their evening meal.

* * *

A. *Sell when you can?* That's awful!
Q. It's supposed to be delightful and self-deprecating. A woman taking her own sex lightly.
A. It isn't!
Q. No, it isn't.
(*Both are silent for a moment.*)
A. Still...it's a great play.
Q. Oh, of course!
A. I mean, what is, if this isn't?
Q. Exactly.

A. Even Homer nods, I guess.

Q. (*sadly*) Even Homer nods.

SOLILOQUY: DUKE SENIOR

There's a young man in the woods who looks amazingly like Rosalind. I asked him about his parentage, and he said something like, "As good as yours, rest assured of that." Great answer! What an old fogy I am, checking into people's genealogy!

I suppose Ros herself will be showing up one of these days. Orlando keeps hinting that they had some kind of understanding before he left for the forest, and if I know Ros, she'll be coming after him. Well, okay. Good. Great! My Ros and Rowland's boy. I'd like to be consulted, though. Any father would.

No, no, that would be great. Ros and Orlando de Boys. Wonderful!

COMMENTARY

At the time he was writing *As You Like It,* Shakespeare had two daughters: Susanna, seventeen, and Judith, fifteen. Although they were raised by his long-suffering wife in Stratford-upon-Avon while Shakespeare himself spent most of his time in London, he had strong feelings about losing his daughters to younger men. That's normal. Many parents have mixed feelings when their children marry. In Shakespeare's times, however, the normal ambivalence was shadowed by a conflict about women. Are women entitled to choose their own men? Or is that an affront to their fathers' authority? In *Romeo and Juliet,* Capulet has a fit when Juliet refuses to marry the man of his choice. If you're mine, he storms, *I'll give you to my friend. [If] you be not, hang, beg, starve, die in the streets.* Hang, beg, die in the streets? Clearly Capulet has gone nuts. In his raging, out-of-control fathers Shakespeare both gives vent to his possessive anger and sees it for the crazy thing it is.

In the tragedies, the father–daughter conflict is, of course, tragic, and Juliet is famously dead by the end of the play. The comedies, however, depend on the free play of female energy. How are the women to assert their autonomy without humiliating their fathers? In *The Merchant of Venice,* Portia's choice *just so happens* to coincide with the terms of her dead father's will. In *A Midsummer Night's Dream*, the suitor favored by the angry father falls in love with someone else, so Hermia gets her man. In *As You Like It*, Rosalind is free to make her own arrangements because her father is in the forest, and patriarchy itself is on vacation, as it were. On top of that, Orlando's father and Rosalind's were close. The friendship between the dead father and the living one creates a halo of paternal approval around the match. As so often happens in comedy, Shakespeare has it both ways. Duke Senior isn't officially *asked* for permission; but given his feelings for Orlando's father, it's impossible that anything could please him more.

"Rowland's boy," he thinks. "Perfect."

* * *

Orlando is in love.

"Rosalind, *heavenly Rosalind*," he thinks all day long. But unlike most lovers, he does not know whether the person he frequently encounters is or is not the woman he loves. Sometimes it is clear to him that Ganymede is not just playing "Rosalind" but actually *is* Rosalind, which is why he agreed to the kiss. But he has his doubts.

By chance he meets Jacques.

"*Rosalind is your love's name?*" Jacques baits him. "*I do not like [it].*" That's Jacques for you.

"*There was no thought of pleasing you when she was christened,*" Orlando answers promptly. Score one for the nice guy! For the most part, though, he is gracious to a fault.

There is one man in the forest Orlando doesn't like. He has never seen this man up close, but even from a distance he finds him repellent. The man seems oblivious to his lovely surroundings, and when he finds some root or berry to eat he shoves it heedlessly into his mouth. Once Orlando saw him digging in a blind, greedy way.

"Disgusting!" said Orlando to himself as the man ate the food without cleaning it off. In spite of the man's dirty habits, and in spite of his ragged clothes, Orlando can tell that he was a courtier.

"I can't abide him," he tells Adam one afternoon. "Isn't that strange?"

Adam lies in the Duke's own cave on a bed of forest detritus. He isn't well. The lords believe he is dying, and on a recent walk, Amiens has tried to say as much to Orlando. Orlando couldn't hear it. Who will he confide in if Adam dies?

"What was he..." says Adam, but can't go on. Orlando sits by his side, hoping he will catch his breath.

"What was he wearing?" Adam finally says.

"Some kind of yellow cloak," Orlando says. Adam's eyes glitter strangely at the news.

"What?" says Orlando. Adam is pressing his hand. "What is it? Tell me, old man!" But the light fades from Adam's eyes, and he returns to his usual state of semi-consciousness. Orlando looks down at him with helpless love.

"Not today," he prays.

The Duke is whispering to one of his men. The courtier glances at Orlando and nods. Quietly he rounds up some of the others, and they sit down outdoors, plucking at their lute strings as if by chance. Soon they are singing a song, and Orlando comes out to hear it. The song is gay on the surface, but the sorrow of things can be glimpsed in its depths. It is neither the gaiety nor the difficulty in the men's songs that soothes Orlando but the combination of both. It is almost time for him to meet his "Rosalind" again. If it weren't for these lovely songs, the disjunction between his grief and his gladness would be too great for him to bear.

SONG

> Under the greenwood tree
> Who loves to lie with me
> And turn his merry note
> Unto the sweet bird's throat
> Come hither, come hither, come hither.
> Here he shall see no enemy
> But winter and rough weather.

SOLILOQUY: OLIVER

Why am I in the forest? I was supposed to make life miserable for others, not to suffer on my own account. And what an ugly forest it is! The dead branches of the pines stick out at all angles, and whichever way I go one of them impales me. During the day I'm covered in a mixture of sweat, humidity, and dirt. At night I huddle in fear by a bush.

One day Duke Frederick called me in on charges of my behavior toward Orlando. Since when does Duke Frederick care how I treat Orlando? The whole thing is just an excuse to seize my lands, which Fred repeatedly threatened to do. And presumably he will, even if I find Orlando and bring him home. Really, I'm beyond plot. All I know is that Duke Frederick turns out to be a bigger bad guy than I am, so here I am in exile, grubbing for roots and growing a beard.

Never mind. *My soul,* I once said, *hates nothing more than* Orlando. Hating Orlando is my vocation, you might say. Here I am in this dank cave, my scrawny arms around my knees, and all I think about is him. I'm obsessed. I do want to find him, but not so he can clear my name, just to hate him some more. Today I found some lines of his on a scrap of paper. *All the pictures fairest lined are but black to Rosalind.* What does he get out of writing that stuff down? No one gets anything out of reading it, that's for sure.

* * *

A. That Oliver!
Q. So *baaaad!*
A. Why does he hate Orlando so much? Sibling rivalry gone nuts?
Q. It's…a joke.
A. He's so overdone.
Q. Slapped into place, you might say.
A. What's the point?
Q. *As you like it!*
A. Huh?
Q. "You"–that's us–need a bad guy. Voilà! Here he is!
A. Why do we need a bad guy, again?
Q. So he can get the good guy in trouble; so the good guys can prevail; so we can have a story, a plot, a play!
A. If you say so.
Q. *If you like it, so.*
A. Huh?

Q. That's in Lodge's preface to *Rosalynd;* addressed to his "gentlemen readers."

A. The gentlemen get the joke?

Q. Yes, they do.

A. I don't.

Q. You will.

* * *

In a secret place in the forest is a bank of mosses, so green in its depths it seems almost black. The mosses are blooming, if that's what mosses do, their exquisite thread-like stalks holding tiny spore capsules at their tips. The mini-forest of stalks catches the light through the trees, and shifting spots are briefly illuminated.

Celia approaches the mosses on a path, swinging a switch in irritation. There is some satisfaction in decapitating the weeds underfoot, but when she finds herself switching at the lovely mosses, she stops for a moment of self-examination.

"What's wrong with me today?" she wonders.

What's wrong is that both her companions, Rosalind and Touchstone, are busy with their own concerns, and Celia is lonely. Rosalind is out from morning to night messing with Orlando, and now Touchstone has found someone to dally with, too. As far as Celia can tell, Audrey, Touchstone's girlfriend, has nothing to recommend her. She's not attractive, and, according to Touchstone, she's downright stupid. Touchstone plans to marry her.

"Excuse me?" said Celia incredulously when he told her.

"I'll get that fellow Mar-text to do the job," Touchstone said happily. "Mar-text, get it? He'll mangle the ceremony, and then if I don't like her afterwards I can say he didn't really do the job."

Celia said, "Whatever next." Apparently you can find anyone you need in the forest. Touchstone has found first Audrey and now this Mar-text. Who the hell is he?

"This is so you can sleep with her?" Celia asked Touchstone.

"Yes," said Touchstone primly. "Otherwise we'd be living in *bawdry.*"

"I see," said Celia. Audrey was engaged to some fellow named William until Touchstone came along. Celia thinks the whole thing is unfair, no matter how stupid Audrey is.

"But mostly," she thinks, "I wish someone would show up for me." Her mind drifts to Mar-text. Maybe he'd do.

"Oh, forget it," she thinks. Herself with Mar-text would be as bad as Touchstone with Audrey.

"I want someone *appropriate*," thinks Celia. She feels jealous of Ros, who will obviously soon marry Orlando, the youngest son of Sir Rowland de Boys. Celia wants someone like that.

It is dinnertime, but the others won't be there, so she doesn't feel like going home. The sun is gone now, and the moss stalks are dim. Celia scratches her leg. She feels bored.

* * *

Orlando is hurrying through the forest, anxious to be on time for his date with "Rosalind."

"If it isn't Rosalind," he thinks, "this is at least good practice." He is smiling, thinking of the way Ganymede/Rosalind seizes upon the slightest infraction of the rules to accuse him of infidelity.

"I'm not unfaithful, I'm just late," he protested last time.

"It's a slippery slope," scolded "Rosalind." He was enchanted.

"I suppose I'll get tired of this some day," he thinks, but he certainly isn't yet.

Just then Orlando steps into a grove where the ragged lord is sound asleep. His mouth has fallen open, and he is sweating in the sunshine. Simultaneously Orlando realizes two terrible things. First of all, a *green and gilded snake [has] wreathed itself* around the sleeper's neck and is threatening his open mouth; and secondly, the ragged lord is none other than Orlando's eldest brother, Oliver de Boys. Orlando flashes back to Adam's mute, piercing look.

"Adam knew!" exclaims Orlando to himself. "It's Oliver!" The snake is surprised and irritated by Orlando's arrival. He unwinds himself from Oliver's neck and slithers off *with indented glides.* Oliver sighs and rolls over, dreaming of killing Orlando. When he moves, a lion springs from the bushes. She has been waiting to see if Oliver is dead or alive, *for [it is] the royal disposition of that beast to prey on nothing that doth seem as dead.* Oliver wakes up in horror. His eyes go straight across the grove to his brother's.

"Orlando!" he shouts. "Help me!" Orlando scrabbles at the bushes, falling, trying to escape. Where is the snake? If he steps on it, he'll die.

"Orlando!" shouts Oliver again. Orlando, upright, pauses at his voice. He doesn't love his awful sibling. Moreover, he has only a short dagger with him, so if he tangles with the lion he might lose. Now he hears a crashing as the lion fights its prey. Orlando turns. He has no sensation of making a decision, but his hand, unbidden, goes for the dagger at his side.

"Fuck!" he cries when he sees what he is doing. "Damn, damn, damn!" And he hurls himself across the grove.

* * *

A. Does this count as one of the times Orlando hurts someone?

Q. Yes.

A. But he gets hurt, too.

Q. Yes.

A. Whereas Oliver, who was being mauled by the lion until Orlando saved him, comes out unscathed.

Q. Don't think too much about it.

A. Or *anything* at this point!

Q. Yes.

* * *

It never rains, but it pours. When Orlando gets Oliver back to the Duke's cave, the Duke's men are looking for him anxiously. Adam is dying, and Orlando must be found to say goodbye.

"I'll get Oliver some food," says Amiens when he finds them. There is no time to be surprised at Oliver's presence, situation, or disgraceful appearance. "You go right in."

"I need to wash," says Oliver. Someone leads him to the stream while Orlando goes to Adam.

Adam is even stiller and more insubstantial than when we saw him last. He is really dying now.

"Oliver..." he tells Orlando with great effort.

"Yes, yes, it was Oliver," cries Orlando emphatically and launches into his story.

"At first I thought I wouldn't save him," he says, racing, "but then I did. I knew who it was. That's what you were trying to tell me, right, old man? I knew it when I saw him."

Adam can't hear what Orlando is saying. He is floating somewhere else, weightless and serene. From time to time he opens his eyes, and a look of anguish comes over him.

"It's okay!" insists Orlando when this happens. "I saved him!" Tears of frustration spring to his eyes.

Now there is a rustling sound, and Oliver comes in. He is wearing a clean huntsman's outfit, brown and green, and his beard has been trimmed with a careful sword. The clothes don't exactly fit, but they're close enough.

"Is he awake?" whispers Oliver.

"I don't know," says Orlando unhappily.

"How will we know when he's dead?"

"How should I know?" says Orlando irritably. Outside the men keep watch. When Adam opens his eyes at last, both brothers scramble to their feet, and Adam has to raise his eyes to see them. To their surprise, he speaks.

"Ah," he says clearly. "The two of you." Orlando quickly puts his arm around his brother.

"Yes," he says, "the two of us!" He looks emphatically at Oliver to prompt him to do likewise, but Oliver is paralyzed by a sudden memory. Once he called Adam *"old dog"* and kicked him away.

"Most true," Adam had answered gently. *"I have lost my teeth in your service."* At that a huge wave of remorse lifts Oliver from his predicament. It raises him from the depths and lands him on dry land, with others of his kind. Dizzy from the journey, he looks at Orlando in amazement.

"My brother!" he wonderingly thinks. Orlando can have everything: the land, the house, the silver plate. Orlando looks back, startled by the change.

"The two of us!" cries Oliver, hugging Orlando to his side. "The two of us!" Adam almost smiles.

"Good," he says before closing his eyes. The two men feel a crazy hope that Oliver's conversion will prolong Adam's life, but it doesn't. Adam drifts off so far they think he's really gone, but then he mumbles something.

"What?" says Orlando, bending down. "What did you say, old man?"

"Take care of each other," says Adam, dying.

"We will," they fervently swear. "We will." They don't need anyone to tell them now that Adam is dead.

* * *

Orlando and Oliver sit down and talk. The cave is dim, but dry and cool. No one interrupts them. The angle of the light coming into the cave changes as the day goes on.

Orlando and Oliver talk without premeditation and without inhibition. They say things they didn't know were there at all to be said; they tell each other everything. They don't mention Adam, but they know they wouldn't be talking like this if it weren't for his life and death. On the other hand, their conversation does not strike them as in any way unusual. It seems the most ordinary possible way to communicate with another person.

Eventually Orlando realizes that he is bleeding again from his wound. The towel it is wrapped in is red. Just then he remembers "Ganymede."

"Rosalind!" he says. He's supposed to meet "her" right now. But he's feeling woozy from loss of blood and isn't sure he can go. In any case, he is late.

"I'll go," says Oliver. "You lie down. I'll show her the towel and explain." Orlando has to agree, and Oliver leaves to find "Ganymede."

* * *

Rosalind and Celia are lounging in the yard, waiting for Orlando. Touchstone and Audrey are giggling on the bench.

"He's late," frets Ros. Celia lies on her back, watching the sky. She knows she should say something witty, or at least offer a cue for Rosalind's wit, but she can't be bothered. A wisp of vapor trailing from a cloud's lower edge slowly turns to air.

"He'll be here," says Celia languidly. Corin sits in a chair tipped back against the house.

"Here's Silvius," says Corin. Silvius nods in greeting.

"This is from Phebe," says Silvius, handing a letter to Ros. Ros reads the letter, but she's genuinely anxious about Orlando and can't think of much else.

"This is a man's handwriting," she finally says. "Phebe couldn't have written it. Did you write it yourself?"

"Not at all," protests Silvius. This goes nowhere. They get into a silly quarrel about Phebe's *hand*, or handwriting.

"*She has a leathern hand, a freestone-colored hand,*" says Rosalind, taking it to the literal level. "*She has a housewife's hands.*"

"She does not!" cries Silvius. Without meaning to, Ros has hit on the very thing to wound him most, a critique of Phebe's hands.

Now Jacques arrives to question Touchstone.

"*Will you be married, motley?*" he asks. He intends to tease Touchstone about Audrey's stupidity and doesn't mind doing so in front of Audrey herself. If she's that stupid, she won't understand the witty repartee.

Touchstone sidesteps Jacques with a comment on marriage in general.

"*As the ox hath his bow, sir, the horse his curb, and the falcon her bells, so man hath his desires,*" declares Touchstone, "*and as pigeons bill, so wedlock would be nibbling.*"

"*So man hath his desires…*" repeats Jacques, amazed. Truly, he can do no better than this. Touchstone is modestly pleased to have out-done Jacques.

Audrey is not as stupid as she looks. Her hair hangs lankly on her forehead, but her features aren't bad, and she grasps quite a lot. She understands that *wedlock*, as Touchstone has weirdly and sublimely said, is both a constraint on desire and a liberation of it; but she also understands that in her case it is a force for social mobility. She would like to get out of the forest, meet interesting people, and move up in the world. Sooner or later the aristocrats will go back to court, and when they do, Touchstone's fiancée, alone of the pastoral characters, intends to go with them.

"Nibbling!" she giggles, poking Touchstone in the ribs. Touchstone blushes. He has indeed nibbled on selected parts of Audrey's person in the past few weeks, but that doesn't mean he wants everyone to know about it.

"Touchstone!" teases Celia. The afternoon goes on in a desultory way except for Ros, who is more and more anxious about Orlando. Either he is blowing her off or he's hurt.

"He's never been so late," she whispers to Celia, who admits it's a first.

Now a stranger arrives. He is wearing brown pants and a green shirt, and over his arm is a bloodstained towel.

"*Good morrow, fair ones,*" he says courteously to Celia and Ros. "Are you the owners of this house?" Celia sits up. Something interesting is happening.

"What can we offer you?" she asks, brushing off her skirt. "Something to drink?" Ros waves her off.

"Do you know where Orlando is?" she demands.

"Indeed I do," he says, and tells the tale. Halfway through Celia guesses who he is.

"Oliver!" she thinks. This could work. Someone from her own social world; aristocratic, wealthy. But does she really want a man who tried to kill his brother?

"*Was't you that did so oft contrive to kill him?*" she asks.

"*'Twas I,*" he answers, shaking his head. "*But 'tis not I.*" In other words, he's reformed. He tells them how *sweet* he finds his *conversion*, and Celia is glad to hear it. Ros, on the other hand, could care less.

"Where's Orlando?" she keeps asking. When Oliver shows her the blood-soaked towel she promptly faints.

"*Why how now, Ganymede,*" cries Celia, "*sweet Ganymede!*" When Ros comes to, she has had enough of "Ganymede" and the whole charade.

"*I would I were at home,*" she says sincerely. Soon, however, she recovers and goes back to her joke. Accused of unmanly behavior, she claims she only fainted as part of her female impersonation, and Oliver is instructed to tell Orlando all about it.

"*I pray you commend my counterfeiting to him,*" calls Ros.

"I will," he calls back. "I will!" Soon he is back in the forest, the trees going by in a blur.

"That Celia," he thinks. "Very pretty." A chickadee flies to a nearby branch. He is hoping for a handout, but Oliver doesn't pause.

"Oh, well," thinks the chickadee. In the forest of Arden there is more than enough for the birds to eat.

At this point there is a lot of business Shakespeare must take care of very quickly. He has been here before. The unions and reunions that end his comedies generally do come thick and fast, straining credulity.

"As if I *couldn't* make things seem plausible if I wanted to," laughs Shakespeare – the all-time master of plausibility. His improbabilities are not a mistake but part of the point. The happy endings of the comedies actually are happy; but they also laugh up their sleeves at the very idea of both happiness and endings.

What remains to be done in *As You Like It*? Celia, of course, must be paired with the reformed Oliver; the Duke must be reunited with his daughter, who must reveal herself as such; Phebe must agree to marry Silvius; and so on. Then they can all go home.

Go home? What about Duke Frederick? Won't he murder them all if they go home?

He can convert. We already have one conversion? So what, now we'll have two! Enter Jacques, not Jacques the philosopher this time, but Jacques the middle brother. Let's have two Jacqueses, too!

"*I am the second son of old Sir Rowland,*" announces Jacques II. He also announces that Duke Frederick has found God and intends to live henceforth as a hermit in the woods. So much for Duke Fred. The rest can be accomplished with equal dispatch.

Now Orlando and "Ganymede" are marveling at the speed with which Celia and Oliver have come to terms. They *no sooner met but they looked; no sooner looked but they loved; no sooner loved but they sighed;* and so forth. Orlando is jealous of his brother's success.

"Just pretend I'm Rosalind," says "Ganymede" for the umpteenth time.

"*I can live no longer by thinking,*" cries Orlando, fed up at last with the game. This seems to be what "Ganymede" has been waiting for. S/he tells everyone to show up the next day at the Duke's where s/he will resolve all their problems.

"At which time," s/he tells Phebe, "I'll marry you if you still want. Otherwise… " and she gestures at Silvius. Phebe eagerly agrees. When Ros reveals herself, Phebe's out of luck; but everyone else, starting with Orlando, is delighted. Rosalind and Orlando; Celia and Oliver; Silvius and Phebe; Touchstone and Audrey. Not a bad haul for one play. Finally the God of Marriage makes a hasty appearance. *"Here's eight that must take hands to join in Hymen's bands,"* he sings. This is not great verse, but presumably the scene can be choreographed to create a sense of festivity. There can be laughter, dancing, throwing of confetti, or what have you. It is not necessary to work this out. The obligatory hoopla can take care of itself.

I have nothing against happy endings in general; or, God forbid, this one in particular. I don't want to see the marriages devolve, as Ros has promised they will; I don't want unhappiness or irony. But…just for a change…maybe something more reserved? Less emphatic. More modest. Isn't that our style these days?

Something says, Come see.

Will you come with me?

* * *

Corin now owns the stone house. The city people gave it to him when they left, along with the money to buy his own flock. Just now, however, the sheep in his yard are not his own but Phebe's. Silvius's. Phebe and Silvius's. Phebe is supposed to have taken them to pasture, but she needed Corin's advice and came here instead.

"I can't get over Ganymede," she says miserably. Her sheep nibble at the remains of the perennial border Rosalind and Celia have left, and they bother Corin as he grinds his new sheep-shearing tools. One tries repeatedly to climb on Phebe's lap.

"Hand me that cutter, will you?" says Corin. He doesn't know whether or not to credit Phebe's account of herself. He has seen her with Silvius several times since they got married, and she always seemed cheerful enough. Once as he approached he saw her remove her husband's hat with unmistakably wifely embarrassment.

"I thought you and Silvius liked each other now," says Corin, grinding. "Silvius always seems pleased as punch."

"Maybe he is," cries Phebe, "but I'm not!" She throws herself back on her chair, shoving off the persistent lamb. "Ganymede" has vanished with the announcement that "he" never existed in the first place, and her mental life is a landscape from which the central feature has been deleted.

One of Phebe's sheep is on the skirting table, and Corin gives it a push. Phebe has been here all afternoon, and Corin wishes she would go. He has the uncharitable thought that when it comes to imposing on other people's patience, Phebe and Silvius are well matched. Now Phebe has a bombshell to drop. She knew all along, she tells Corin, that "Ganymede" was a woman.

"No, you didn't," says Corin shortly.

"I did," insists Phebe. Now Phebe thinks she's bi. She is sitting tensely upright, her dress frothing over her chair. When Corin glances up at her, she meets his appraising eye.

"What do I know," he thinks. "But if you're bi, you should wear something else!" It is not just the dress, but the pinafore on top that strikes him as inappropriate. In the fading light its color is more bluestone gray than blue.

Q and A are excited by the return to the topic of homoeroticism. They can't agree on whether, as one critic has said, Phebe's crush on "Ganymede" is truly "femme–femme love," as one critic has called it, but they do agree that Shakespeare can't be serious about androgyny, since Ros is all-girl at the end of the play.

"I mean, she faints at the sight of blood," says A. "What more could you ask?" Corin cannot hear Q and A, but beyond Phebe's unhappy, unstoppable voice, he does hear a hermit thrush start singing.

"Oh, holy, holy, holy," sings the hermit thrush; "ah, purity, purity, purity." The voice of the hermit thrush has been called "flute-like" and "crystal-toned." Because of this, and because it is rarely seen, it often stirs its listeners to longing. Meanwhile, at court, Celia gathers fruit from espaliered trees along a wall. As she nips off a shoot to train the tree, she is thinking of the forest, where the trees grow tall without human assistance.

"Here or there," she thinks, caught in dreams. She'd like to be in both places, not alternately but at once. Tiny gray mist pearls form on the leaves and twigs of the espaliered trees.

"Oh well," thinks Corin, letting go. He understands that Phebe is not just self-absorbed but really sad.

"She's not alone," he reflects. "We all make our loved ones up." He thinks of a barmaid in town who looks at him directly when she puts down his drink. Perhaps he will go into town this evening to see her.

"Go on," he tells Phebe, sitting down near her. Phebe instantly feels the change. Two of her sheep doze off, their spindly legs folded beneath them.

"Eeh, sweetly, sweetly, sweetly," concludes the hermit thrush, and soon Phebe, too, comes to a stopping place. The song of the hermit thrush is like "a theme with variations in different keys and has invited comparisons to human musical compositions."

THAT WAS THEN

Of course I had predicted that Orlando and I would split, but I didn't really mean it at the time. *Men are April when they woo, December when they wed,* I told him during our courtship. This had the desired effect of stimulating Orlando to further protestations. Not me, he passionately swore, believe me, I'll love you forever. Reader, he didn't. And now he's gone off with Little Bo Peep.

"If she's a shepherdess," said Celia, "I'm Marie Antoinette."

"Celia!" I said, laughing, but trying to be stern. "Marie Antoinette was later!"

"By about a hundred and eighty years," agreed Celia, smoothing her skirt. "And change." True. *As You Like It,* 1599; Marie's theme-park farm, 1783. But Celia's joke got me thinking how you could mix things up and get away with it. After Orlando left I didn't have the heart anymore for the tra-la-la of comedy, but I didn't want to, like, *die,* like Desdemona and Cleopatra, and so forth, so I didn't want to be in a tragedy, either. I thought a history play might be a nice middle ground. So one day I whispered fervently, "I don't like it anymore," and the whole world around me, shepherds, meadows, forest and all, began to sag. I repeated, "I don't like it anymore," and the forest crumpled into broken lines of print, like computer-generated art. By the third time I said, "I don't like it anymore," I was somewhere else.

"What's this?" I wondered, slightly dazed. I was in *Henry IV, Part One,* as I soon understood. Goodbye contented and discontented shepherds; hello kings and counselors, treaties and plots. People were beside themselves with anger and ambition. Once I spoke up, however, I got lots of attention, dating all three of the principal men: King Henry himself; his oldest son, Hal; and the fiery would-be usurper Hotspur, scourge of the North. Henry was a nicer guy than you'd think, but he was a good twenty years older than I, and soon I left him for Hal. The king felt it keenly for a while, but then it got to be summer, and the Scottish marches were in revolt. He felt better when he'd put them down.

Everyone thought Hal and I would be a perfect match, but we weren't. Yes, we laughed a lot; but something was missing.

"That's enough irony now," I told him once. All these guys could take seriously, and that only in a pinch, was their fathers.

"How about directing a little sincerity toward *me*," I complained. Finally I threw a bottle of sherry at him, after which things went quickly south. He cleaned up the wine and swept the broken glass neatly into a dustpan; then we had humiliating make-up sex, and in the morning I left for good.

You know who I loved from that play? Hotspur. That guy was seriously fun. He had no perspective whatsoever, no irony, nothing to cloud his pure, deep blue conviction that this was It, I was It, this was Real. He was like that about everything, of course; totally into his role. He and *his* dad were starting a war against Henry.

"But you supported him for king against Richard," I protested. Richard had been the prior occupant of the British throne, corrupt but legitimate.

"That was different," glowered Hotspur. Or, that was then, or whatever.

"Okay, then," I said. I was having too much fun to complain. At first I used to tease him the way I did Orlando, but then I stopped. If I mocked and teased either he wouldn't get it or he'd be hurt and mad. Orlando had been so mild and imperturbable that it never occurred to me someone could take things so hard. I wanted to say, "But this is my great role, being in love but having a sense of humor about it; everyone loves it, why don't you?" When I saw that he really didn't, however, I stopped joking and pretended I, too, was convinced about Us—which I almost partly was. Soon after that, of course, Hotspur decided he needed to go back to Kate. He and his father were running her brother Mortimer for king, so breaking up with her had never been in the cards.

"What's this about?" I asked him once. "You people are *already* fabulously rich and well connected. How will you be better off with

Mortimer as king?" Hotspur was offended, of course. Rich and well connected? That had *nothing to do with it*. It was a matter of Honor.

"Honor?" I said dubiously.

"Honor!" he said vehemently.

"Okay," I said quickly. "Honor." Does everyone remember Hotspur's famous line on this subject? No? Here it is:

By heaven, he swears, early in the play, *methinks it were an easy leap to pluck bright honor from the pale-faced moon—or dive into the bottom of the deep…and pluck up drowned honor by the locks!*

That's a great, impassioned, half-silly line, full of Hotspur's fire and dash; but what I like best is its reference to "honor's" hair, or *locks*. It reminds me of the way, when aroused, he would gather my hair in one of his hands and kiss me, yanking hard. Only Hotspur—Henry Percy of Northumberland—could pull that off. Sometimes when we were in bed, when we'd already made love enough and thought to stop and either get up because it was morning or go to sleep because it was night, sometimes I'd kiss him…just for fun…or maybe it *wasn't* exactly for fun, maybe I wanted more.

"What the fuck have you done," he'd soon say roughly, shoving my hand to his groin. "What the fuck have you done?" Well, let me tell you how things stand now. I've changed plays again. It's a little elegiac here, but still fun. It's fine. But if I could go back, if I could check in from time to time with one thing from the past, that would be it. Hotspur and I would be in bed, and Hotspur would be twisting my hair and kissing me hard.

"What the fuck have you done?" he'd be saying in my ear. "What the fuck have you done?"

CLEOPATRA AND ANTONY

In the beginning Cleopatra and Antony are quarreling.

Listen to the news from Rome, urges Cleopatra, but Antony says no. The messengers from Rome shift from foot to foot.

Hear them, Antony, Cleopatra insists. This is odd, since what she really wants is for Antony to stay in Egypt, and the news from Rome may require him to leave.

Who knows, she says ironically, maybe *Fulvia* is angry with you.

How, my love? says Antony, frowning.

Fulvia, says Cleopatra, not kindly. You know, your wife. Or perhaps that *child*, Octavian, has some *errand* he'd like you to run. Octavian Caesar is Antony's much younger partner. Together they avenged the death of Julius Caesar and took over the world some years ago. It's galling for Antony to share power with someone so young, but Octavian is the old Caesar's heir, so there's nothing to be done about it. *The scarce-bearded Caesar*, Cleopatra sneeringly calls him. Antony is rattled without knowing why.

Let Rome in Tiber melt! he cries to cut things off. I could care less about the news from Rome!

Really? says Cleopatra.

Really! says Antony. He sweeps an arm at the messengers. Scram! he tells them. *Speak not to us!*

Yes! thinks Cleopatra, mentally punching the air with her fist. The messengers bow and leave, their faces frozen into expressions of a deference they do not feel. They do not approve of Antony's romantic sojourn in Egypt, and neither do their superiors.

Now what, sweetheart? inquires Antony, feeling lighthearted. I'm at your disposal. One thing the lovers like to do is to dress down and wander in the streets, observing *the qualities of people.*

Last night you did desire it, he reminds Cleopatra. I did? thinks Cleopatra. But strolling the streets will be fine. Anything's fine that doesn't involve the messengers from Rome.

Sounds good, she agrees.

Okay, then, says cheerful Antony. Let's go!

So they do.

EVENING WALK

The streets of Alexandria were well worth wandering in the first century B.C.E., being crowded, colorful, and varied. There were Jewish merchants, Phoenician traders, Egyptian priests, and Greek courtiers. The whole town bordered the sea. Later in the play there are hints that the pleasures of Egypt may be excessive or even disgusting, involving too much eating, drinking, and getting laid; but at this point they are innocence itself. I myself love an unplanned walk, preferably with someone I'm close to. Faces and gestures flick by as in a movie; I love to share impressions or keep them to myself.

"Oh, a wedding," I said to my companion once. The city we were strolling was a mishmash of cultures, like Alexandria; the couple could have been Cuban, Puerto Rican, Guatemalan, Chilean, or some combination of which we had no idea. Palm fronds waved above the guests as they poured out of the church, blocking our route. We didn't say out loud that this was the point of our walk, but each knew the other knew it, too.

Good luck, good luck, we mutely wished the stocky, strapless bride and her groom. Antony and Cleopatra, as everyone knows, run out of luck in the end. But this is the beginning of the story, not the end; and so far the famous couple is troubled by nothing more than a minor disagreement.

Come, my queen, says Antony, sweeping her off the stage. For the rest of the night they will be both actors and spectators in a world that is less dramatic but no less satisfying than Shakespeare's. While his relies on marriages, murder, and mayhem, theirs needs nothing more than *the qualities of people* to hold their attention. *Exeunt,* followed by their train.

Good for Antony and Cleopatra! And phooey on the news from Rome!

PUSSY-WHIPPED

DEMETRIUS: Which is to say…phooey on *us*!

PHILO: The messengers!

DEMETRIUS: Yet we're the real beginning of the play.

PHILO: Standing around before the leads come out…

DEMETRIUS: …cluck-clucking over Antony.

PHILO: He's gone soft, we say.

DEMETRIUS: Down here in Egypt.

PHILO: Lost his punch.

DEMETRIUS: (*shaking his head*) *Sometimes when he is not Antony* he lacks the properties that ought to go with being Antony.

PHILO: He ought to have his mind on business. Reorganize the Eastern kingdoms.

DEMETRIUS: Fight the Parthians, take Caesar's back. Instead he's, like, Boy toy-in-Chief.

PHILO: (*getting carried away*) Pussy-whipped!

DEMETRIUS: (*coolly, as if offended*) I don't believe we have that term yet.

PHILO: *Strumpet's fool,* then. Is that Shakespearean enough for you?

DEMETRIUS: Indeed. But she's not a *gypsy,* you know.

PHILO: Did I ever say she was?

DEMETRIUS: Yes.

PHILO: (*remembering*) Oh, yeah. But…that's what they called Egyptians back then.

DEMETRIUS: Cleopatra isn't Egyptian!

PHILO: Excuse me? She's the queen of Egypt, Dee!

DEMETRIUS: She's Greek.

PHILO: No.

DEMETRIUS: Yes. The Ptolemies were a foreign dynasty. They liked to dress up as Egyptian gods for ceremonial occasions, but otherwise they didn't mix much with the locals…and they certainly didn't marry them.

PHILO: Well, whatever. The point is, Antony shouldn't mix so much with *her.*

DEMETRIUS: You got that right.

PHILO: She's bad news.

DEMETRIUS: Or something.

EGYPT, GREECE, AND ROME

In the first century B.C.E. Greece made Rome nervous. Its military and political power was long in the past, but its culture, even in its late, Hellenistic form, was clearly superior to Rome's. To assuage their cultural anxiety, Romans lost no opportunity to badmouth the inheritors of Periclean Athens. Cicero, for instance, coined the term "Graeculus," which means "Greekling" or "dirty little Greek." Antony's romantic involvement with a Hellenistic queen was a boon for Octavian when their partnership dissolved. By appealing to Roman anti-Hellenism, Octavian's spinmeisters were able to alienate many of Antony's supporters.

Shortly after Antony's death, Virgil writes in praise of Rome. Although the Greeks might be better at artistic or intellectual endeavors, *yours, my Romans,* he writes, *is the gift of government.* What does he mean by *government?* Passing legislation? Building roads? The Romans certainly excelled at these things, but Virgil has something else in mind. For his speaker, "to govern" means *utterly to crush the intransigent,* showing mercy only to *the conquered.*

Utterly to crush the intransigent?!? If that was Rome's *bent,* as Virgil calls it, no wonder so many nations scrambled to stay on its good side, kowtowing or seducing to avoid being crushed. For many years Egypt was Rome's best client state, dutifully sending tons of wheat and raising armies to fight Rome's wars. Then, as now, the governments of client states had their way with their local populations as long as they minded their p's and q's with You Know Who, which the Ptolemies certainly did. When a high Roman official came to visit in 112 B.C.E., for instance, Cleopatra's great-grandfather wished to show him consummate respect.

And give him a view of the sacred crocodiles at their feeding time, Ptolemy VII's prime minister admonished a provincial potentate. This more-or-less charming injunction, written on a piece of papyrus, has survived to this day. From these and other documents we may conclude that Egypt itself had a kind of mistress status with respect to Rome. It was a valuable source of support, but it knew its place. Does Cleopatra, who goes by Egypt's name, know hers?

LEAVING EGYPT

Antony must have changed his mind, because now he is deep in conversation with the very messengers he formerly dismissed. Of course the news is bad. It seems that Fulvia, presumably enraged at Antony, has started a couple of wars, one with her husband's brother Lucas and one with his partner. While Antony has been relaxing in Egypt, moreover, the Parthians have successfully invaded Syria and parts of Turkey, territories that should be Rome's. It is Antony's job to keep the Parthians in line, and he feels deeply ashamed.

These strong Egyptian fetters I must break, he mutters to himself, *or lose myself in dotage.*

And PS, your wife is dead, says another messenger, arriving just behind the others.

What??

It's all here in a letter, says the messenger. She died in Sicyon. Antony is shaken, not just by Fulvia's death but by the sudden grief he feels on learning she is gone. His friend Enobarbus can't grasp the news.

Sir? he says when Antony tells him.

Fulvia is dead, repeats Antony.

Fulvia? says Enobarbus incredulously.

Dead, repeats Antony. He is baffled, as he often is, by his own instability of purpose and emotion. *The hand could pluck her back that shoved her on,* he wonderingly says. As a Roman he should be steady under all conditions; as a man he wants a core he can call himself. Who is he if he loves and hates by turns? That question underlies the play as a whole.

Now Antony must go; but first he must tell Cleopatra. He finds her in the palace and bravely begins.

Most sweet queen, he says, but she interrupts.

Sweet queen, my ass, she says. The time for the sweet queen stuff was when you wanted to stay, not now that you want to go. *Eternity was in our lips and eyes!* Did you mean all that or were you just full of shit? If you're leaving, you jerk, just *bid farewell and go!*

No, no, pleads Antony. Listen up. Fulvia is dead.

Cleopatra stops in her tracks.

What? she says. I don't understand. *Can Fulvia die?* This is partly a genuine expression of wonder and partly a (really funny) joke on herself. Cleopatra is nothing if not entertaining; and now she rallies to entertain both Antony and us with more taunts and threats. Can she undermine his resolve, as she did earlier?

No, she can't.

Stop now, he says strongly when he's had enough. I'm going, and that's it.

I see, says Cleopatra. But who can say if he'll come back? Fulvia may be dead, but there are more women in Rome than Fulvia, and they tend to fall for handsome Antony, married or not.

Not that Rome is the only place with willing women! thinks Cleopatra. Does anybody seriously think that Antony refrains on campaigns? Not to mention the fact that he himself could *die* in godforsaken Parthia, or wherever he goes for the glory of Rome. Or drown on the passage home, or back; or anything. It's scary.

Courteous lord, she pleads, suddenly sincere, *one word.*

What? says Antony, impatient.

Sir, you and I must part, she tries, *but that's not it.* Cleopatra, the great ventriloquist of her own personality, is for once at a loss. *Sir, you and I have loved…but there's not it.* What is it that lovers want from one another at the moment of parting? Blessings? Reassurance? Some wafer on the tongue to carry back to their uncertain lives apart?

"Take care, be good, I love you," a famous parrot is said to have told his trainer the night before dying. "See you in the morning." Perhaps that's all there is to say.

Something it is I would—she tries; but then she gives up. *Oh, my oblivion is a very Antony,* she laments, *and I am all forgotten!* Here, for once, Cleopatra means what she cannot say. With an effort, she lets go.

Upon your sword sit laurel victory, and smooth success be strewed before your feet! she concludes. That is…since you're going, good luck! A parrot could say that, but Antony has no taste right now for what only Cleopatra can say.

Fine, he says; I'm outta here. *Away!* Goodbye Egypt, goodbye Cleopatra. Antony's mind is already in Rome.

ENOBARBUS

If anyone rivals Cleopatra as an entertainer, it's Enobarbus. He is a gifted ironist, a foil to the sincere, often-stumbling Antony. When he understands that Fulvia is really dead, he comforts his boss with an inspired riff.

Why, sir, he cries, *give the gods a thankful sacrifice. If there were no more women but Fulvia, then had you indeed a cut, and the case to be lamented; [but] this grief is crowned with consolation: your old smock brings forth a new petticoat, and indeed the tears live in an onion that should water this sorrow.*

Cleopatra as Antony's new petticoat! Tears that live in an onion! In a play full of idealizations (of love, honor, war) Enobarbus is the reader's best friend as well as Antony's. Without him we might take his boss as seriously as Antony takes himself.

SOLILOQUY: OCTAVIAN (IN ROME)

Where the hell is Antony? The veterans from the last war still haven't been paid; the landowners we evicted are enraged; our enemies are flocking to Sextus Pompeius. On top of which, unbelievably, I had to fight a war with Antony's freakin' wife! *Let us grant, it's not amiss to tumble on the bed of Ptolemy;* but only in your spare time, buddy; only in your spare time! Have his brains gone soft from the heat? How much better is Cleopatra than your basic Livia or Salvia or Tertulla? God help me, but I want him to be Antony again; the Antony of Philippi, for example, a battle for which he's still so loved by one and all that I can't lift a finger against him. Let him pull himself together or step the fuck aside!

Fat chance of that, of course. If I want him gone, I'll have to kill him myself, beside which this last little war will look like a walk in the park. For the love of God, pal, pull your share of the load! He was supposed to be raising money in Egypt for a Parthian campaign. Anybody seen any signs of a Parthian campaign? Unless you count the incursions *they've* made against *us.* Antony, get your butt home from Egypt and let me hear from you right quick!

Unlike Octavian, I'm in no rush to get Antony home. In fact, I've returned in my thoughts to the evening walk, a retrogression in terms of plot. The French have a word for someone who wanders the streets, observing: it's *flâneur*. The *flâneur* is not lost, but he has no particular destination, either, and no requirements for what he'll see along the way.

Where might the lovers have gone? An artist's rendering of the ancient city shows a broad, red road with monumental buildings on either side. One would have been the world-famous Library of Alexandria with its thousands of papyri; another might have been the zoo. The Royal Greek Quarter, reserved for the ruling elite, was a fantasyland of palaces, arcades, fountains, and gardens, all with a view of the sea. But *flâneurs* need anonymity, so Antony and Cleopatra must have headed somewhere else. Possibly they walked in the Jews' quarter, near the Gate of the Sun; or perhaps they went to the native Egyptian quarter on the other side of town. The Rhacotis District, as it was called, was poor and left no traces in marble or bronze; but perhaps it housed the warehouses and workshops for the Ptolemaic monopolies of papyrus, wool, salt, cloth, scent, and oil. Perhaps it was noisy and busy, like the immigrants' Lower East Side. Did people holler out of windows, cook food on the street? We'll never know. I do, however, have a mental image of the native quarter of Alexandria twenty centuries later, when E. M. Forster was there. In a photo I've seen from that time the buildings are covered in crumbling stucco; awkward add-ons and cantilevered rooms try to maximize their occupants' access to light. Some bentwood chairs on either side of a café table bring a little current of Parisian or Viennese chic to the local scene. Under the picture a quotation from Forster praises the quarter for its *gentle charm, especially at evening. The best way of seeing it,* he adds, *is to wander aimlessly about.*

Where were we before this detour? On the verge of meeting Caesar. Back we go to Rome. Antony and Octavian are on terrible terms, so the atmosphere is highly charged.

Will Antony make nice? someone nervously asks Enobarbus before the meeting. Please *entreat your captain to soft and gentle speech.*

No way! says Enobarbus loudly. I hope he lets Caesar have it!

Enter the Great Ones, with more generals and aides.

Welcome to Rome, says Octavian coolly.

Thank you, says Antony. Period.

Sit, says Octavian. What could outdo this for monosyllabic discourtesy? How about, You first?

Sit, sir, says Antony sharply.

Nay then! says Octavian. Like the shape of the negotiating table after Vietnam, the question of who sits first threatens to sink the talks. Caesar and Antony glare for a moment; then Antony flicks his cape with a tiny movement of the wrist—and sits. They both flick and sit, extremely tense. Then Caesar begins.

You taunted a messenger I sent, he angrily says. What the hell was that about? Antony considers.

Sir, he says, that was an unfortunate event, and my behavior left much to be desired. But your messenger barged in *ere admitted,* and I wasn't myself at the time. *Three kings I had newly feasted then!* The next day *I told him of myself; which was as much as to have asked him pardon.* Don't you think that was enough?

I did want of what I was, says Antony. To *want* is to lack; hung-over, Antony lacked "what he was." The "real" Antony, as everyone agrees, is gracious, kind, and has a magic touch with his subordinates. In practice Antony can be as petty, selfish, and mean as the next world-conqueror, but his behavior should not affect our understanding of who he really is. In fact, what is consistently appealing about Antony is his talent for making amends. He doesn't skimp, but he doesn't grovel, either; he "tells us of himself" without abjection or appeal. Antony may not be the deepest or smartest of Shakespeare's heroes, but none is more disarming.

This time, however, his charm doesn't work. Antony, says Octavian, has broken his oath.

I have? says Antony. What oath was that?

To lend me arms and aid when I required them, says Caesar; "aid" being, basically, money. This is serious indeed. As the old Republic was dying a violent death, the Great Ones were constantly meeting in Tarentum or Brindisi or Rome itself and agreeing to shift arms, ships, men, money, and territory from one of them to the other. You give me Sicily and I'll give you Syria; Lepidus can have Libya and you can have Armenia. I'll send nine Gallic legions, and you give me three hundred ships with experienced rowers. Oh, and by the way, I want a bodyguard of one thousand crack troops for my wife. And nine thousand talents to pay debts incurred in the East. You have my word for it, they would tell each other; and then, when the time came, they either would or wouldn't send the promised ships. In this case, it seems, Antony didn't; but he claims it all just slipped his mind. I *neglected* to send *arms and aid* in a timely manner, he says. That's all. And, by the way, the whole conversation is getting on his nerves.

That's it now, he says, standing up. *Truth is that Fulvia, to have me out of Egypt, made wars in my name, and I'm sorry.* But I knew nothing about it and you can't blame me. Now, as I said, that's it.

I do not much dislike the matter, but the manner of his speech, mutters Caesar, discontent. Some kind of deal is a strong necessity for all concerned. Everyone buzzes around.

Why don't you marry Caesar's sister? Agrippa soon asks Antony. That would *knit your hearts* like nothing else. This seems a bit bizarre, but the Romans often did marry each other's daughters and sisters for political reasons.

I could, says Antony thoughtfully.

And Cleopatra? Octavian says sardonically.

I am not married, Caesar, says faithless Antony.

Fine, then, thinks Octavian. That should work. Octavian's sister, Octavia, was by all historical accounts an extremely good egg who ended up raising everybody's children: her own by another marriage, the ones she had with Antony, and Antony's children from his alliances with both Fulvia and Cleopatra. I count at least nine, but there may have been more. Clearly she deserves better than the minimal role she plays in an extravaganza starring Cleopatra, but in *Antony and Cleopatra* that's what she gets. By the time she comes onstage the deal is done, and Antony is promising, in his lovable way, to reform.

Read not my blemishes in the world's report, he tells his new fiancée. *I have not kept my square, but that to come shall all be done by the rule.* That sounds great, but (*a*) where does that leave Cleopatra, and (*b*) oh, really? As readers, we're torn. Do we want to believe him or not? And can we, if we do? His words spin round and round.

After the negotiations end, Enobarbus stays onstage with Agrippa and Maecenas, whom he hasn't seen since he left with Antony for Egypt.

So, says Maecenas when they have some privacy. It seems you had yourselves a time down there. *Eight wild boars roasted whole at a breakfast, and but twelve persons there; is this true?*

That and more, says Enobarbus. You bet. But, you know—feasting was the least of it.

Everyone knows what he means.

They say she's something else, nods Maecenas.

You've never seen anything like her, says Enobarbus. She's something totally else. For the rest of the scene he raves on about Cleopatra's charms while the others make brief interjections of amazement and envy. *The barge she sat on,* begins Enobarbus, *like a burnished throne...*

THE BARGE SHE SAT ON

DEMETRIUS: *...burned on the water.*

PHILO: (*hesitantly*) Dee...?

DEMETRIUS: What?

PHILO: What water?

DEMETRIUS: Huh?

PHILO: What water did the burnished barge burn on?

DEMETRIUS: The River Cydnus. Antony was in Tarsus at the time, and Cleopatra sailed downstream to meet him there.

PHILO: All dressed up, I bet.

DEMETRIUS: Yes...but the speech features the boat. Purple sails, silver oars...The wind is *lovesick* for the sails, and the water is aroused by the oars' little slaps.

PHILO: (*laughing*) Really?

DEMETRIUS: It's erotic as hell. Cleopatra lay in a pavilion, blushing and being cooled by little cupids with rainbow-colored fans. *Silken tackle* swelled at the *flower-soft* touches of her ladies' hands.

PHILO: (*frowning*) Ship's tackle doesn't swell when you touch it. If it did, it wouldn't fit through the blocks.

DEMETRIUS: True; but what *does* swell when ladies touch it with their *flower-soft* hands?

PHILO: Oh. I see.

DEMETRIUS: Swells.

PHILO: That it does.

DEMETRIUS: Shakespeare didn't write this part, you know.

PHILO: What, he said to someone, Here, pal, I need the sexiest speech ever written; it should focus on a boat; can you have it by Tuesday?

DEMETRIUS: No, no; he found it in Plutarch. It's the most famous case of plagiarism in all of Western lit.

PHILO: Purple sails? Silver oars?

DEMETRIUS: It's all in Plutarch's *Lives*, translated into English by Sir Thomas North.

PHILO: Sir Thomas...

DEMETRIUS: North.

PHILO: Who remembers the humble translator?

DEMETRIUS: Shakespeare got all kinds of things from North. Like, when the barge arrives, Antony invites Cleopatra to dinner. No way, she says. You be *my* guest.

PHILO: You go, girl! An early case of check-grabbing!

DEMETRIUS: Okay, figures Antony. He's psyched. He comes to dinner *barbered ten times over; and pays his heart for what his eyes eat only.*

PHILO: *And pays his heart for what his eyes eat only.* Is that Sir Thomas North?

DEMETRIUS: North's good, dude; but that's Shakespeare.

PHILO: (*shaking his head*) *And pays his heart for what his eyes eat only.*

PASS IT ON

In the beginning there was Plutarch. Not Shakespeare, the middle-class son of a provincial glove-maker; not Thomas North, the second son of an aristocrat who turned to literature when he couldn't find a place at court; not Jacques Amyot, whose French version of Plutarch's *Lives* was the basis of North's translation into English. No. All of those people came later, and Plutarch is the Only Beginner of the story.

Who, or what, was Mestrius Plutarchus, whom we call Plutarch? He was Greek, for one thing; not Greek like Cleopatra, whose family had lived in Egypt for generations, but Greek as in born and raised in Greece. On the other hand, he was partly Roman, too, since Greece at this time was not a nation but a province of Rome. Plutarch was a perfect provincial: conservative, devout, serviceable, and unrebellious. Although nostalgic for Greece's lost glory, Plutarch was pragmatic about his Roman overlords, advising his countrymen to cultivate their friendship; or, as we might say, kowtow. Plutarch came from a good family (*which he is not reluctant to talk about,* says one source wryly). He was educated in Athens and went on official business to Rome, where he may have lived a single degree of separation from the Emperor himself. But he chose to return to Boetia, a region mildly ridiculed by his fellow countrymen for its boorishness. It was and is a flat, undistinguished landscape of which almost nothing can be said but that it is now home to an immense number of military tanks. It grew wheat. There Plutarch was born in Chaeronea—a *poor little town,* he remarked humorously, *and yet I do remain there willingly, lest it should become less.* A big fish in a very small pond, Plutarch willingly undertook *what little administrative work was still entrusted to provincials.* Let the Romans dispense justice, make laws, and collect taxes; Plutarch was willing to *see to the stones, sand and lime* if a little general contracting was all Chaeronea needed when they got through with it.

It's our good fortune, of course, that Plutarch was content to lie low and write, since his work is both indispensable as history and a pleasure to read. But Mestrius wrote his *Life of Antony* a hundred and fifty years after the events it describes, and he was none too scrupulous with the facts, even when he knew what they were. If Plutarch is the foundation of Shakespeare's story, he's a murky, shifting kind of base. Like Shakespeare, he took what he liked and made the rest up.

In my opinion Plutarch got some of his information from his grandfather, of whom he was very fond. And where did his grandfather get *his* information? Maybe from other old Greeks. If you've ever been to Greece, you've seen those old men sitting outside tavernas drinking coffee, talking, killing time. I once spent several summers in Greece, and several winters, too. Now I own a painting in which half a dozen Greek old-timers loaf together on a clear fall day. In the foreground a man in a worn cap gazes off past the viewer, not meeting her eye. That could be Plutarch's grandfather, listening, grateful for the thin November sun. The beginning of Plutarch's story, I believe, peters out into the anonymous, unreliable, all-day conversations of taverna-sitters like these. They are telling the stories they got from their fathers, some of which concern Antony and Cleopatra. Did you hear they wandered in the streets at night? asks one Greek man of another. Someone tells of the street brawls Antony sometimes provoked; someone else says people only pretended not to see through his disguise. The grandfather soaks it up all day, and at night he tells his grandson what he heard.

And sometimes, writes Plutarch in his *Life of Antony, when [Antony] would go up and down the city disguised like a slave in the night, and would peer into poor men's windows and their shops, and scold and brawl with them within the house, Cleopatra would be also in a chambermaid's array, and amble up and down the streets with him, so that oftentimes Antonius bare away both mocks and blows.* Centuries later, Shakespeare turns this passage into a one-line hint of the lovers' city walks; and centuries after that, his one-liner strikes a chord in me.

Who is the Beginner of the tale? And whom can you believe?

SOLILOQUY: CLEOPATRA

Was I mad when I learned that Antony had married Octavia? Of course I was. But did it turn me into the crazy, helpless bitch in Shakespeare's play, hitting and threatening the messenger? *Thou shalt be whipped with wire and stewed in brine,* he has me scream, *smarting in lingering pickle.* *Lingering pickle* is good, but if I'd wanted revenge, I could have taken it on Antony himself! The Parthians were in Judea then, practically on my doorstep. If I'd cut a deal with them, Antony would have been toast. But he and I stuck together in matters of foreign policy, whatever else was going on. Does Shakespeare's Cleopatra even *have* a foreign policy? No. She's just Mrs. Hell-Hath-No-Fury-Like-a-Woman-Scorned.

I was pregnant then with Alexander Helios and Cleopatra Selene—not that I knew at the time we'd have twins. I did know I was more uncomfortable than I had been with Caesarion, who was a breeze. I was throwing up a lot. I'm not saying it was a pleasant time for me; but this was not, as they say, my first barbeque.

Caesarion was Caesar's son; that's Caesar as in *Julius* Caesar, of course, not that stupid little shit Octavian. Everyone knows that before Antony I had an affair with Julius Caesar. He was older, of course; but that had its upside. If he died before I did, as in all likelihood he would, perhaps I'd rule Rome through his son! I wasn't banking on it, but you never know. But Caesarion was barely two when Caesar was assassinated, so there was no question of fighting for the succession. We were living in Rome at the time, near the Janiculum Hill. I got out of town as fast as I could, terrified for the safety of my son. One of my brothers, who was with us, died on the trip. Now *there* was a horrible time.

So get this straight. I didn't *like* watching from Alexandria while Antony had a two-year honeymoon in Athens; and I didn't like it when their child was born. But I didn't panic. Sure enough, when Antony was finally ready to fight the Parthians, he sent for me. He needed money, food, men, and ships, as usual. We met in Antioch and took up where we left off. By the time their second child was born, Antony was back where he belonged, with me.

JULIUS

The first to refer to her former love affair is Cleopatra herself.

Did I, Charmian, she theatrically asks her lady-in-waiting, *ever love Caesar so?* The point is how much more she loves Antony.

Yeah, you did, says cheeky Charmian. She clutches her heart and staggers around the room, pretending to be Cleopatra during her Caesar phase.

Caesar, Caesar, what a guy! she moans. Cleopatra threatens to give her *bloody teeth* if she keeps it up. The next time Julius comes up, things are less lighthearted. Defeated and feeling betrayed, Antony throws the whole thing in her face.

I found you as a morsel cold upon dead Caesar's trencher! he shouts. A trencher is a wooden plate, and Cleopatra is a limp piece of pizza. Of course she doesn't like the insult; but she's in the doghouse at the time, so she lets it go.

UP A LAZY RIVER

DEMETRIUS: Shall I tell you how they met?
PHILO: Who?
DEMETRIUS: Cleopatra and Julius Caesar.
PHILO: Was a barge involved?

DEMETRIUS: In this case, the barge came later. First they had to fight a war with one of her brothers, who wanted the throne.

PHILO: While Julius...

DEMETRIUS: ...thought he'd be better off with her.

PHILO: Hence the hookup?

DEMETRIUS: In the morning the brother walked in on them and threw a temper tantrum.

PHILO: Really?

DEMETRIUS: (*reading from a book*) *Hastening out into the streets, he tore the royal diadem from his head and dashed it to the ground in a spectacular rage, appealing for popular support against the couple.*

PHILO: Drama king!

DEMETRIUS: Those were dramatic times. Once there was a major fire in downtown Alexandria. Cleopatra could have seen it from the palace, where she waited for Caesar to come home at night.

PHILO: He was out fighting? Not running the war from some secure location?

DEMETRIUS: (*laughing*) No, indeed! Plutarch says he was *shot at from all sides.* Once he had to abandon ship and swim two hundred yards, fully armed. At fifty-two!

PHILO: Impressive!

DEMETRIUS: He had some papers in one hand, which he held overhead while everyone tried to kill him.

PHILO: (*thoughtfully*) The sidestroke, then.

DEMETRIUS: Then it was over, and they'd won. Goodbye to fire, drama, and being shot at from all sides; hello to a long, slow trip up the Nile.

PHILO: Whose idea was that?

DEMETRIUS: Cleopatra wanted to show him the antiquities.

PHILO: (*waving his arms*) Different music! Different lights! Cue up the herons and cattle egrets!

DEMETRIUS: They took along a couple of legions just in case; otherwise, it was your basic honeymoon cruise: the bride pregnant, the groom married to someone else, the river broad and calm.

PHILO: Crocodiles, temples, pyramids...

DEMETRIUS: Flocks of sacred geese...

PHILO: The *felladin* running along the shore to get a glimpse of them...

DEMETRIUS: The barge before the barge!

PHILO: (*humming*) Up a lazy river by the old mill stream...

DEMETRIUS: (*singing along*) That lazy, hazy river where we both can dream...

Both: (*getting enthusiastic*) Blue skies up above, and as long as we're in love...up that lazy river, with me!

ATTENTION TO DETAIL

The barge Cleopatra and Julius Caesar took up the Nile was *of immense size,* according to a modern writer. It was *faced with ebony, trimmed with gold and hung with purple silk.* In 1999 a replica of its bow was built for a $28 million ABC Cleopatra miniseries, along with six models of the whole barge, emphasizing authenticity and paying *pointillistic attention to detail.* The problem is that no one has any idea what the details of the barge could possibly have been. Of the two ancient sources, as opposed to the more imaginative modern ones, one says merely that such a trip occurred and the other that *Caesar ascended the Nile with four hundred ships, exploring the country in the company of Cleopatra and generally enjoying himself with her.* That's it. Nothing about silk, ebony, or gold. We can't even be sure of the four hundred extra ships, since the author of the amusing second version, written long after Cleopatra died, may have gone in for the lunatic, baseless precision of the 1999 miniseries.

The lack of information about the barge—and the eager confidence with which so many have "recreated" it—reflects a larger problem. Almost *all* information about Cleopatra is as shamelessly invented as the barges that she sat on. Although Plutarch's *Life of Mark Antony* is no pillar of historical research, there is no text on Cleopatra by anyone with a fraction of Plutarch's credibility. The ancient sources on Cleopatra, as one writer crisply puts it, *(a) have no footnotes; (b) conflict [with each other]; (c) are almost entirely hostile; and (d) for the most part, postdate her reign.* History is written by the winners, and in the battle between Cleopatra and Octavian, Octavian won. In the absence of objective sources everyone makes Cleopatra up. Obviously, says one scholar, she never loved Antony; *she seems to have adored him,* claims another. The historical Cleopatra is a Rorschach blot, inviting the wildest projections—including Shakespeare's, and mine.

What are we to make, for instance, of Plutarch's claim that Cleopatra knew many languages? She didn't use an interpreter, he says, when speaking to *barbarous people, but made them answer herself.* In fact, he says, getting a little carried away, she knew the languages of *the Ethiopians, the Arabians, the Troglodytes, the Hebrews, the Syrians, and Medes and the Parthians.* That's a lot of languages! Was Cleopatra a kind of idiot savant for languages, picking them up as if they were so many hats? Alternatively, did she spend her mornings being tutored by some foreign slave, memorizing exotic grammar and vocabulary? Neither explanation rings a bell; but the language thing has been used over and over as proof of her statecraft. Whereas her father and forefathers spoke only Greek, Cleopatra was able to speak to her allies and subjects directly.

Cleopatra's forefathers had their own ways of communicating with the local population. On the occasion of his coronation, for instance, Cleopatra's great-great-grandfather, Ptolemy V, had a stone incised with both Greek letters and Egyptian hieroglyphs, reminding its readers that he was *a king like the Sun, the living image of Zeus, son of the Sun, a god sprung from a god,* and so forth. All right! This wasn't any old stone, moreover, but the Rosetta Stone, which taught the modern world to read Egyptian hieroglyphics. Cleopatra, by contrast, is undecodable, defying characterization even as she invites it. Assured of that, we all take a turn, cooking her up as whatever we need her to be.

PRELUDE TO WAR

Antony and Octavia are in Athens, where they've spent two pleasant years. Now, however, the marriage is wearing thin. Antony is furious at Octavia's brother, who's in Rome.

Not only that, Antony fumes, *that and thousands more, but he hath waged new wars 'gainst Pompey...* and so forth. It is not clear why Octavian's new war with Pompey is so offensive, but it is. In fact, it's the last straw.

I've had it, he tells Octavia forcefully. This is war.

Please, no! cries Octavia. Whom would I root for? My brother? My husband? *The good gods will mock me* if I pray for both! Antony is unmoved. Octavia's gods mean less to him each day.

Choose between us, he tells her coldly. If she wants to talk to Caesar, she may do so; but Antony will be raising an army in the meantime.

The Jove of power make me most weak, most weak, your reconciler,
prays Octavia.

You can spend what you like on the trip, says Antony, leaving the room.

Who cares what I spend?! thinks Octavia, distraught. Luxury travel is
not the point. It is clear that Antony has no investment in her diplomatic
mission.

Cut to Rome, where Octavian is as angry at Antony as Antony, a scene
or so earlier, was at him.

He has done all this and more, Octavian rages to Maecenas, *in Alexandria.* Antony has done all *what*? Oh, never mind. Like Antony's griev-
ances with Octavian, Octavian's with Antony can be left vague. But...*in
Alexandria?* Didn't we just leave Antony in Athens?

I'll tell you the manner of it, Caesar complains. *I' th' marketplace
on a tribunal silvered, Cleopatra and himself were publicly enthroned.*
Caesar is describing what came to be called the Donations of Alexandria,
an elaborate ceremony conferring kingdoms and titles on Cleopatra's
children. So in the space of a couple of scenes Antony has not only made
it to Egypt but also reconciled with Cleopatra and organized some major,
title-conferring event! How can this be? Octavia hasn't isn't even made
it to Rome!

In real life there wasn't such a rush. Between parting from Octavia
and proclaiming Cleopatra's children *kings of kings* the historical Antony found time to invade both Parthia and Armenia. But neither the
Parthian disaster (in which Antony lost twenty-eight thousand men)
nor the consolation prize of Armenia is of any use to Shakespeare, so
he leaves them out. Also omitted is Antony's reunion with Cleopatra,
of which we never hear a word. We know that in real life it was warm,
because it resulted in little Ptolemy Philadelphus, now two and the
recipient of some of the kingdoms Antony is handing out. But before
the make-up sex, did Cleopatra have a few choice words to say about
Antony's marriage to Octavia? What terms did she set for the reunion?
Plutarch doesn't say, and Shakespeare doesn't either.

Skip to the Donations of Alexandria, he mutters to himself halfway
through act 3. I don't question his choice. North's Plutarch is open on his
desk, as it is on mine. Both of us have deadlines.

Unto Cleopatra, scribbles Shakespeare, Antony gave Egypt; *made her
of lower Syria, Cyprus, Lydia, absolute queen.*

Let Rome be thus informed, says Maecenas when the news reaches him. By this time both he and Agrippa are squarely behind Caesar and hard at work on Antony's destruction. The Donations of Alexandria, properly publicized, should be very useful in the propaganda war against him. *The final, foulest breath of the free speech of the old Republic,* it has been called; and it yields nothing in sophistication, ruthlessness, or mendacity to contemporary political mudslinging. Caesar's people for the most part used Cleopatra as a surrogate for Antony, spreading word that the foreign queen intended to invade and conquer Italy itself. This wasn't true, but it worked, the politics of fear being what they are. The Donations of Alexandria were spun as a disastrous giveaway.

Back in Rome, Octavia arrives, a little late.

What are you doing here? Caesar demands. And why did you creep into town like a waif?

To come thus was I not constrained, Octavia says hastily, *but did it on my free will.* My husband would have paid for a more lavish trip, I can assure you.

Your husband! scoffs Caesar. Do you even know where your husband is?

My lord, in Athens, says Octavia simply. Her brother shakes his head. He's in Egypt, sister dear, he says. *Cleopatra hath nodded him to her.* Octavia is stunned.

What? she says. I don't believe you!

He hath given his empire up to a whore, says Caesar crudely. Octavia feels sick.

Ay me, most wretched, she cries, so Maecenas tries to comfort her.

Each heart in Rome does love and pity you, he croons. Is this true? In any case, Maecenas will be sure to let each Roman know just how badly Antony has treated his Roman wife.

My dear'st sister! Caesar somewhat insincerely concludes. This story has legs.

ENOBARBUS TO AGRIPPA

You must know the Donations of Alexandria were a farce. Antony and Cleopatra got themselves up as gods, as they love to do. They were Isis and Osiris; or perhaps Dionysus and Aphrodite instead. They have these all-purpose robes they wear when they're pretending to be gods, Egyptian, Greek, or what-have-you. The children sat on lower thrones, absurdly dressed. One was supposed to be the overlord of the old Persian territories, so he had a peacock feather in a turban, like a pasha; another was in the Macedonian purple cloak and booties. All the children were betrothed to some Eastern prince or princess; who can remember which. What nonsense! When the baby cried, the older ones tried to hush him up. Antony's own heir, as you know, is none of Cleopatra's children but Fulvia's first born. Is Antonius Marcus Jr. Roman enough for you people? This whole thing about Antony installing Cleopatra in Rome is fearmongering bullshit, and you know it. It was hot in the gymnasium, and we were all glad to get out.

Oh, well. Never mind. When plans for war reach a certain point, reality can wait. Well, fine, then. But Agrippa, I never thought I'd be fighting *you*. We won't both live to see the end of this, I'm sure; this may be the last time it's even safe to write. How to sum up our years of friendship? Which one of us will die?

SOLILOQUY: CLEOPATRA

In 33 B.C.E., Antony asked me to raise two hundred warships and meet him in Ephesus.

Now? I asked—through a messenger, course. What I wanted just then was a trip up the Nile.

Now, said Antony. Antony had never seen the Upper Nile, and if we lost the war he never would. But business is business, so I raised the fleet and went to Ephesus.

Up the Nile people lived just as they had for fifteen or twenty centuries, planting when the river ebbed and harvesting from the fertile silt it left behind. The priests up there loved us Ptolemies. As well they might, since we always sent them tons of dough! But they believed in me; they thought I was divine; and in their towns and temples, so did I. The very year I came to power their sacred bull died, and a new one had to be installed. I was invited to row the new Buchis across the river at Hermonthis, and somehow that made me a goddess even as it made him a god. It was a bright, hot day, and the bull was dazzling white. In the boat he looked at me with human eyes, as if there was a secret between us.

"I'm Buchis now," he seemed to say. "You're Isis." The Upper Nile was where I fled some months later when my brother threw me off the throne; and it was where I went on that triumphal trip with Julius Caesar after he restored me to it. Now I wanted to go there again, before the war. I thought it would be good luck to be the people's living goddess once more, blessing and blessed; but Antony said no. So, okay. To Ephesus I went. When the time came to fight, we fought.

ACTIUM

No sooner do the opposing sides in *Antony and Cleopatra* suit up in battle regalia, shouting things like, *Strike not by land!* or *Set we our squadrons on yond side o' th' hill!* than we come to the Battle of Actium, which history has agreed to call the end. September 2, 31 B.C.E. is the official end not only of the war between Antony and Octavian but of the Ptolemaic dynasty, the Hellenistic Age, and the Roman Republic. What came next was the Roman Empire, which would last in various states of success and failure for the next five centuries. But in Shakespeare's play Actium is just the first in a series of battles, most of which Antony loses.

O, whither hast thou led me, Egypt? cries Antony after one defeat. Apparently she fled in the middle of a sea battle, and Antony pursued her.

I little thought you would have followed, protests Cleopatra.

Thou knew'st too well, Antony says hotly, *my heart was to thy rudder tied by th' strings, and thou shouldst tow me after.* Does this make sense? In a fight for his political and biological life, would Antony chase after Cleopatra like a teenager whose girlfriend has flounced out of the soda shop? Antony probably lost the Battle of Actium because he couldn't feed his troops, not because Cleopatra lured him away. When the time came for his men to row like hell out of the Gulf of Ambracia and ram Caesar's ships with their bronze-plated quinqueremes, they were too sick and hungry to do much damage.

Before Actium, Antony was adored by his men. His love affair with his legions was as famous and consequential as his love affair with Cleopatra, and may have been unique in human history. But Antony abandoned one hundred and fifty ships at Actium. Five thousand men died, three fifths of Antony's troops. After that his people left him in droves. After that he couldn't win.

SOLILOQUY: ENOBARBUS

When I saw he couldn't win, I, too, deserted Antony. May the gods forgive me! Antony did, to my eternal chagrin.

Enobarbus, a soldier told me a few days after I had joined Caesar's camp, *Antony hath after thee sent all thy treasure with his bounty overplus.* I didn't believe it.

I give it thee, I said sarcastically.

No, said the soldier. *Mock not.* They're unloading the mules as we speak. Finally I understood. Antony had sent everything of mine, and many gifts as well.

O Antony, I cried, *thou mine of bounty, how would'st thou have paid my better service when my turpitude thou dost so crown with gold!* I had made an irreversible mistake and felt nothing but regret.

A SPACIOUS MIRROR

What? says Antony when he learns of Enobarbus's defection. *Is he gone? O, my fortunes have corrupted honest men! Write to him gentle adieus and greetings. Say that I wish he never find more cause to change a master.* What are we to make of this? Antony behaves badly; then well; then badly, then *magnificently!* His almost Christ-like treatment of Enobarbus, for instance, follows hard upon his worst behavior to date. Caesar has sent a messenger to corrupt Cleopatra, and Antony has come upon a most suspicious scene. Cleopatra is allowing her hand to be kissed and saying hum and ho when the messenger suggests she defect.

Take hence this jack and whip him, bellows Antony. *Whip him, fellows, till like a boy you see him cringe his face and whine aloud for mercy.* Cleopatra has indeed been flirting with defection, but the messenger is not to blame, and Antony's behavior is repellent.

If Caesar doesn't like it, he brutally says when the whipping is done, *tell him he has Hipparchus, my bondman, whom he may at pleasure whip, or hang, or torture, as he shall like, to quit me.*

Which is the real Mark Antony: the moral idiot who sacrifices Hipparchus or the devoted friend who forgives Enobarbus? Between Actium and Antony's end, his identity is in flux. Generous, selfish, sentimental, resolute, magnificent, simple...finally Antony himself is baffled by his changes.

Eros, thou yet behold'st me? he asks an aide during a rare contemplative moment.

Indeed I do, answers Eros. He is aptly named, since he loves his master
very much. It is twilight; the two are looking toward the palace from a
promontory by the sea.

And yet, says Antony slowly, what is this "me" that thou behold'st?

Eros looks at him inquiringly. Antony looks at the sky.

Sometimes we see a cloud that's dragonish, says Antony; *a vapor
sometime like a bear or lion.* Then the cloud *dislimns;* and all is *indis-
tinct as water is in water.*

That's true, thinks Eros. Where is this going?

Here I am Antony, his master continues, *yet cannot hold this visible
shape, my knave.*

Eros nods. He understands, as do we, that this is the philosophical crux
of the play. Things change; and even the one who knows his own changes
changes. The grave, simple, meditative Antony is as quickly dislimned as
the rest, and we never see him again.

Antony's changeableness may be particular to him, or it may illustrate a general truth about the nature of things. It may also be seen in
historical context. The artists of the European Renaissance, of whom
Shakespeare is an outstanding example, were exhilarated by the new
possibilities for art. While the Christian Middle Ages required human
experience to be placed in a religious context, the humanist Renaissance
found whatever men and women felt and thought and did worthy of
representation for its own sake. Visual artists filled their sketchbooks
with faces reflecting all states of mind and soul: fear, bliss, anger, cru-
elty, peace, and greed. Shakespeare, like the others, delighted in human
variety per se, depicting his heroes in one extremity after another. With
Antony he pushes the envelope, allowing him moments of real ugliness
as well as many forms of beauty.

His taints and honors waged equal with him, says Maecenas at the
end; but taints and honors are both beside the point. The point is the
variety and power of his many guises, not their moral valence. Antony
has been a *spacious mirror,* as Maecenas puts in, and the more we see
of him, the more we see ourselves. The humanist's bent is to find that
worthwhile.

As *Antony and Cleopatra* winds down, five or six characters kill themselves, starting with Enobarbus.

I will go seek some ditch wherein to die, he miserably says, and does.

Do you hear something? says one sentry to another.

O thou blessed moon! cries Enobarbus, remember I repented! By the time the sentries approach, it's too late.

The next to kill himself, Eros, is even more abrupt. Antony has lost yet another battle to Caesar and is raging yet again at Cleopatra.

This foul Egyptian hath betrayed me! he cries. *The witch shall die!* But then the witch sends word that she is dead, and Antony believes it. The combination of grief and defeat is too much for Antony, who says, in effect, I'm done.

Unarm, Eros, is how he puts it. *The long day's task is done, and we must sleep.* Eros has promised to kill Antony should the need arise, and now, says Antony, it has.

No way! says Eros. God forbid! When softness doesn't work, Antony pulls rank.

When I did make thee free, Antony sternly reminds his former bondsman, *swor'st thou not then to do this when I bade thee?*

Yes, I did, says Eros. And I will. *But let me say before I strike this bloody stroke, farewell.*

'Tis said, man, and farewell, says Antony, impatient. Let's go!

Why there, then! says Eros; but instead of killing Antony, to Antony's horror he kills himself.

O valiant Eros! he says. *Thrice-nobler than myself! Thou teachest me what I should and thou couldst not.* He falls on his sword and shortly thereafter dies of the wound. At the end, Cleopatra, too, takes her own life.

Husband, I come! she calls before dying.

Egyptian pharaohs of the early dynasties took escorts with them when they died—"escort" being a euphemism for someone who was killed and buried by the pharaohs' sides. In *Antony and Cleopatra* Shakespeare uses escorts to magnify the passing of his two main characters. The suicides of Enobarbus and Eros surround the dying Antony; Cleopatra's ladies-in-waiting, dying just before and just after Cleopatra, create a similar ripple around her as she goes.

Charmian, is this well done? reproaches one of Caesar's guards when he finds Cleopatra dead. Caesar had been hoping to display Cleopatra in his triumph back in Rome, and his guard is disappointed by her death.

It is well done, says Charmian firmly, *and fitting for a princess descended of so many royal kings.* At that, to underscore her point, she applies an asp and joins her queen.

Ah, soldier! she cries in her death spasm. She has only him to call to as she dies.

SOLILOQUY: CLEOPATRA

After I died, things went as you might expect. Caesarion fled south to the Upper Nile and was captured and killed on the road. The other three were given to Octavia to raise, which she dutifully did. They lived out their lives obscurely, married to lesser potentates. I have various feelings about that, as you can imagine; but my deepest grief is for my oldest boy. He was Horus to my Isis, the Divine Child to my All-Powerful Mother. Together we ruled not just Egypt, as it seemed, but the whole earthly realm. Whatever we once ruled, we didn't anymore. I died, he died, and Egypt was annexed to Rome.

After Caesarion, the one I think of most isn't Antony, as you might think. It's Buchis, the bull. I remember the day I rowed him to his installation the way other women remember their wedding day. The sky was intensely blue and the bull intensely white. He and I were both young and hopeful, but I wasn't much of an oarswoman, so it was a tippy ride. I was seated, of course; but Buchis was standing up, and nervous. He kept seeking a point of balance, glancing my way and spreading his feet. I was dimly aware of the dull, wide river and the calling of the sacred geese, but mostly I was focused on the bull.

Can you keep this thing a little steadier? he seemed to ask as I raised the dripping oars and put them down again.

I'll try, I told him silently. And I did. Why does that persist in my mind when more important matters don't? I'll try, I tell Buchis in my thoughts each day. I'll try. Strange to spend eternity talking to a bull!

With Cleopatra died the Hellenistic world, and Rome was thenceforth unopposed. What was lost when Hellenism died? The Hellenistic monarchs were as oppressive as the Roman emperors that followed them. They nickeled-and-dimed their local populations with equal enthusiasm and success. By Cleopatra's time, moreover, the great Hellenistic philosophers and scientists were gone, and the culture was plagued with artificiality and self-repetition. But Hellenism was the liberal arts division of the ancient world, and those of us who work that field should note, at least, its passing. Antony, who studied as a young man in Athens, remained a Philhellene for his entire life. His big idea was to join Rome's genius for technology, engineering, and material science to Hellenism's bent for literature, scholarship, rhetoric, and pure research. He wanted the Hellenistic Eastern kingdoms, over which he ruled, to be Rome's partners, not its provinces. As heirs of the ancient world ourselves, we have a retrospective stake in his defeat. Would things be different if he'd won?

He lost. Caesar buried him near Cleopatra, as he had wished, and went on to lay the foundations for centuries of Roman rule. Eventually, of course, Rome, too, was overcome, although it's hard to say just when. Did it end with the Battle of Adrianople, in 378 C.E.? The sack of Rome in 410 C.E.? In 476 C.E., when the last Roman emperor was deposed? Of all the suggestions scholars have made, David Markson's is the most appealing. Rome may have ended, he says (in his great non-novel, *The Last Novel*) when its last two citizens had their final street corner conversation in Latin. Presumably this took place in the far corners of empire, long out of date.

Take care, be good, one may have called in Latin to the other. See you in the morning! But morning never came for one or the other of these friends; and with that the language, the era, and the empire died.

THE TEMPLE OF POSEIDON

We don't know when, exactly, the ancient world came to an end, but I can say with some precision when my interest in it began. I was seventeen at the time, almost Cleopatra's age when she first came to power. I was enrolled in a program of classical studies that bored me to death. The program was taught in Greece itself, and we students were taken to its hallowed sites. Through the winter and spring of that year I sat on blocks of fallen marble, too young to know how little I cared for what the earnest, gesticulating adults were pitching. When summer came at last, I dropped the boring past and headed for the islands with my friends. We drank retsina and wandered, slightly drunk, into the sea; then we stripped and lay in our rooms through the heat of the day. At night there was an ever-changing selection of new best friends to dance and stay up with. We went home to do our laundry and make plans; then we set out again. But we traveled cheaply, and cheap passage on the boats was rough. One night, returning to Athens from Paros, my cabin was airless, seasick-y, and hot. I went on deck to breathe and wait for dawn. Some power of attention within me had been sharpened by the rigors of the night, and I was wide awake when our ship rounded Cape Sounion, the Temple of Poseidon perched on its cliff. The sea was beginning to shine, as if it, too, were waking up. At that age I had no conception of myself as someone who had memorable encounters with art or nature. My life just flowed, like a child's. But the temple on the headlands was and is one of the most beautiful things in the world, a miracle of siting, proportions, and materials; and that day, it was addressed to me. It was small, unguarded, high on its hill. It seemed to have spent centuries in silence, waiting for my startled eyes. It was a wonder; absolute. I who perceived it was a wonder to myself.

Who built that? I thought. Was it meant to be seen from the sea? Who paid for it, who cared for it, who came? Those were the kinds of questions my teachers that year had wanted me to ask; now they'd arrived, too late. Perhaps it's just as well. If I'd had questions they would have had answers; and that would have been that.

Did Plutarch see Sounion? Did Antony and Cleopatra? The temple wasn't as old as the Egyptian tombs and pyramids; but it was as far in their past as, for instance, Plymouth Rock is in ours. Built around 440 B.C.E., it had seen four hundred winters when Antony and Cleopatra sailed past on their way to Greece. Did those two look up and feel, as I did, a sudden sense of the past?

Shakespeare's *Antony and Cleopatra* itself is about the age of Plymouth Rock; or rather, since the rock itself is eons old, it's roughly contemporary with what the rock represents, the landing of the Mayflower pilgrims. Like the Temple of Poseidon, the play is both old and young. Byron carved his name into one of the temple's columns; perhaps I've carved mine in the play. Is this an act of vandalism or interpretation? Linda, was this well done? I hope it is, since it's been *sweating labor,* as Cleopatra says of her own entertainments, *to bear such idleness so near the heart.* In any case, I can't have done much harm. *Age cannot wither nor custom stale* the play; nor can any act of mine. As for the other threats it faces—competition from alternative media, the decline of literacy, and so forth—I'm not concerned. Yes, things change. Some day the peak of Mount Everest will be leveled flat, and Plymouth Rock will be no more. In the meantime, google any five words from *Antony and Cleopatra,* and the whole play comes up on the Web. Its pleasures will detain the most determined multitasker. For this sublime antiquity, there is no end in sight.

AN INCARCERATION OF HAMLETS

Denmark's a prison. *Hamlet*, II, ii, 247

SOLILOQUY: HORATIO (ACT 1, SCENE 1)

I was skeptical about the ghost, so they told me to come see for myself. It was after midnight and cold, but the streets were oddly active. I was full of dread. Norway was contesting our right to certain lands we had lately won; shipbuilders and armaments makers were working through the night to prepare for war.

I met Marcellus on the way. When we got to the ramparts, Barnardo greeted us, full of agitation. His mind was on the ghost, not war.

Tush, tush, 'twill not appear, I insisted; but, as everyone knows, it did. Or did it? Are ghosts real or not? This one seemed real. It gestured and mouthed and moved here and there. Perhaps it had something to tell us.

Speak to me, I tried. Silence; so I tried again.

If thou are privy to thy country's fate, I demanded, *which happily foreknowing may avoid, O, speak!* To my annoyance, a cock crowed just then, signaling daylight, the curfew for ghosts. Hamlet Senior disappeared.

It faded on the crowing of the cock, Marcellus needlessly observed. Now he was in a contemplative mood. At Christmas, he reflected, the cock crows all night long, keeping witches, goblins, demons, and ghosts at bay.

The nights are wholesome then, he sagely said.

So have I heard and do in part believe it, I told him. That sums it up. If someone tells you he saw a ghost on the ramparts of the city, believe it, but *in part.* With that we went off to tell Hamlet. It was his father's ghost; his play. I mean, if the play were about me, it would be called *Horatio,* not *Hamlet,* right?

It isn't.

In a 2002 episode of *This American Life* called "Act V," a group of prisoners in a Missouri prison are staging *Hamlet* under the direction of Agnes Wilcox of Prison Performing Arts. Horatio is played by Derrick "Big Hutch" Hutchinson, who is doing time for armed robbery. Big Hutch, says *This American Life* reporter, Jack Hitt, is indeed big, with "a smooth, bald skull and hooded, threatening eyes." He has a big reputation in the yard, too, acknowledged as "a whale among minnows"; but his fellow actors claim it's a role. They stop short of saying he's a sweetheart, but "in Shakespeare," as they refer to their time in the program, they see a different man.

I'm not just a whale, but a *blue* whale, Hutch insists. The blue whale outranks even killer whales. But Horatio, he says, is a chump. He's Hamlet's yes-man, answering *aye, m'lord* and *yes, lord* to whatever Hamlet says.

"I mean, if we're friends," argues Hutch, "we're going to communicate better than that. You're going to tell me your deepest secrets. I want to know what you and Ophelia did last night." Now, Hamlet and Ophelia didn't do anything last night. When we first see her, Ophelia is being scolded by her father and brother not to do anything with Hamlet—tonight or any night. She promises not to, and as far as we know, she never does. But Hutch has a point: in the friendship with Hamlet, Horatio is definitely the junior partner, feeding Hamlet lines. In act 5, scene 2, for instance, Hamlet asks, *Wilt thou hear me how I did proceed?* and Horatio, typically, answers, *I beseech you.* Eight lines later it happens again. *Wilt thou know the effect of what I wrote?* asks Hamlet.

Aye, good my lord, says faithful Horatio. And so it goes.

Does this make Horatio a chump? I think not. A chump is a kind of person, and Horatio for the most part is a dramatic convenience rather than a person with qualities. *Hamlet* includes seven soliloquies by its main character. Without Horatio to break up the dialogue Hamlet might get on a roll whenever he opens his mouth. In any case, this is a play with one whale so big that everyone, not just Horatio, is a minnow by comparison. Hamlet's murderous uncle has his moment of regret; Ophelia has her madness when Hamlet kills her father; Laertes has his vengeful rage; but nothing compares to the full-court press of Hamlet's inner life. By turns uneasy, heartbroken, enthusiastic, conflicted, bitter, depressed, enraged, hardhearted, contemplative, self-hating, confused, excited, and serene, Hamlet rises to every occasion with linguistic, intellectual, and emotional energy that equals or surpasses that of any character in any language ever. When he's not staging a play, stabbing a courtier, and generally making things happen, Hamlet *is* what happens, a seemingly infinite well of responses to events. He likes Horatio and takes a moment or two to praise him; but he's much too busy to work, as it were, on the relationship. Yes, it's unequal. No, Hamlet can't deal with it now.

"Don't wait till I get to the end of act five and I'm getting ready to drink a cup of poison and you stop me," objects Big Hutch. "You know, let me know down the line, man, that I'm really your friend." Sorry, man. Hamlet is otherwise engaged.

Q AND PRISONER A

Q. In your portrayal of Hamlet, do you emphasize his endless responsiveness?

A. Sometimes. It's complicated, man.

Q. How so?

A. First off, Hamlet not always *respondin'* to shit. Sometimes he stirrin' shit up.

Q. True.

A. Plus, he don't *need* nothin' to respond to sometimes. Sometimes he just mad.

Q. Like when?

A. First time we see him, Hamlet watchin' his uncle make out like he king. Hamlet sittin' there thinkin', what the fuck? Ain't this guy king; my *father* king. That point he don't know nothin' about Claudius killin' his daddy. He just mad.

Q. But his father's dead.

A. Yeah. Hamlet confused.

Q. Claudius tells him to cheer up.

A. *To persever in obstinate condolement,* Claudius say, *is unmanly grief.* That don't cut no ice with H.

Q. Wow.

A. What?

Q. You said that really well.

A. What I say well?

Q. That line.

A. That? That's nothin'!

Q. *Obstinate condolement* is something, I'd say.

A. Dude: I play Hamlet in the play. I say the whole thing.

Q. Amazing.

A. Yeah. A dick wad like me.

Q. Please!

A. No, it's true. But you know what? I got a book in my room called *Shakespeare for Dummies*. I got two dictionaries; three editions of *Hamlet*; recordings, tapes, CDs…I even got a coffee mug with Shakespeare's face on the side. So I a dick wad, but now I a dick wad *and* Hamlet; both.

Q. Well, good for you!

A. (*modestly*) Thanks!

(Q *and* A *both smile.*)

Q. The queen wants her son to cheer up, too. Everyone loses his father, she tells him. *Why seems it so particular with thee?*

A. Hamlet already good and pissed at his momma.

Q. (*nods*) For remarrying so fast.

A. Gertrude one horny bitch.

Q. Please.

A. Sorry.

Q. (*pause*) What happens next?

A. Hamlet ask Gertrude, What you mean, *seems?* You think I'm *actin'* sad? I ain't actin'! I *real*, bitch. I real.

Q. Do you have to call her a bitch?

A. Yeah.

Q. (*sighs*) Okay.

A. *I have that within which passes show.*

Q. What?

A. He tell the queen, *I have that within which passes show.*

Q. Which he does!

A. Yeah; but then why he have to say so?

Q. Are you implying…

A. I ain't implyin' nothin'.

Q. Then what do you mean?

A. I mean, Hamlet worry, man. He worry, I havin' the right feelin's for what's goin' down? I havin' *enough* feelin's? So when the queen says *seems*, it hits a sore spot. I ain't sayin' he *ain't* real. I just sayin' he got issues.

Q. I see.

A. Yeah. Whole play, until the end, Hamlet worried.

Q. That's true.

A. Gertrude don't mean nothin' by *seems*. She just want him to cheer up.

Q. Fat chance.

A. Yeah.

Q. Gertrude, now.

A. She want life to go on.

Q. "Can't we just have Christmas?"

A. What?

Q. That's what my friend Katie says about her.

A. Who Katie?

Q. That's not the point. "Can't we just have Christmas?" is how Katie characterizes Gertrude's attitude throughout the play.

A. Yeah, man. Katie right.

Q. That's wittier than calling her a bitch, don't you think?

A. Gertrude one horny bitch.

SOLILOQUY: HORATIO (ACT 1, SCENE 2)

When we returned the next night with Hamlet, the ghost appeared on cue. Marcellus and I hid behind some buttresses and heard the whole hair-raising thing. Hamlet's father, he told Hamlet, was in limbo, *doomed for a certain term to walk the night.* Perhaps he could upgrade after that, but for now it was gruesome.

I could a tale unfold, he moaned, *whose lightest word would harrow up thy soul, freeze thy young blood, make thy two eyes, like stars, start from their spheres,* and so on. Hamlet responded in his sweetest, simplest vein.

Alas, poor ghost! he cried. That's Hamlet, sometimes. Pure gold. But after the ghost told his son what he had come for, things changed.

Revenge, revenge! moaned the ghost, and Hamlet came unhinged.

I'm on it! he swore. In fact, I'll think of nothing else until I do! My mind will go blank except for *thy commandment*. Goodbye simplicity, hello excess.

O all you host of heaven! he howled after the ghost had left. *O earth! What else? And shall I couple hell? O villain, villain, smiling, damned villain!* Then, oddly, he whipped out his notebook and made a note.

That one may smile and smile and be a villain, he scribbled fiercely. Certainly that applies to Claudius, who's quite the hypocrite; but was this a time for making notes?

At that we ran up with a *Hillo, ho, ho!* and he snapped into focus to deal.

Don't tell what you saw tonight, he said forcefully. Swear on your life!

We won't, we swore. But suddenly he was dancing around us, performing all the ways we could leak the story while pretending not to. Don't hint, he said, don't fold your arms like this and shake your head and say, *"Well, well, we know,"* or *"We could, an if we would,"* or *"If we list to speak,"* or *"There be, an if they might."* He was wired, but brilliant, alive. We swore there'd be no such *ambiguous givings out*, as he put it. He told us he planned to act half-mad to throw people off, and we said okay. I was relieved the ghost had spared his life. When he told me what the ghost had said, I pretended I didn't already know. I can smile and smile and be a villain, too, I guess – or at least dissemble.

Q AND PRISONER A

A. It's like Hamlet lookin' for a role and his daddy say, have I got a role for you.

Q. What do you mean?

A. At first, Hamlet like *unemployed*, you know? He just sittin' around the palace havin' feelin's. When the ghost say, *Revenge,* he come to life. Now he got somethin' to do.

Q. His father casts him for the play?

A. Yeah. He gonna be the Revenger, man.

Q. That was an outdated role by Shakespeare's time, you know. Like...I don't know, the sheriff in an old Western.

A. Beats sittin' in the wings!

Q. That it does.

A. So his daddy give him his role, and he say, Yeah! Lemme at 'im!

Q. Horatio seems to think he overdoes it.

A. What he overdo?

Q. The excitement. He could be covering up.

A. You think he *don't* want to do it?

Q. Do you know what ambivalent means?

A. Means he want and he don't want.

Q. Right.

A. Maybe. But he glad to have somethin' he *'sposed* do, even if he mixed up about doin' it.

Q. Hence the famous delay.

A. Look, man. They says, you'll be Hamlet, or Othello, or Lear, and you say, thank *you;* but that don't mean you Lear or Othello right off. You want to be Lear but you don't want to be old and stupid; you want to be Othello but you don't want to kill your nice wife. So you does the work. The character change, you change, you get it wrong, you give up, you get mad; then you do it right.

Q. So Hamlet's an actor? Looking for a way to play his part?

A. Ain't easy lettin' what's inside out.

Q. Even when what's inside *passes show?*

A. That's what ain't easy to show.

BIG HUTCH: VERBATIM FROM THE TRANSCRIPT OF
THIS AMERICAN LIFE

I don't see the conflict. I don't see what Hamlet is dealing with, man. Aw, I should kill the king now. I shouldn't kill him now. What's the hullaballoo about? I couldn't see somebody raping my daughter or something and just sitting around. No, no, no, no, no. I got to *do* you, man. And that's just [SMACKING SOUND], you done. That's why I think Hamlet's an old minnow, too. If I'm strong enough to believe in ghosts, then I'm strong enough to believe what that ghost tells me. If I'm strong enough to believe you're a ghost, then I'm sure you know what happened to you.

Q AND PRISONER A

A. Hutch say that?

Q. Yeah.

A. Where Hutch now?

Q. St. Louis. Out of jail. He cleans parking lots and garages at night.
A. I gotta talk with him, man. "I gotta *do* you." (*shakes his head*) Gimme
a break.

ACTING THE TRUTH

Prisoner A, whom I invented, plays Hamlet by himself, as actors normally do. In "Act V," Hamlet is played by four different men.

"They're all on stage at the same time," explains Jack Hitt in the
broadcast, "taking turns delivering the lines. This small gang of Hamlets, which mutters to itself and laughs at its own jokes, nicely captures
that fractured quality of Hamlet's different personalities." Is "fractured"
another word for "ambivalent"?

At the high-security Missouri Eastern Correctional Center, the Hamlets worked together. They would assemble after lunch on Sundays and
go down to the track.

"You'd hear this chatter of somebody giving their lines," says Chris
Harris, one of the Hamlets, "the rest of us with our heads down in the
books walking the line. Now, there are benches that are all throughout
the inside of the track. So there are people that actually watch us. So
you'll hear this Old English–style speech. You know, 'Ho, Horatio,' and
these people are like, ho, what?"

I loved the idea of a muttering gaggle, so I called Agnes Wilcox to
ask her if that indeed was how the role was played. No, she said. The
Hamlets took turns, line by line, and when one spoke the others were
silent. When I pressed her for specifics, she offered this staging of English drama's most famous lines:

> HAMLET 1: To be?
> HAMLET 2: Or not to be?
> HAMLET 3: That is the question.
> *They all look at Hamlet 4, who shrugs and shakes his head.*

That's great, I told Agnes.

Make sure you say it was *fun,* she urged. Clearly it was. But…why
always Shakespeare? If the point is to have fun with something difficult, why not sometimes Sophocles or Aeschylus? Or August Wilson or

Tony Kushner or Chekhov? Any of these would also be a worthwhile challenge.

"I see Shakespeare as a gateway drug," said Agnes when I asked her. Presumably Shakespeare's immense prestige, over and above the quality of his work, is a factor. Agnes tells of walking with a cluster of Shakespeare actors past a group of card-playing inmates who looked up from their game as if at a powerful gang. Jack Hitt, whom I also contacted, told me that for the men of "Act V," Shakespeare was "a second hand-code"; a secret language. When Jack asked an inmate about his crime, "*I could a tale unfold*," the prisoner intoned, fixing Jack with a terrible eye,

> *...whose lightest word*
> *Would harrow up thy soul, freeze thy young blood,*
> *Make thy two eyes, like stars, start from their spheres.*

Borrowing Shakespeare's linguistic beauty to describe one's own experience is empowering for us all. For men in prison, mastery of his work can be a veritable claim to transformation.

SHAKESPEARE BEHIND BARS

Three years after *This American Life* aired "Act V," Philomath Films released Hank Rogerson and Jilann Spitzmiller's documentary *Shakespeare Behind Bars*. Named for the Shakespeare program at the Luther Luckett Correction Center in La Grange, Kentucky, the movie follows the lives of twenty inmates as they rehearse a production of Shakespeare's *The Tempest*. One of the most likeable is Jerry "Big G" Guenther, who killed a cop in a drug bust at twenty-one. Big G, like Big Hutch, is indeed big, with thinning flax/gray hair worn in something between a mullet and an aging biker's ponytail. He works in the laundry, where he can be seen reciting Shakespeare and folding clothes. His early prison mentors, he says, were hustlers. They taught him every known way of "getting over on the *poh*-lice," but "in Shakespeare" he learned something new. Now a scrawny youngster named Rick has joined the troupe, and Big G is his official mentor. By his own account, Rick has "been into every kind of dirt" that prison has to offer, but he's intrigued by Shakespeare and ready to change.

What if he doesn't change? asks an interviewer. If he gets sent to solitary, who will play his part? Big G smooths a pair of khaki pants on the dryer and glows as if he has a delightful secret.

"He's not going to the hole," he warmly says, "because he's a different person now than he was six months ago." We see Rick mopping huge turquoise and yellow linoleum squares; wringing out the filthy mop; hanging it on the wall next to eight or nine other filthy mops. Unfortunately, Rick *does* go to the hole and has to be replaced. Big G is at a loss for words.

"It's...disappointing," he finally says, folding; folding. But he cheers up when asked to comment on inmates as actors. Confident, leisurely, and amused, he stands in a doorway to explain. If it weren't for his girth, his shapeless prison shirt, and his awful haircut, he could be a lecturer at a local university.

"I've often thought that convicts are used to lying and playing roles," he says,

> but acting is the opposite of that, because it's to tell the truth, and to *inhabit* a character. And that's scary for me, for the rest of the guys in the group, to open themselves up, to connect their inner selves to the inner part of these characters that they're inhabiting and just bare themselves, you know, for the yard and for everyone else to see.

Who would have thought a high-security prison was the place to develop a sophisticated understanding of the actor's craft? There are professional actors who could learn from Big G's discussion of the place of truth onstage.

Q AND OPHELIA

Q. What did you do with Hamlet last night?
O. I didn't do anything with Hamlet.
Q. We heard he came to your room with *his doublet all unbraced.*
O. That wasn't last night.
Q. Whenever. What did you do?
O. Nothing, I tell you. Although...
Q. Yes?

O. That night I *thought* we would do it.

Q. In spite of promising…

O. …not to. But when I saw him like that…*pale as his shirt, his knees knocking each other…*

Q. Mmm. Hot guy!

O. (*annoyed*) Do you want to hear it or not?

Q. Sorry.

O. He *needed* me.

Q. (*nodding*) That'll do it.

O. (*pause*) He grabbed my wrist and looked at my face like I've never been looked at before. My blood was pounding. My knees were weak.

Q. And?

O. And nothing. After a few heart-stopping moments, he made his way to the door, his head turned back to look at me. Then he crossed the threshold and fled.

Q. Darn!

O. I wanted to run after him and say, "Sweetheart, what's wrong? Tell me, stay, I love you," but I didn't.

Q. Too well brought up.

O. Or something. Jesus!

Q. What? What? Stop that with your nails!

O. What?

Q. Stop scratching your face!

O. (*looking at her nails*) Oh, fuck.

Q. That's creepy!

O. (*intensely*) Q, what I did next was the worst mistake of my life. All those people dead, it was all my fault.

Q. *Your* fault? You're the innocent victim, O. Pawn of the patriarchy, etc.

O. (*inhales*) I told my father what happened.

Q. So?

O. Oh, he said, that explains Hamlet's weirdness. He's out of his mind with lust; or love. Let's tell the king.

Q. So?

O. They made a plan to spy on us, which I'm pretty sure Hamlet knew they were doing at the time. That was supposed to show the king it was all about me, which it wasn't.

Q. So?

o. An act or so later Hamlet killed my father.

q. That was an accident.

o. There are no accidents.

q. He heard a noise in Gertrude's room. He thought it was Claudius and blindly stabbed through a curtain.

o. He hated Polonius. *Thou wretched, rash, intruding fool, farewell!* he said to my father's fresh remains.

q. That's not nice.

o. No; although it's not untrue. I loved him, because he was my father; but *intruding fool* isn't wrong. Even Laertes knows that.

q. O...

o. What?

q. Why *did* Hamlet come to your room that night?

o. Presumably because he'd seen the ghost.

q. And wanted to tell you?

o. But couldn't, because he didn't trust me. Oh!

q. (*grabbing O's wrists*) Don't start!

o. He was afraid I'd tell Polonius. Which I did! It's all my fault!

q. That's nuts!

o. (*normal voice*) Well, I do go crazy by act four.

q. Just don't act crazy now!

o. (*shaking her head*) I can't believe I ran and told my dad.

WITNESSING

For her book on prison Shakespeare, *Shakespeare Inside*, Amy Scott-Douglas visited several prison programs, including those in Missouri and Kentucky. She, too, reports on Shakespeare as a phenomenon. Some inmates, she says, regard Shakespeare as "a sort of secular redeemer, a savior who is tolerant and loving and accepting of everyone." The old-timers "line their cells with books, quote from plays as if they were scripture, and witness to the men on the yard in an effort to bring others to Shakespeare." An inmate named Floyd Vaughn describes an event from his program in 2001.

Jerry Guenther and Sammie Byron were doing one of the skits where Brutus and Cassius go at it inside their tent, and they was doin' it in the bullpen. And it was so good that...I can't put it into words. Everybody on the walkway just stopped and watched the whole process. And I thought, "Wow." And as soon as they seen me, sitting there, and I clapped for them when they was done, they said, "Bingo. We got you."

"We got you." Like a missionary who's saved a soul.

Not everyone is in favor of prison Shakespeare. One volunteer in a prison program was asked by a guard, "Why do you want to teach these guys to be even better actors so they can do a more thorough job of fooling us?"

"Here they are," another dissenter complains, "criminals, doing something they're enjoying while their victims and their victims' families suffer." Politicians who cultivate the "tough on crime" vote encourage this sort of thing. Perhaps the best answer to all this comes from Curt Tofteland, the director of the Kentucky Shakespeare program. "If I could get all of the victims together in one place," he says, "I'd work with them. But I can't. So I work with the offenders."

Q AND PRISONER A

A. Now Hamlet runnin' around the castle, actin' weird.

Q. Feigning madness.

A. Old Claudius, he worried.

Q. Why?

A. He worried Hamlet knows what he did.

Q. Which he does.

A. The king send for Hamlet's good buddies, Rosencrantz and Guildenstern.

Q. Good Jewish buddies, from the sound of them.

A. Jewish rats.

Q. Are you anti-Semitic, A?

A. Not that I knows about it; but maybe Shakespeare, he was.

Q. You think?

A. Some. They all was, back then.

Q. Yeah.

A. Whatever they religion, Hamlet glad to see them; but then he get the feelin' somethin' up. Wait, he say, you workin' for the king? You come to spy on me?

Q. *If you love me, hold not off,* Hamlet pleads.

A. Dude can be sincere when he want to. Kinda wistful, you know?

Q. *Be even and direct with me,* he begs, *whether you were sent for or no.*

A. Rosencrantz take Guildenstern aside. *What say you?* he ask, real quiet. Hamlet watchin' to see whatall they gonna do.

Q. *My lord,* Guildenstern admits, *we were sent for.*

A. But don't say why.

Q. No.

A. They spyin' on him, all right. Hamlet real cool with them after that.

Q. For all the good it does him.

A. Oh, he gettin' his licks in.

Q. Still…

A. Yeah. They bad.

Q. They're awful.

SOLILOQUY: A TRAVELING PLAYER (ACT 2, SCENE 2)

We ran into Hamlet and his friends near an artificial lake he was think-ing of jumping into. We were on our way to Elsinore Castle, and from the manicured look of the paths and trees, we were already on the grounds.

What a piece of work is man! we heard Hamlet groan to Rosencrantz and Guildenstern as we came up. Hamlet's quite a piece of work him-self—we all are—but he didn't mean it like that. He meant, look how great "man" is, but I don't care; I'm depressed. We were pleased to see him anyway, because when Hamlet's there he makes sure we get good beds and enough to eat. Hello, we said, and he cheered right up. He loves our work.

Remember that play of yours? he eagerly said. I don't think you did it more than once; no one appreciates real theater these days. Damn, it was good! Remember that speech, Pyrrhus something something some-thing? Then he recited a whole swatch of the play.

That was a big moment for me. I had written that play myself; it was about the Trojan War. It had *pleased not the million,* as Hamlet put it, so it had closed quickly. In the speech Hamlet remembered, a Greek named

Pyrrhus had just killed Priam, and Hecuba, Priam's wife, was running up and down. I listened for a while, delighted; and then, almost unconsciously, I stepped in.

When she saw Pyrrhus make malicious sport, I declaimed when Hamlet paused, *in mincing with his sword her husband's limbs...* and so on and on. I don't know what got into me, but I was suddenly white hot. Under that enormous elm, clad in traveling clothes – the horses snorting and jerking the carts, the troupe impatient to get back on the road – I was as good as I've ever been. In fact, there was no "I." There was nothing but Pyrrhus, Priam, and Hecuba; and finally, nothing but grief.

It would have brought tears to heaven's eye, I said, shaken on Hecuba's behalf, *and passion in the gods.*

Look, cried that moron Polonius, he's got tears in his own eyes. *Prithee no more!* If even Polonius was moved, I'd done well.

Actors are superstitious. If they do well on a rainy Wednesday, they anxiously watch the sky before a Wednesday performance, hoping for rain. What did the trick this time? Hamlet's admiration? The impromptu spirit of the moment? The weather, the lake, the elm? Forget it, I told myself. Whatever had come together this time never would again. But for a moment I *was* a Trojan soldier shattered by Hecuba's loss. That's what an actor lives for. That's what we've got. The rest is just trudging from town to town, hoping for decent treatment.

WEEP FOR HECUBA (ACT 2, SCENE 2)

The players leave, and Rosencrantz and Guildenstern leave with them. Hamlet muses out loud, as he often does.

Look, he miserably says, how that player – in a mere *fiction;* in a mere *dream of passion* – could *force his soul* to do his bidding; which I can't.

What's Hecuba to him, or he to Hecuba, he asks, *that he should weep for her.* I, on the other hand, *the son of a dear father murdered,* just brood and mope and don't do shit. He decides to write a play that will force his uncle to reveal himself, and he does. The players duly perform it; Claudius duly reveals himself; and nothing changes.

Am I a coward? asks poor Hamlet. He cannot find his way into his role.

SOLILOQUY: PRISONER A

Hamlet always beratin' himself for not takin' out his uncle ASAP; we got a guy here, killed the friends who did his daddy before they lef' the house. And guess what? He gonna die in prison. Two life sentences, and he don't even get to *see* the parole board. Ever.

I don't know how they came up with that sentence, he tole us, shakin' his head. Dude, you killed two people, we tole him. I mean, yeah, it sucks; don't nobody deserve to *never* see the parole board; but nothin' good gonna happen for the brother here if he keep on blamin' the judge. He loved Shakespeare, and we thought he gonna be able to finish; but he in the hole now. Some dumb shit. Tattoos. Stealing. Dumb shit.

Q AND PRISONER A

Q. The guy in the hole blames the judge?

A. Yeah.

Q. But he shouldn't, you think.

A. Gotta stop blamin' other people. That come first.

Q. What comes next?

A. Then you blames yourself, of course. You blames yourself for hurtin' someone; and you blames yourself *real bad* for fuckin' up your life. You thinks of all the people hurtin' because of what you did. They hate you, and you thinks they got a point.

Q. Is that good?

A. It's a start.

Q. What comes next?

A. If you lucky, sooner or later, you apologizes to the others in your heart (*touching his heart*); then you forgives yourself.

Q. What if you've killed someone?

A. What I said.

Q. I'm saying, what if what you've done is unforgivable?

A. Forgive that, too.

Q. I don't see how.

A. Blame and forgive. Blame and forgive. It's a cycle, man. Got a life of its own.

Q. I see.

A. Finally you worn out. It want to start up again, but you just say, later man; I eatin' now. Or I workin', or I in the hole, or I playin' cards with my friends.

Q. And then?

A. I don't know, man. Then whatever, just like in regular life. Like in the play.

Q. What do you mean?

A. The whole way through, Hamlet askin' himself, I kill the king or not? I a man if I don't kill the king?

Q. But he's not *blaming* himself.

A. Yeah, he is. He sayin', why I ain't killed the king yet? When I gonna?

Q. That's true.

A. At the end he ain't sayin' that no more. He don't know whether he gonna kill the king or not. He just figure, whatever happen, that'll be what was *gonna* happen.

Q. (*remembering*) *If it be now, 'tis not to come.*

A. *If it be not to come, it will be now.*

Q. *If it be not now, yet it will come.* (Q *and* A *look at each other and nod.*)

A. *Let be.* That's what Hamlet say when he done blamin' the king *or* himself. *Let be.* That don't mean he don't kill the king.

Q. One last thing.

A. What?

Q. What if you didn't do it?

A. Do what?

Q. Whatever.

A. You didn't do it and you here anyway?

Q. That happens, you know. More than you'd think.

A. Yeah. I know.

Q. What do those people do?

A. Inside? In they heads?

Q. Yeah.

A. (*shaking his head*) I don't know nothin' 'bout that, man. I don't know nothin' 'bout that.

MURDERERS PLAYING MURDERERS

How bad are the men of "Act V" and *Shakespeare Behind Bars*? Many of them have qualities we associate with good citizenship. They may be well spoken, intelligent, self-aware, collegial, even witty. But, "This is 'Shakespeare Behind Bars,'" Big G points out when Rick goes down. "It's not Mary Poppins Productions." None of the inmates claims *not* to have broken the law. Jack Hitt tells of learning their crimes only after getting to know and like the inmates in "Act V." After reading their case records at the St. Louis records depository, he dreamed he was at a dinner party where the hostess, a long-time friend shot a guest in the face. "And the next thing I knew," he says,

> I was sitting up in my hotel bed, panting like a sprinter. It didn't take Freud to figure out what it meant. Someone I knew and liked was a murderer.

What a piece of work is man! How can we kill our wives, husbands, lovers, enemies, children, friends...or random people on the street...and then go on to love Shakespeare? Perhaps we've changed. That's what the inmates tell Jack, in any case.

"I'm no longer the criminal I used to be," says Danny Waller, who plays the ghost. "I know that I will not do any other crimes out there." On the other hand, he doesn't argue for his own release.

"I took a man's life," he says. "Do I deserve to be out there? I cannot say." Is the "I" who "cannot say" the same "I" who "took a man's life"? Danny both is and is not the man who committed the crime.

Q AND PRISONER A

A. Hamlet always sayin', who I am if I don't do this thing? We always saying, I ain't the thing I done!

Q. Right.

A. You done a crime, that's what you *are*. Long's you in prison, anyways. You get out, maybe things change.

Q. But Hamlet *is* a coward if he can't revenge.

A. That's what he think, man. Ain't necessarily so.

Q. What do you mean?

A. Killin' Claudius, by the time he do it, just the icing on the cake. Hamlet show who he is while he just rushin' around *thinkin'* 'bout killin' Claudius.

Q. So in the end he doesn't need to kill Claudius at all?

A. Yeah, he do.

Q. Why?

A. Cake gotta be iced, man. Don't nobody sing "Happy Birthday" if it ain't.

Q. Wow.

A. What?

Q. You've really thought about this play.

A. (*spreading his arms in a mocking way*) What else I got to do, my brother? What else I got to do?

SOLILOQUY: GERTRUDE (ACT 3, SCENE 4)

After the players performed his play, Hamlet went from bad to worse. He was crazed when he came to my room, and I truly feared for my life. I admit that Claudius storming out of the performance looked bad, but I hadn't had a chance to discuss it with him yet, so I wasn't sure what it meant. Hamlet knew, of course. It meant Claudius was guilty of fratricide. But what he wanted to discuss was not Claudius's guilt but how in the name of God I could go from being his father's wife to being Claudius's.

Could you on this fair mountain leave to feed, he roared, barely restraining himself from grabbing me, *And batten on this moor?* I was terrified.

So sorry, I said; yes, you're right; and whatever else he wanted to hear; but the fact is, my two husbands had a lot in common. They were brothers; they had similar interests and similar quirks.

Not only are you married to that thug, shouted Hamlet, you're *sleeping* with him! Big surprise. Children never like to think of their parents' sex lives. *Honeying and making love over the nasty sty!* is how he put it; and worse. The fact is, Claudius was very nice in bed. It wouldn't behoove me to compare him in that regard to Hamlet's father; but he was very nice.

How did I feel when Hamlet killed Polonius that night? No one's ever asked me that before. He was so mad he had to kill *somebody*; maybe I was just glad it wasn't me. In any case, it didn't fully register until later, when Ophelia came in barefoot and mad. She was singing and distributing flowers.

My brother shall know of it, she said in a pause between nutty songs. That didn't sound mad to me at all. My blood ran cold. Now Laertes would have to kill my son.

I'll lug the guts into the neighbor room, Hamlet said on leaving my room. That was boorish, to say the least; but I was in no position just then to reprimand him.

LAME (ACT 5, SCENE 2)

Before fighting the duel that will kill them both, Hamlet offers Laertes an apology of sorts. If Hamlet, he says, speaking of himself in the third person, *does wrong Laertes* while mad,

> *Then Hamlet does it not...*
> *Who does it then? His madness. If't be so,*
> *Hamlet is of the faction that is wronged;*
> *His madness is poor Hamlet's enemy.*

What sort of an apology is that? "So sorry, I wasn't myself at the time; and believe me, I'm as much a victim of what I did as you are!" Danny Waller's sense of self-difference is far more nuanced than this. In fact, Hamlet never really repents of killing Polonius, even after his girlfriend dies lamenting the murder.

We forgive him anyway. Why? Because Shakespeare wants us to. He signals this in many ways, but one of the most important is by having Laertes lead the way.

Exchange forgiveness with me, noble Hamlet, says Laertes as the two men face death. *Mine and my father's death come not upon thee.* However inadequate Hamlet's performance of remorse, it satisfies his accuser, who offers not just earthly absolution but a prayer for Hamlet's soul. God is not to punish Hamlet on Laertes's behalf; and, by extension, nor should we.

PERFORMING REPENTANCE

In *Shakespeare Behind Bars* an inmate named Howard comes up for parole. A metal door beneath a plain black-and-white sign reading

PAROLE BOARD ROOM marks the site of his failure to get it.

"They gave me sixty months," Howard stolidly says when it's over. "So I'll be in Shakespeare another five years." Unlike Laertes, most parole boards require repentance before showing mercy. But how do they know the repentance is real? Can't repentance be performed? We don't see Howard plead his case, but another inmate, Leonard Hood, does repent onscreen. The interview takes place around a bare, circular table on which Leonard rests his handcuffed wrists. He is in the green hospital pajamas worn by men in solitary confinement. Leonard has never before spoken to the media, but the *Shakespeare Behind Bars* crew believe he is "ready," and he is. He urgently parses the last lines from *The Tempest* to make his point:

> *As you from crimes would pardoned be,*
> *Let your indulgence set me free.*

"Indulgence" means "redemption," he explains, leaning tensely forward. He longs to be redeemed, which is to say, paroled. He wants to make amends and be remembered for something other than his crimes.

"What's the worst thing you ever did?" the interviewer asks at length. For thirty long seconds Leonard is silent. Tension mounts. His eyes close; his face gives up.

"I sexually molested seven girls," he finally says. The camera cuts to his handcuffed wrists.

When I first saw this scene my only question was whether the filmmakers had the right to probe this deep onscreen. Leonard seemed helpless and raw.

"It may be too much," I said. My companion, on the other hand, was unconvinced.

"He sees the cameras running," he said. "Who knows? It could be an act."

"Don't be so cynical!" I said; but he might be right. There's no state of mind that can't be enacted, no matter its status as "truth." Later, in a confusing montage, we learn that Leonard is guilty of some new violation of the rules. Over a shot of a departing bus an onscreen title informs us of his transfer to a maximum-security facility.

Q AND PRISONER A

Q. What did you do, A?

A. Yeah, you gotta ask. I knew you would.

Q. You'd rather I didn't?

A. Yeah.

Q. Don't answer then.

A. What the fuck.

Q. I'm sorry, A.

A. What the fuck. You asked. (*inhales*) I killed a man. Wasn't even high, just out of my head. Tied him up; put him in the back seat; shot him dead.

Q. Why?

A. No reason.

Q. That's crazy!

A. I was crazy, all right.

Q. But you don't seem crazy at all.

A. I ain't. Crazy then; not crazy now. Parole board didn't get it; gave me ten years.

Q. Ten years! How long ago was that?

A. Nine years ago. Nine years, eleven months, and thirteen days.

Q. So you're coming up again soon!

A. Real soon.

Q. What happened at the hearing? If you remember.

A. Two things I think about every day: what I done, and what happened at the hearing. I remembers, all right.

Q. Well?

A. (*waves a hand*) You ain't got time to hear it.

Q. Yeah, I do.

A. Yeah? (*looks at* Q)

Q. I'm listening.

A. (*silence; then*) Okay, but I gotta stand up.

Q. (*pushing his chair back*) Stand up, then.

A. (*standing*) Okay. (*inhales*) So. I get in the room, victim's supporters already there. (*gestures along the wall, as if that's where they were*) Judge come in, we all stand. Proceedin's start. Whole time the lawyers talkin' I lookin' at this young woman by the wall. Well, she ain't all that young anymore; but she frozen in time. The others still angry, want me dead, but she look *sad*. I look to see, she got a wedding ring? Found someone new? But she don't. She look so sad it make me cry. I so sorry, I tole her when my turn came to talk. I don't know whatall I said, but I talked on and on. I thinkin' of her, I swear, tryin' to say what might help. But right in the middle, my face all wet, I think, what this look like to the parole board? I gonna make parole? I sure wisht I hadn't a had that thought just then! Parole board don't know what I'm thinkin' of course; or maybe they do. Maybe they think, he not really cryin' because he sad; he in Shakespeare, he know how to cry. It ain't true, but how they gonna know? Then that thought come outta nowhere, damn, this look good! I sure wisht I hadn't a had that thought! (*shakes his head; exhales; sits down*)

Q. (*after a pause*) So you weren't paroled.

A. No, man. I wasn't.

Q. Too bad.

A. Yeah.

Q. That's all you have to say?

A. (*irritably*) What you want me to say?

Q. Are you angry?

A. I was then.

Q. And now?

A. (*looks at Q with some irony*) Shit, man, I'm what they call a model prisoner. I'm in every program they got; workin' on a college degree. I so fast in the Data Lab I got a job waitin' for me when I get out. What they want? I know what I done. I feel remorse. Then I have this awful thought, this look good just now? Maybe they could hear what I thinkin'. Maybe invisible letters on my forehead say, this guy *actin'*.

Q. I didn't know you had a Data Lab here.

A. There's lots you don't know.

Q. What do you do there?

A. Keys in data 'bout marriages, deaths, and divorces for the state. Like I say, got a job with the company waitin' for when I get out. *If* I get out.

Q. When's your next parole board hearing?

A. Like I say: soon.

Q. How do you prepare for it?

A. I tries not to think about it twenty-four seven.

SOLILOQUY: HORATIO (ACT 5, SCENE 2)

When Hamlet told me how he disposed of Rosencrantz and Guildenstern, he was unrepentant. Claudius had shipped him off under the
supervision of his former friends, who had a letter to the king of England to have him executed. One night Hamlet tiptoed into their cabin,
found the letter, and rewrote it to order *their* executions instead. Then
he escaped on a pirate ship that conveniently pulled up. The pirates liked
him, so they brought him home. Done!

We were walking the halls of the castle.

So Rosencrantz and Guildenstern go to't, I said after a moment. It was
the lightest possible suggestion that he might feel remorse. He turned
to me in surprise.

Why, man, he exclaimed, *they did make love to this employment.
They are not near my conscience.* Well, I suppose you could call it self-
defense. In any case, I dropped the topic.

Why, what a king is this! I said. I meant Claudius, of course.

Don't you think I should kill him? Hamlet compulsively asked.

He'll soon hear from England what you've done, I said. I was really
worried, but he refused to take precautions.

What will be will be, he said, or words to that effect.

True enough, I said. If he was feeling calm, far be it from me to disturb
his peace. I walked alongside him in silence.

Q AND PRISONER A

Q. Hey.

A. What?

Q. What about the war?

A. What war?

Q. The war against Norway. What's that even about?

A. Fortinbras up in arms about some land his daddy lost to Denmark. Old
   Hamlet won it fair and square, but Fortinbras young, he want it back.

Q. Why don't we hear more about it?

A. Because Fortinbras's uncle call it off in act two!

Q. His uncle?

A. Fortinbras's daddy die, so his uncle get to be king. He real mad when
   he hear what his nephew doin'; tell him to cease and desist. Fortinbras

gotta have somethin' to fight about, so he go after some dumbass piece of land in Poland.

Q. Who cares?

A. Exactly. Hamlet hear about it, first he say, I can't believe it, man. What he want that for? Can't farm it, can't do nothin', who cares? Then he say, ain't that great? Dude fightin' over nothin'. I can't even fight when my daddy's been done by that stupid piece of shit now sittin' on the throne.

Q. Same old, same old.

A. Dude's a *rare and delicate prince*, he says; and I'm a mook.

Q. (*shakes his head*)

A. Hamlet don't let no opportunity go by.

Q. For self-flagellation.

A. Same old, same old.

SECRETS

Prisons these days are more and more about retributive justice, less and less about rehabilitation. The Shakespeare programs are an effort, at least, at redressing the balance. They seem to work, although to different degrees, of course, for different participants. Alumni of the programs say everything from "It saved my life!" to "It was something to do." What interests me here is not the degree to which the programs may or may not succeed, but the contrast between opposing approaches to theater as rehabilitation. Curt Tofteland's process encourages his actors directly to share their past as they engage with the play, while Agnes Wilcox more or less explicitly excludes it.

In Shakespeare Behind Bars in Kentucky, the men are fond of saying their roles chose them, rather than the other way around. Their roles chose them, Curt encourages them to think, to help them reflect on their crimes and the state of their souls at the time of their offense. Sometimes this yields dramatic results. A prisoner named Sammie, for instance, serving time for having strangled his girlfriend, had a breakthrough playing Othello. When he "strangled" Desdemona, played by his good friend Mike, Sammie finally "got" what he had done.

"Then I was able to see, in the face of someone that I cared about," Sammie says, "exactly what was going on with them." He is in tears as he talks. "There's no excuse for what I've done," he chokes. The men are familiar with each other's transgressions, and if we watch the movie, so are we. Big G, as we've seen, shot a cop; Leonard abused young girls; Hal, who plays Prospero, dropped a hair dryer into his wife's bathwater, electrocuting her to death. The actors help each other come to terms with the awful things they've done, suggesting connections and celebrating epiphanies.

Agnes Wilcox works differently. Not only does she refrain from using her actors' crimes to shed light on their roles and vice versa; she makes a point of guarding the past with silence. When Jack Hitt looked up their cases in the St. Louis depository, Agnes was upset, and so were some of the men.

"I felt I'd betrayed them all," he told me.

What are her reasons for taking this approach? Perhaps she wants the program to be a space of freedom from a prisoner's identity as "criminal." Perhaps she feels that her actors' development as actors will of itself promote their development, and that indirection is the surest path to growth. On the other hand, many acting teachers and directors do insist on "secrets" per se. In a training manual called *Acting Is Believing*, the very word is listed as a theatrical term.

"Found in all great acting," say the authors, a "secret" is "a character's *private* history that arouses an audience's strong curiosity about his inner life." Actors are urged to keep the "substitutions" they make from their own memories strictly to themselves.

"DO NOT SHARE your substitutions," says the great acting guru Uta Hagen, "with anyone, ever. It will change the way they perceive you." Perhaps Agnes believes "substitutions" are more powerful if they are also "secrets." Perhaps she thinks her actors in particular need protection from other people's perceptions of them.

"I am not privy to their discoveries," Agnes told me firmly. "Everyone takes what they need from the play."

FLASHBACK (ACT 3, SCENE 2)

Now Rosencrantz and Guildenstern are dead; but earlier in the play something transpired between them and Hamlet that is worth remembering here. After Claudius stormed out of the play-within-the-play, it came to a halt, and players and audience dispersed. Hamlet was chatting with Rosencrantz and Guildenstern when traveling players came drifting through the castle, some with recorders from the performance. When they passed by, Hamlet was inspired to an improvisation.

O, the recorders, he said, relieving the players of one of them. He turned to Guildenstern and asked, *Will you play upon this pipe?* Guildenstern said he didn't know how.

I pray you, urged Hamlet.

I can't, said Guildenstern again. Weirdly, Hamlet persisted.

I pray you, he said.

Believe me, I cannot.

I beseech you… and so on. Finally Hamlet came to the point:

Why, look you now, how unworthy a thing you make of me! You would play upon me; you would pluck out the heart of my mystery; you would sound me from my lowest note to the top of my compass; but you cannot play this pipe. Do you think I am easier to be played on than a pipe?

The key word here is *mystery.* What is a person's "mystery," his "secret"? Is it a handle by which we can have him? In the case of the prisoners, is it their crimes?

"What's the worst thing you've ever done?" the interviewer asks Leonard. Hamlet, if he were unfortunate enough to be incarcerated in Kentucky for his crimes, wouldn't answer the question. He wouldn't confess onscreen; he wouldn't discuss his past with his director, his fellow actors, or the media.

Do you think I am easier to be played on than a pipe? he would say. In other words: fuck off.

Q AND PRISONER A

A. Hamlet mysterious all right.

Q. Say how.

A. First, he love Ophelia or not?

Q. Well?

A. She got some old valentines he wrote her, but he don't say one sweet thing to her, whole play. Plus, he kill her daddy, don't think how she feel.

Q. Yeah. Would it have killed him to say, So sorry, sweetie. Believe me, I didn't mean to do it.

A. Plus, why he write that play?

Q. To test the ghost's word, of course.

A. He doubt the ghost? Then why he act like he don't?

Q. Good point.

A. He never tell Horatio or nobody, Hey, ghost could be lyin'.

Q. Just the opposite! He's pro-ghost all the way!

A. Then out of nowhere, he write this play. Second...

Q. Yes?

A. Why he tell his momma to stop havin' sex?

Q. So she won't be tempted to tell her husband the truth about Hamlet. That he's not really mad.

A. They gotta have sex for her to tell him that?

Q. You know, A...pillow talk!

A. Listen...she stop havin' sex with him, Claudius gonna *know* something up.

Q. (*laughing*) True.

A. Three, why he delay?

Q. Hutch's question.

A. Yeah.

Q. Because if he didn't, there'd be no play. If the ghost says, kill, and he kills...that's it! Boom, done.

A. That ain't what you'd call motivation.

Q. *All* revengers delay. It's a crucial feature of the genre.

A. Dude, we don't know shit about Hamlet. We don't even know if he a good man! We *like* him, yeah, but he do things good men don't. He mysterious, all right.

Q. As opposed to Laertes, who isn't.

A. Mysterious.

Q. Or Fortinbras.

A. Those brothers kinda simple. Laertes hear Hamlet killed his father, he come tearin' home from wherever he been screamin' bloody murder. He never, like, looks within.

Q. "Kill Hamlet." That's Laertes.

A. Fortinbras, too.

Q. Wants just one thing: win wars for Norway.

A. (*shaking his head*) The two of them runnin' around wavin' they swords every time someone look at them cross-eyed.

Q. Whereas Hamlet…

A. You don't know what he'll do next. Can't *pluck out his heart*, like he say; can't stop tryin'.

Q. He's unfathomable, then.

A. (*sitting back*) He mysterious, man. Like I say.

SOLILOQUY: GERTRUDE (ACT 4, SCENE 7; ACT 5, SCENE 1)

I thought Hamlet *did* love Ophelia. I thought he meant to marry her, although I could be wrong. What do I know? I "just want to have Christmas," just as Katie said.

When Ophelia died, I had to tell Laertes.

Your sister's drowned, Laertes, I told him. There was no way to soften it. She fell from a tree she was garlanding. Why she was unattended I don't know, since we knew she wasn't well. She fell in a brook and sang to herself for a while; then she drowned.

Sweets to the sweet, farewell! I said at her funeral, throwing flowers on her coffin. *I thought thy bride bed to have decked, sweet maid, and not have strewed thy grave!* She was a sweetheart, all right. I hope Hamlet loved her.

A PIECE OF WORK

Is privacy part of mystery? If so, the mystery of the prisoners in "Act V" and *Shakespeare Behind Bars* is severely compromised by invasions on their privacy. Body cavity searches, for instance, are required before they can attend rehearsals. Edgar Evans, an actor in "Act V," says it's worth it.

Agnes makes us feel human, man. When I go in there I have to take my clothes off and get butt naked and bend over and spread my cheeks so some man can look up my butt. You know, all the humiliating things that they do to us here. And when she comes in and does what she does, for all that minute, those two and a half hours—I at least can feel human in here. I think this is taking me to be sane. For just one day. Just one day I'm sane enough.

What is it about Shakespeare or prison theater that "takes a man to be sane"? Whatever the magic, it works in even harsher conditions as well. Laura Bates, a professor at Indiana University, runs yet another Shakespeare program, this one for men who live in "segregated housing" at the Wabash Valley Correctional Facility in Indiana. "Segregated housing" means that the men live in "the hole" on a more or less permanent basis. The prison is a super-maximum facility for "the worst of the worst," men who have either tried to escape or committed violent crimes in prison itself. Forbidden to associate with each other, the inmates can neither rehearse nor perform the plays as a group; but they read Shakespeare in their cement cells, and Professor Bates has permission to hold discussions once a week.

"This place is *great*," says one enthusiastic participant, gesturing at his eight-by-ten-foot cell. "Great for reading Shakespeare." Another participant says the program is a necessity. Otherwise, what he calls "living in your bathroom" for six years, as he has, could drive you nuts.

Professor Bates's students, like Agnes's actors, go through a lot to get to class. "To come to the Shakespeare group," she writes,

a prisoner must place his hands through the cuff port in his steel cell door and be handcuffed behind his back before his door is opened. He must be frisked and, perhaps, strip-searched. With his hands and feet bound, and a leather leash attached to his chains, he is escorted by two officers to the area, where he is again locked into an individual cell. I sit in the middle of a narrow hallway with prisoners in four side-by-side cells on each side of me, a total of eight. For two hours, they kneel on the concrete floor, with shackles still on their legs, and communicate to each other through the opened cuff ports in the steel doors.

This appalling scene can be seen, bizarrely enough, on YouTube, leather leash and all. The truncated faces seen through the cuff ports are mostly young and engaged. They are grappling with the question Professor Bates has posed for the day: Is Macbeth motivated by conscience or ego? An inmate named Leon Benson is asked how long he's been in the program.

"It must be, what," he says, looking toward another cell for help, "seven years?" At that his young face lights up. "Seven years!" he exclaims, in a delighted voice, as one might say, "Thirteen years!" or "Two years!" or "Forty years!" on realizing the length of one's fruitful marriage. We give ourselves credit for sticking with something good.

What a piece of work is man! says Hamlet. *How noble in reason! How infinite in faculties!* And yet some men end up leading others around on leather leashes; and some end up being led. What a piece of work.

There's more to my story, so I need to go on; but my story's just a story, and at this point one might wish for something else. The power to make changes, perhaps. Something else.

SOLILOQUY: HORATIO (ACT 5, SCENE 2)

After Hamlet got back from England, it was only a matter of time before Claudius would make his move. I said as much, and Hamlet agreed.

It will be short, he said. *The interim's mine.*

Short indeed. That very day a nitwit named Osric showed up to say the king wanted Hamlet to "play" with Laertes, "play" being a euphemism for "duel." All very friendly, of course.

Let the foils be brought, Hamlet amicably said; but later he confessed to some unease.

Well, yeah, I said. All in good fun? Both Claudius and Laertes wanted him dead, but Hamlet and Laertes were going to "play" like gamboling cubs?

If your mind dislike any thing, I told him strongly, *obey it. I will fore-stall them and say you are not fit.* Of course he refused.

Let be, he said. So I let be. The result, you might say, was a pile-up of corpses. The king had persuaded Laertes to poison the end of his sword, but in a scuffle the swords were exchanged, and each man fatally wounded the other. Claudius had taken the precaution of poisoning some wine as well, so if Hamlet didn't die from the sword fight he'd die from the conviviality. In the middle of the swordfight, however, Gertrude toasted her son with the poisoned wine. Oops!

Kerplunk.

O my dear Hamlet! she called from the floor. *The drink, the drink! I am poisoned.* Finally, it seemed, she saw the light: Hamlet good, Claudius bad. Of course it was too late. Hamlet grabbed the goblet and forced the rest down Claudius's throat.

Here, thou incestuous, murd'rous, damned Dane, he cried. *Drink off this potion.* Then everybody died.

Was this revenge at last? Perhaps; but the ghost was nowhere to be seen, and no one was thinking of Hamlet Senior. Hamlet was "revenging," if that's the word, his own and his mother's deaths as much as his father's. Before he died, he asked me to *report [his] cause* to the world.

No way, I said, seizing the poisoned goblet. I'm going with you. I can't explain the state I was in at the time. The carnage, the horror, the loss of my best friend . . . I seemed to have nothing left.

O God, Horatio, Hamlet cried, *what a wounded name, things standing thus unknown, shall live behind me!* I beg you, stick around and *tell my story!*

A wounded name. Our "name" is our most precious possession, our story. Now, at the threshold of death, Hamlet wanted his name to survive him whole, and I was its only hope. I let him have the cup; too late. His hand went slack. The goblet fell, and I heard its rim and base take turns tattooing the floor.

Gonegonegone, said the bouncing cup. Gonegonegone. The wine spilled out completely, veining with red the veined white marble floor.

Now the play is done, and I'm still here. I've been telling Hamlet's story now for four hundred years, and I must say, people like it. In fact, apart from tales in scriptures and myth, it may be the greatest story ever told.

"So I went to the ramparts," I begin each time, "and there was the ghost." I'm often struck anew by Hamlet's greatness.

"Wait, wait," I want to say, "listen to the amazing thing Hamlet said about death. Listen to how he confronted his mother; teased Polonius; competed with Laertes at Ophelia's funeral."

Forty thousand brothers, he shouted, leaping into his girlfriend's grave, *could not make up with all their quantity of love my sum.*

"I won the lottery," I think, dazzled. "I got the best part: teller of the tale."

Most days, I admit, aren't like that. Most days I just do it, as one does anything, making a conscious effort at freshness and sincerity when I remember to do so. But my favorite moments come when the story is neither fresh nor stale, neither a burden nor a gift. At such times there's no Horatio at all; not even enough to tell his friend, I'm here, my lord; I'm listening.

Aye, m'lord, I kept telling Hamlet. *Yes, my lord;* go on. Hutch thought that was too little, but at best, it's too much. Then the story's neither mine, nor his, nor yours. It's just itself. I disappear.

I disappear.

The story tells itself.

PHONING BIG HUTCH

"Having seen every performance, I can testify, " says Jack Hitt in *This American Life.* "In the last show the actors rose above their talents." The real surprise was Hutch. "I always thought," says Jack,

> that Hutch was plagued by what you might call the Jack Nicholson syndrome. The actor's persona is bigger than any role he might play. But in that last performance, Horatio has Hutch under control and the audience in his hand.

Good night, sweet prince, says Horatio as Hamlet lies dying, *and flights of angels sing thee to thy rest.* On the website Hutch does sound full of sorrow and love. I called Derrick Hutchinson to congratulate him on his performance and ask some questions. These days he drives a street sweeper, working at night and sleeping during the day. After fifteen minutes I got to the point.

"Do you still think you'd have to kill someone who raped your daughter?" I asked. I didn't say "do" or "take care of " or "whack" or "take out." I said "kill."

"You bet," said Hutch instantly. You don't mess with family. He explained that he wouldn't touch a woman or an old person, but someone in the yard? A hustler? Someone already bad? Yeah, he's a target.

"Okay," I said. Okay. As Big G would say, this is Prison Arts, not Mary Poppins Productions. Also on my mind was Hutch's participation in the alumni group Agnes coordinates in St. Louis. Ex-cons from her program perform for possible donors to the Prison Arts Program once every three or four months.

"Is it fun?" I asked.

"Fun??" echoed Hutch. "Not at all!" It was work, and annoying work at that. Too much rehearsal, he said. And his fellow actors never know their lines.

"I work fourteen hours a night," he said. "I have about a three-hour window, you know what I mean? If I can learn lines on my schedule, so can you. I don't want to go there and you don't know your lines." It's worthwhile, he said, because it's a positive thing. "But if you don't put out effort then you really wastin' my time."

"So why do you do it?" I asked.

"If it wasn't for Agnes," he swore, "I wouldn't deal with you." Admiration for Agnes seemed to be universal among the people I contacted. Jack said he had had to struggle against the temptation to make "Act V" a paean of praise to her talent, persistence, and wit.

"I don't know why," said Hutch, "but I like that little short lady. That's why I do it. I like her."

May *flights of angels*, Hutch tells the dying Hamlets, *sing thee to thy rest*. A flight of angels; a pounce of cats; a pitying of doves; a busyness of ferrets. Agnes's production calls for a new collective noun. A self-hatred of Hamlets? An intelligence of Hamlets? A vivacity, an intensity, a mutability of Hamlets? You decide.

PAROLE

A. I gotta go.

Q. Why?

A. My parole hearing this morning.

Q. That's great!

A. Be great if I make parole.

Q. I'll walk you to the board room.

A. (*pointing*) See that sign?

Q. You mean we're here?

A. Been here for a while.

Q. Just be yourself, and you'll do fine!

A. (*irritated*) Just be myself?!? Shit, man...what we been talkin' about this whole time?

Q. I just meant...

A. (*waving a hand*) Forget it.

Q. Well…good luck.

A. An' don't say good luck!

Q. (*startled*) Why not?

A. I'm an actor, you know.

Q. (*relieved*) Oh, I get it.

A. You says…

Q. I know: break a leg.

A. Yeah.

Q. Break a leg, then.

A. (*indifferently*) Thanks.

Q. (*fervently*) May flights of angels sing your praises in the judge's ear. (A *meets* Q*'s eye*) Oh, A, may you break a leg!

(A *nods. The door opens to admit* A.)

THE GROSS CLINIC

April 5. "Do you like that one?" I asked Nick yesterday. It was Thomas Eakins's painting *Max Schmitt in a Single Scull.* Another artist might have painted the oarsman straining at the oars, a vein standing out in his forehead and sweat darkening his clothes, but Max is seated in the drifting boat, both oars in one hand. He looks at the viewer with no particular meaning.

Nick considered the painting. "No," he said. "It's borderline dull." He went off to look at something else, and I stood there thinking of Bob.

"I guess he worked all day and then went rowing," he might have said. I would have heard in that Bob's profound approval of the scene before us: the brown trees, the red canoe, the clear, quiet light on one side of the river, the shade on the other. Because Bob was there, I would have become conscious of the painter himself, his patient, careful presence suffusing the picture like the light itself. The river was calm, and the trees along its banks were clearly reflected on its surface.

"I want my real husband back," I thought. But it's been eight years since I lost Bob, and I've been married to Nick for three.

"Get a life!" I told myself. Bob was somewhere in the painting, reaching me from far away. I stood in front of it, trying to warm myself in his long and vanishing rays.

I got Bob interested in Eakins when I showed him *The Gross Clinic,* which portrays a surgeon in the middle of an operation. For the occasion Samuel Gross wears a dark, rumpled suit and vest, a far cry from the ill-fitting blue pajamas Bob wore during surgery. But Bob identified with the look on Gross's face, absorbed and passionate, blood on his hands. The violence of surgery is transmogrified by its passage through the great man's brain and heart.

"I'm a plumber," Bob's friend Lou used to say. "I fix hearts like plumbers fix toilets." Not Bob.

Once I woke up on a Sunday morning to find Bob on his way out of the house.

"I need eggs," he said.

"There are eggs in the refrigerator," I said from bed. I didn't want him to go.

"I need lots of eggs," he said. He came home with six-dozen eggs, and spent the morning at the sink peeling them all. He was trying to get all the shell off without breaking the thin membrane between the shell and the egg.

When I told Lucille about it she said, "You mean cooked eggs, right? Hard-boiled?"

"*Raw*," I said. "Uncooked." Bob was practicing to remove a thin bone from someone's body without breaking the mucous membrane behind it. He stood at the sink tapping the eggs as if he were a demolitions expert defusing a bomb.

"But in a kindly way," I told Lucille. "As if the eggs could get hurt." He didn't stop when he got it right. Egg after egg would be gently stripped of its shell and rest exposed in Bob's large, beautiful, wonder-working hands. You could see the yolks lolling around in their thick, translucent whites, relaxed, ready to become alive or not.

"Look," he said, when he got the first one whole. Half an hour later I came into the kitchen and saw there was the same pleasure in it for him every time.

I can't imagine Nick doing *anything* for that long at a stretch. Nick is always finishing up, snapping stuff into a drawer, clicking things shut. Most people who do what Nick does spend the day at their machines, but Nick works at something for fifteen minutes and then runs out for food or supplies. Later he'll be working again. Books being reshelved, files stashed away, the camera whirring shut, moving on, that's Nick.

"Nick!" I want to say. "Alight!" It feels as if he's on some line or belt that's moving at a different pace from me.

Actually, there's nothing wrong with being in motion. It's just his style. But…where's the *gravitas* in Nick?

Eakins looked at things for a long, long time. He looked at his sitters so long they grew old under his gaze, so he painted them old. "Eakins, I wish you were dead!" Gross once said after an interminable session. But that's where Eakins gets his famous insight, from looking. Even at the zoo Nick moves too fast.

I first noticed Bob because he was looking at me. He was a resident; I was a fourth-year medical student. I had come into an on-call room to get some sleep, and instead I was having a nervous breakdown, howling and crying without restraint. Bob came down from the upper bunk to help.

"I didn't know there was anybody here!" I bawled. There was nothing in the room but the bunk bed and a telephone – no windows, no table, no tissues on the table for medical students who were cracking up. I blew my nose again and again into the sheet, making the dim, squalid scene truly disgusting. Bob thought I was crying from fatigue, or from the recent death of a patient, or from guilt over a fatal mistake, and he tried to comfort me.

"Just don't take drugs to get through it," he said. "That's the worst." We were hunched on the lower bunk. I didn't care how many of my patients I killed anymore, but I couldn't tell him that; so I complained in a lying, evasive way, and Bob answered without making any impression at all. Then we gave up, and I just cried in long despairing waves, now wilder, now calmer, until I couldn't cry anymore. Bob leaned against the metal bunk frame and watched me cry.

"That's it, now," I said, blowing my nose with finality. What I meant was, you can go. I'm not going to kill myself. But nothing happened. I blew my nose some more and looked up. There was Bob, gray in the face from his own interminable shift, looking right at me through his brown eyes. I hardly knew him. Suddenly I felt exposed.

"Go away!" I said before I could stop myself. Bob looked surprised, but didn't look away. I met his eyes.

"No, stay," I said quickly. We looked at each other in silence. "I don't like this," I finally said.

"Crying?" he asked.

"No, being a doctor," I said.

"That's bad," he said feelingly. "When you feel that, it's bad."

"You don't understand," I said. "I've always hated it!"

"Then why are you here?" he reasonably asked. I told him about Professor Birkholtz, my college biology teacher. To him the human body was the weirdest, most delightful thing in the world, a patchwork of clumsy and elegant solutions. Every failure, every jury-rigged or redundant system just made him feel how far beyond us it all is and excited him all the more. Studying with Professor Birkholz had made me feel that being a doctor would be an adventure. But medical school was nothing but nomenclature, and I was ashamed every day that I didn't quit.

"Then quit!" said Bob.

"After all this money and work..." I helplessly said. The time wore on, and for some reason no one disturbed us. His beeper didn't go off and neither did mine. Eventually I fell asleep, and when I woke up he was gone. I felt as if I had been sleeping for hours, protected as if by a ring of spear grass in a field. The dim hump of my body under the sheets was comforting to behold, and the bland, cramped space was my home.

"When was the last time I woke up naturally?" I thought. Later it turned out that I had turned my beeper off by mistake, and I got in a lot of trouble. I didn't care. By then I had something else to think about, and it was Bob. I kept seeing his thoughtful eyes, brown in the colorless room. The rest of his body came back to me in pieces, as my interest in it developed. Of course, he wasn't thinking about me romantically after the performance I had put on, so I had to pursue him at length. Finally I convinced the chief resident that I had an irreconcilable personality conflict with my team leader and got switched to Bob's.

"Edwina!" he said uneasily, when he learned what I had done. He knew why I was there and didn't think it was a very good reason.

"Don't worry," I said, pretending to misunderstand. "All that's behind me." I worked hard to impress him with my newfound commitment as a healer, insightful, thorough, and kind. I also tried to impress him with the sexy scraps of clothing visible through the opening in my white coat, with notes and messages, with my amazing capacity to show up in the cafeteria just when he arrived. What I really wanted was to run into him again in the on-call room, and finally I did.

"This is precisely what these rooms are not for," Bob mused after we'd made love. When I thought of the on-call room after that it seemed to me like a field of paint in which the apparently neutral colors—dun, white, steel gray—turn out to conceal within them flaming red and the whole rainbow of colors of flesh. Three months later I quit, safely engaged to Bob.

I have never been so lost to myself as I was in medical school, not even when Bob died. By then I was older and could find my way back on a daily basis, however briefly, to a sense of reality.

"I am a woman whose dear husband has died," I would say to myself. "It is my turn to grope in the dark. Although I don't know why I should do so, I will pick up this book and put it on the bookshelf; then I will eat cereal with milk." It was hell, but I was there in hell with myself. In medical school "Edwina," who would soon be a doctor, was an outsized, over-colored, cardboard figure, like something outside a store.

Bob really was what he thought he was. He knew what to do with himself. That's the beauty of a profession: not only can you earn a living from it, but it tells you what to *want*. Bob wanted more mastery of more procedures, more technical support, more access to research, more patients, more students. And somewhere in there, of course, more money and success. But for someone like Bob, money and success are just a by-product of all the rest.

Art history is obviously a better profession for me than medicine, and thank God I got my degree and found work; but I'm not, like, gung ho—like most of my colleagues. I don't have a field; I just like to think in an unsystematic way about whatever catches my attention. That must be okay with the Powers That Be at the museum, because they want me to do the gallery talks on Eakins, our biggest show of the year. I'm flattered, of course, but anxious, too. On the one hand I'm not sure what I'll say, since I'm no expert on Eakins; on the other hand, I'm afraid working him up will keep me too sad at having lost the husband I could share him with.

Of course, there's no question of not doing it. I'm not *that* unprofessional.

Eakins loved professionals. All the men he painted had *become* their professions, all his scientists, cellists, clergymen, professors, and so on. In France it was called the *portrait d'apparat*, but the French paintings focus on the subject's success whereas Eakins made his successful men look shabby. Leslie Miller, a famous professor of classics, had to wear a sack coat he used for biking. Of James Holland, an Anglican dean, Miller said, "[Eakins] made the poor Dean go and put on a pair of old shoes that he kept to go fishing in, and painted him shod in this way when he faced a distinguished audience." The pleasures of professional dedication only show up as occasional grace notes: a glint of red in the string of a cello; a rainbow-colored diffraction device in the hand of a ramrod-backed, wing-tipped physicist; a luscious pile of women's clothing in the studio of a black-suited sculptor. In *The Writing Master* the sober, hardworking subject, who happens to be Eakins's father, produces luxuriant curlicues on thick, curled parchment. Perhaps Benjamin Eakins, whose success and dedication to his craft generated the income to support his beloved grown-up son, was the prototype for all those other admirable, successful, work-worn men.

And then there's Nick. What does Nick do, exactly? He's sort of a software consultant; he's sort of a photographer; he's sort of an intellectual. He's someone in whom obsessions come and go. These days it's cosmology. Suddenly he's talking about Jupiter, dark matter, walls of galaxies, and so on. Where did it come from? Last year it was Chinese history, and there were elaborate charts of the dynasties up in the bathroom. Green for the Sung, yellow for the Han.

"Look at that!" he'll suddenly say on a walk, interrupting himself or me. I'll look, and some undistinguished-looking bird will turn out to be a peregrine falcon or a great green-sided flycatcher. Whatever. When Bob talked about something I didn't care about, I listened, planning to care; but with Nick it's just bait and switch.

April 16. Nick is having another show. Is it meaningful to have a show in a camera store? Does it make any difference that the camera store is downtown? These are imponderables. As is the question of why I care. Anyway, if I want to worry about someone's little career, I suppose it should be my own.

In *The Gross Clinic* a patient lies on an operating table with his feet drawn up and his naked buttocks and thigh facing the viewer. With shocking precision the painting shows the incision in his thigh, the gleaming retractors, the blood on the white cuffs of the crouching attendant physicians. Samuel Gross, standing, his forehead like a cliff, is holding a bloody scalpel while he lectures. *The Gross Clinic* is typical of Eakins in that it shows someone pausing in the middle of an action, like the rower in *Max Schmitt*. Like Schmitt, Gross is totally present in the pause, concentrated, and, in some sense, alone.

I do love the silence of this painting. Everything in the scene is a demand for words, the students listening, the wound held open, the physicians waiting for direction; but Gross isn't trying to speak. He's in that space between one flow of language and another, not so much collecting his thoughts as waiting. His silence guarantees the significance, the weight, of what will come. And this is happening not only in public, in an amphitheater where everything focuses on him, but in the presence of a naked fellow creature, who wears nothing but a pair of gray socks to keep his feet warm. Gross was famous for all kinds of courageous medical explorations, of which this operation was one; but for me what's admirable here about Gross is not what he's doing but what he isn't doing. He's still.

Sometimes when Bob was telling me about his patients he would come to a silence. At first I would say things like, "Well, do you think she has a chance?" or "Have you done an MRI?" I never got much of an answer. Bob would say yes or no and once again fall silent. If I persisted he would turn to some task, clearing the table or sorting the mail. Once I noticed that he was deadheading some pink begonias on the kitchen table.

"I did that yesterday," I said. "You're pinching off perfectly good blossoms."

He looked at me blankly. Then he said, "Okay."

"I'll be quiet," I said. He stopped beheading the begonia plant and said, "Okay." I sat there with him, wishing he would say something, generating more and more thoughts about his patient. But when Bob started talking again it wasn't about that.

"What was that silver thing we saw last week at the museum?" he asked.

"What silver thing?" I said.

"It looked like a spacecraft landing," he said. In the museum store we had seen a lemon juicer, shaped like an egg pointing down and resting on three spidery legs. The cup for juice went underneath.

"I want to get it for you," said Bob. It had delighted me, although I hadn't thought to buy it myself.

What connected Bob's possibly terminal patients to the delightful lemon juicer we had seen together? Nothing, perhaps. But in the grave silence surrounding his patients' mortality, often Bob found peace. He touched some existential ocean floor. When he re-surfaced his arms were full of gifts, and he wanted to give them to me.

Does this mean that Bob was the Truly Caring Doctor everyone dreams of finding? No. No one can actually care about as many people as a doctor has patients. Coming out of a movie once we were accosted by a man in his sixties who challenged Bob to remember his name.

"I'm sorry," said Bob as politely as he could. "I have no idea." It turned out that Bob had cut off the top of his head so he could have his brains fixed up. The man kept knocking angrily on his bald, knobby skull. He thought that someone with whom he had been so weirdly intimate should remember the experience, but all he did was make Bob nostalgic for his days as a rural doctor, when he got to do all kinds of surgery he had no training for.

Then Bob got mortally sick himself. I wish I could say that his talent for spiritual depths kept him sane going through it, but I can't. He was angry, afraid, and unwilling. The drugs sometimes made him crazy, and he took violent offense at minor things. Once at the hospital I opened a window he wanted shut or vice versa.

"Forgive me," I pleaded. "I'm doing my best."

"You think you know best," Bob shouted. "That's always what you think." It was so crazy and unrelenting I felt I had lost him already. The only place I could be alone was the hospital chapel, a blind room over a parking lot. I sat amidst the interdenominational platitudes and thought bitterly of Bob's prayerful silences.

"Fat lot of good they're doing now," I thought. On the wall was a brown textile embroidered with a crude sunflower and some words from Mother Teresa. It was meant to be simple and universal, but I took it as a massive insult.

Once in the hospital I read Bob a story in which everything went wrong. The characters were looking for something they could live by, but things just got worse and life went on. Bob was flat on his back, so I couldn't see his face. When the story was over I thought, "Whatever possessed me to choose such a story?" But after a minute Bob said, "Yes; what a relief."

"What do you mean?" I said.

"That's the way it is," he answered–in his normal, beloved voice. He meant, it's a relief to hear the truth, not some pointless consolation.

"Oh, good," I said, tears springing to my eyes. It was not so much that I had succeeded in pleasing him as that Bob was being himself.

"Who wrote that?" he asked.

"Chekhov," I said.

"Next time read me another Chekhov story, will you?" said Bob. Bob's taste in art was narrow but deep. If he had lived long enough he would willingly have listened to every play and story Chekhov ever wrote. God knows I would willingly have read them to him.

April 23. That's enough now about Bob. No more.

April 26. I mean it. No more.

April 27. Eakins, then.

At a time when impressionism was all the rage among his peers – spontaneity, love of the instantaneous – Eakins went in for a kind of painstaking realism. It was a matter of telling the truth. You should be able to tell the time and weather from a painting, he thought, "what kind of people are there, and what they are doing, and why they are doing it." So meticulous was his attention to realistic details that in *Max Schmitt,* for instance, scholars claim we can tell the exact moment it depicts: 7:20 P.M. in early June (or mid-July), 1871. There's another dimension to Eakins's truth-telling as well. From the time he went to Paris in his early twenties, he championed the truth of the body, sometimes to the point of scandal. Paris was as good a place then as now for a large boy from Philadelphia to figure out that there's more to life than pleasing his father, so we must assume he took advantage of it in more ways than one; but the revelation he writes of took place in his life classes. There he was promoted from the plaster casts used in Philadelphia to real, live, naked models, men and women both. He never got over the experience.

I see Eakins in Jean-Léon Gérôme's Paris studio, aroused and engaged. It's winter, and the students have put their woolen gloves near the wood stove to dry them while they work. The model is not young but she has a wild mass of red hair, and Eakins (or rather Tom, since I'm developing a closer relationship to him) is thrilled to be drawing her breasts, hands, stomach, and thighs exactly as they are. He is also aware that Gérôme, whom he calls "my Master," will soon be by his side, looking at his work. The prospect is dangerous but full of the pleasure of being looked at oneself. Various smells fill the room: the steam rising from the gloves, bodies, and clothing of his neighbors; paint, turpentine, singed wool. Eakins is stirred to do things with paint that he could not say. He feels a new sense of his own powers, along with an indignation at having been kept from them for so long.

He was also indignant at the soft porn of his day. He hated those pictures of "naked women, standing sitting lying down flying dancing doing nothing which they call...Venuses." Why not paint naked men? he wondered. Anything but these "smiling smirking goddesses of waxy complexion amidst the...purling streams running melodious up and down the hills especially up." Streams should run downhill. Naked men and women should look like naked men and women.

In Eakins's paintings they do, to a fault. In 1880 he painted one of his students on a rooftop posing as Jesus on the cross—looking for all the world like a student posing on a rooftop as Jesus on the cross. And although I like Eakins's naked women well enough, I much prefer the ones in clothes. I love the way their formal, ruffled dresses contrast with something about them that is emphatically plain, real, and imperfect. A woman in a Sargent painting *is* her clothes. Paint flows, fabric flows, subject and clothing merge. But in Eakins's work women's dresses bunch or pull in odd places, however luscious their texture, color, and drape. There are real bodies underneath, and they don't conform to the expectations of their tailors. The contrast is even greater with their faces. In *Portrait of Mrs. Edith Mahon*, for instance, Edith is wearing an important black dress with big velvet bows on either side of the décolletage. If you cover up the face, she looks like some bossy, rich lady who gives the servants a hard time. But Edith's face is middle-aged, and the shadows of her life are in her eyes. The muscles in her face are going soft. Once you see her head, you know she just put on the first thing she found in her closet to pose in. Her mind is on other things.

April 30. Friends came for lunch on Saturday, and Nick took pictures of us all. As usual, I had mixed feelings about his doing so. On the one hand, I want to take him seriously as an artist, so I like to see him work; on the other hand, it's the ruination of any social situation when the rest of us are partly posing for Nick. On top of which we were sitting outside, pretending not to be cold. The sun was glaring through the bare trees but it didn't warm the air. April in Massachusetts – the final disappointment. I was nervously chatting and eating too many corn chips while Molly (cute but very pesky these days) kept knocking things over.

"Molly, no!" Karen kept saying. Someone was always handing her off.

Then last night I came home to find one of the pictures from Saturday blown up and taped to the bedroom door. It's a black and white portrait of me as Mrs. Edith Mahon, looking at the camera from the bottom of my heart. My face looks its age, transparent, like a glass of water. The bare sycamore is gesturing behind me; it seems I've come to terms with life and death.

I didn't know what to think. My first response was, "That's it?" I was angry and flattered at once. It was exciting to think I might have that much bare existence, but is it okay to have just as much beauty as I have, with no possibility of more? And what about Nick's methods? Eakins saw into his subjects through an interminable act of looking, but Nick did this in a split second, on a day when my mood was the opposite of the one it implies. I was scattered, not whole. Is Nick mocking Eakins, who is, after all, *my* subject?

Whatever I'm working on seems to show up in Nick's photos. Sometimes he'll mimic a particular painting, as here; sometimes he'll make a vague reference to an artist's style. He's like a bird that's not fussy about its nest: twigs and leaves, of course, but also dog fur, dental floss, cattail fluff, confetti. I leave my books around, and Nick reads them in snatches.

"Where did you find Mrs. Edith Mahon?" I asked this morning.

"She's all over the house," he said, wolfing his breakfast. Then he went out running.

May 7. I'm having second thoughts about *The Gross Clinic*, whose heroic realism turns out to be flawed. One of Gross's assistants, for instance, is impossibly sized. He sits behind Gross holding a retractor in his left hand – which couldn't possibly belong to the same person as his right knee, which emerges on Gross's right. Also to Gross's right is a dark-clad woman in a convulsive state, one claw-like hand raised to ward off the sight of the surgical butchery. She's the patient's mother, it seems, so she's legitimately stressed at seeing him sliced up; but her gesture is wildly excessive. This isn't the moment of incision or danger or anything sudden. Of course her discomfort is there to contrast with Gross's monumental calm; but a simple hand to the eyes would be much more believable.

Even more disturbing is that I'm having second thoughts about Eakins himself. In 1886 the great man was fired from his job at the Philadelphia Academy of Art for sexual improprieties. He said he didn't do it.

"I never in my life seduced a girl," he wrote in despair, "but what else can people think of all this rage and insanity." According to one story he was a martyr to his artistic principles, which dictated teaching from naked models as he himself had been taught. Stuffy, conventional Philadelphia couldn't take it, so some of Eakins's students helped found a new school where he could teach. But other students and witnesses tell an equally plausible story. Indeed, I don't know what to think.

May 10. I told Nick how Eakins was unraveling for me and why.

"Bear down on the errors," he advised me. "The secret's in what doesn't fit." He meant well, but it didn't help. Then last night he didn't even mean well. He was reading one of my Eakins books and laughed out loud.

"What?" I said.

"A Canadian student of Eakins's," Nick told me, looking up, "asked an American why they always called him Eakins instead of *Mr.* Eakins. The American student said, 'What? Do you say *"Mr.* Jesus" in Canada?'"

I didn't laugh. Nick looked up.

"Sorry," he said, and left the room.

We're not getting along these days at all. It started when I asked Nick to show me some tools on Photoshop. We scanned in *The Gross Clinic,* and Nick cloned its various parts. Soon we had Gross's amazing head all over the screen, where, of course, it didn't look so amazing anymore. Ditto the patient's buttocks, socks, and sliced-up thigh. Then we started over again, leaving the picture whole but changing the direction of the light. In a subtler way, this, too, completely ruined the painting. It had been my idea to use *The Gross Clinic,* but I saw now it had been a mistake. Nick was zooming along excitedly, demonstrating new techniques. I couldn't keep up. *The Gross Clinic* was dismembered in a dozen different ways.

"That's enough now," I kept saying. "I can't take it in anymore."

"Just one more thing," Nick said, absorbed. Eventually I left. He looked up, surprised, but some new possibility drew him back, and he went on playing with the picture.

Later we worked on Nick's show. We spread out a hodge-podge of collages, abstractions, extended frame sequences, depth-of-field prints, mixed-media pieces, and a few forays into social commentary. It made my heart sink.

"I really liked those pictures you used to do of people's gestures," I said tactfully. "Why don't you do more of that?"

"Edwina," said Nick. "We've been over that."

"Sorry," I said. "Whatever." But then I realized that he intended to include the picture of me as Mrs. Edith Mahon.

"You can't use that," I said without thinking.

"What the hell," said Nick. "Why not?"

"It's too personal. Or too impersonal, I don't know which."

"Well, that's clear," said Nick.

"You were making a joke," I said, groping. "It's not about me at all."

"What makes you think that?" said Nick.

"That wasn't going on at the time," I said. "All that collectedness."

"Everything's going on all the time," argued Nick. "You just have to know what you're looking for."

"Well, you weren't looking for me," I said vehemently. I thought, "You never are!" But when I saw Nick's face, I felt bad. "Well, fine," he said. "If you don't want it up, I'll leave it out." The day did not improve from there.

Should we call it quits before this gets worse? If I'm just mad at Nick for being Nick, we'd both be better off without it.

No, that's too grim. Get a grip, Edwina!

May 16. No progress on Eakins; worse and worse all week with Nick.

May 22. Major fight yesterday. I couldn't stop saying mean things.

"I'm done," Nick finally said, and went to his sister's. I'm mad he beat me to it, but—fine, then. Fine. Whatever.

May 31. Not fine at all, as it turns out! I'm sick with confusion and impending loss.

Eakins went through some dark times, too. The Philadelphia Sketch Club, where he went after the Academy fiasco, *also* expelled him; this time it was clearly unjust. His sister Fanny and her husband William were his closest allies going through it; William wrote a long, eloquent affidavit on Eakins's behalf. But then Fanny's oldest daughter, Ella Crowell, went to live and study with Uncle Tom. She apparently fell in love with him, and later came home and killed herself. The Crowells didn't feel so good about Tom after that. They told him not to come down to their farm anymore. Now it was Susan Macdowell, Eakins's wife, who was up in the night writing in her husband's defense.

I've been up in the night myself. The take-away is that I've behaved pretty badly. It's not just this business over the portrait; I didn't give Nick a chance. I don't want to apologize, because that would look as if I were trying to get him back, which I may not even want; but yesterday I called him at his sister's.

"Edwina?" said Melanie. "Oh, thank god." I don't know what she thought I was going to say, but she started yelling for Nick.

"What is it?" he said in some alarm when he got on.

"Nothing," I said. "I don't know why Melanie got so excited. It's just that I've changed my mind about that picture you took of me."

"Really?" said Nick.

"I think it belongs in the show."

"Yeah?" said Nick.

"Yes," I said, "it's a strong picture no matter how I feel about it."

"But you don't like it," said Nick.

"I don't know anymore. But I know it belongs in your show."

"When I took it, you know," said Nick, "I thought you would like it." At that something happened to me. It was as if the plane I was riding hit an air pocket, and might just keep falling. Why exactly *hadn't* I liked the picture? Maybe it meant something I hadn't understood. Suddenly it seemed as if things were happening too fast. "I'm sorry," I said, and then, beginning to panic, "I'm *really* sorry."

"No," said Nick, correctly hearing the general apology I hadn't wanted to make, "we both screwed up. I guess you weren't ready to get married again. If you ever will be."

"What is that supposed to mean?" I said. "It sounds hostile."

"That's to be expected," said Nick. "We're splitting up." I suppose that was witty, but it wasn't what I wanted to hear.

"What do you mean, if I ever will be?" I demanded. Nick knows me far better than he lets on. Does he think I'll never get over Bob?

"Nothing," said Nick, "I suppose I will use the picture, if you really don't mind."

"I really don't mind," I said. The picture was the least of it now. We said good-bye and hung up.

June 7. Yesterday I went to see Nick's show. I wore my blue dress, and when I saw a tall man with springy blond-gray hair leaving the gallery, I thought it was Nick. Apparently I was expecting to see him.

The show is in a real gallery. It's upstairs from a camera store and owned by the same people, but it's a regular art space with expensive, exotic flowers and white walls. The windows were open, and no one else was there. Some lilacs were blooming right outside, and I kept walking through currents of scent.

There I was as Mrs. Edith Mahon, framed at the last minute and hung with the rest. The person I was in April and I looked at each other for a long time. After a while I was also aware of the other pictures in the room. They looked different. Something was going on between them, or among them, that seemed to wake them all up.

"Have you seen the review?" asked a young man I hadn't noticed before. He came out from behind a desk and handed me a newspaper article in a plastic protector. "Do you know the artist? We're so excited by the show."

Spare me, I thought. I'm really not here to buy anything. "There's a review already?" I said.

"And two more in the works," he said. He was wearing large black glasses on his thin face, which gave him a kind of exaggerated look to begin with, and then he launched into the wildest praise of Nick's work. When I'd had enough I tried to go.

"Would you like a copy of the review?" he asked. "I can make you one in a second."

"Sure," I said. I didn't think about the review again until this morning, when I read it; but since then I've thought of little else. It's written by the *Advocate's* best critic, and it's just about perfect. The show, she writes, is an example of what postmodernism ought to be but rarely is: free and even incoherent play in an "impossible" conjunction with the high seriousness of modernism. She particularly likes the photo of the artist's wife, which she says shows how much feeling he has for her and how clearly he sees her anyway. The crazy variety of styles is at the same time an amazing, lunatic display and a serious commentary on the tradition of photography itself. After this exhibition Nick's work will surely, *must* surely, receive the recognition it deserves.

Whew! Is this babe for real? I may be incompetent to judge the worth of Nick's work, and I *know* I'm incompetent to judge the worth of this review. But that doesn't mean I can stop thinking about it!

June 17. "I've found an essay that does what you said," I told Nick on the phone. I was determined to be friendly and decent.

"What's that?" he asked guardedly.

"Bear down on Eakins's errors."

"I said that?"

"You said to focus on his *failures* of realism, remember? You said they held the key."

"Okay," he said.

"It's a great essay," I told him. "You were right!"

There was a silence. Then Nick said flatly, "I'm happy for you," and I flared right up.

"Then try not to sound as if you couldn't care less," I said, hurt and mad. Of course we never recovered from that.

The Eakins essay, on the other hand, is superb. Eakins, argues the author, was divided, and his conflicts result in opposing ways of painting. Much of it has to do with his dad. Eakins's father was well to do, and he loved his eldest son.

"You learn to paint the best you can, Tom," he said. "You'll never have to earn your own living." So on the one hand Eakins felt good about paternalism, male authority, and all that; but there were also, as there always are, disruptive feelings: anger; unauthorized desires; refusals.

Eakins's profound, exacting realism comes from one side of the conflict; his distortions come from the other. The essay leaps around Eakins's early work, making wild connections that turn out to be valid. Eakins's father, Benjamin, was a writing master and the subject of one of Eakins's most affectionate portraits. Benjamin's bent head, like Gross's in *The Gross Clinic,* is domed, highlighted, gray-haired, impressive; he is working on a large, formal document. The scalpel in Gross's hand, argues the essay, is like the writing implement Benjamin uses for his calligraphy. Tom himself is in a corner of *The Gross Clinic,* taking notes with *his* writing implement. It doesn't hurt that one of the meanings of "to engross" is "to write in a clear, attractive script, as a public document or record," which is what Benjamin does in the portrait. So there's Benjamin Eakins, engrossed in his engrossing work; Tom engrossed in Gross; and Gross, with blood as bright as nail polish on his scalpel, engrossed in his teaching/slicing task. Suddenly fathers, sons, pens, pencils, letters, and numbers show up all over Eakins's work, like Gross's head on Nick's screen the day he showed me Photoshop. Suddenly Eakins's strong feelings for and against all the authoritative older men he painted have everything to do with his inordinately principled realism and his violations thereof.

This feels new. The old Eakins was wearing thin.

June 25. Nick came over, and then he came again; and again; but we're not resolving things. Yesterday, saying good-bye, having arrived at our usual impasse, I felt panicky. We were standing at the door.

"How's the Eakins going?" asked Nick. Maybe he was delaying, too.

"Oh, the Eakins," I said vaguely, too tense to give him a real answer.

"Right," said Nick, as if he should have known I'd blow him off.

"No, I mean..." I said, but Nick was walking down the driveway to his car. I trailed along.

"'Bye," I called, but Nick's face was set. Some sparrows flew up from the hedges when he started his car.

And that's it. We hash and rehash, and nothing changes. Then I cry, or call friends for advice, or go for long, distressing walks. And then... I go back to Eakins. I'll be ready to talk next week, whatever happens with Nick. I just don't know if he'll be there.

June 30. Yesterday I went to have a look at *A May Morning in the Park.* The reproductions of it suck, so I needed to see the original. But when I got to the Eakins exhibit, whom should I find there but Nick, in front of *Baby at Play.* The baby in question is none other than Ella Crowley, she who fell in love with her Uncle Tom and subsequently killed herself. There she was in a child's embroidered dress and red-striped sandals, seriously selecting a small wooden block. She had no idea at the time the misery that would befall her twenty years later; and Nick, for his part, had no idea I was there. He was taking notes, like Eakins in *The Gross Clinic.* Presumably he planned to use something he saw in his work.

"What are you doing here?" I asked when he finally noticed me.

"Looking at the paintings," he said. Duh.

"But you don't like Eakins," I said. *Baby at Play,* as many people have pointed out, might as well be called *Baby at Work.* Ella seems not so much caught in a moment of concentration as preparing to write a doctoral dissertation about the block she is staring at. There is a small block structure nearby, and one would like to assume that the new block will join it soon; but in fact construction seems to have come to a halt, with no plans to resume it.

"Where are you getting that?" said Nick coolly.

"You said he was too quiet," I said. "'Borderline dull.'"

"I said that about *one painting,*" Nick exploded. "That's your problem, Edwina. You make things into all or nothing." Maybe because it was morning, and the nearly empty museum felt airy and spacious; or maybe it was because I could tell I had been very glad to see him; but for whatever reason I was suddenly interested in what he had to say. I sat down on the brown velvet hassock to hear more. He stood above me, gesticulating.

"You totalize," he insisted.

"Shh," I said, not meaning that he should stop but only that he should lower his voice. Nick understood, and warmed to his theme. In an energetic whisper, he told me many terrible things about myself, and I listened with great absorption. There was something virtuosic, for one thing, about the way he derived my entire personality structure from the unfounded assumption that he disliked Eakins's work; and, more importantly, there was something enjoyable and reassuring about the mere fact of his talking so much about *me.*

"You could be right," I said, but Nick went on and on. "You could be right," I kept saying. A feeling of joyful self-abandonment was welling up. Why shouldn't Nick be the new authority on who I was? And why shouldn't I just *be* the deeply flawed, exasperating woman he described? Who cared?

He loves me anyway! I thought. Can you believe it? I felt loved; finally, I wanted him back. Could I tell him that?

Not right away, I thought. It would be like saying he's cute when he's mad! To stall for time I gestured toward *Baby At Play*.

"Well, do you like this one?" I asked him waving my arm at the near-moribund baby. Nick stopped talking and thought about it.

"Yes," he said. "I do." It wasn't Ella's intense stillness that he liked but the moving shadows across her face; the painted wooden horse running off into the bushes; and the splayed, abandoned doll near the broken flowerpot. I don't know how any of this connects to Nick's current work, but I knew it would show up in some weird, unpredictable way.

"Nick," I said on impulse, "can I tell you what I'm going to say?"

"About Eakins?" he asked.

"Yes," I said. So I told him about all the fathers and sons and writing implements; and about the way Eakins's anger found an outlet in the strange distortions of size, perspective, and timing; and also in the color red. Nick said something about the reds in *The Gross Clinic* that was almost right but not quite, so I talked some more to clear things up. The longer I talked the more Nick relaxed. My expansiveness on Eakins seemed to affect him just as his knowledgeable analysis of my faults had affected me.

He knows! I thought as I talked on. I don't even have to say it! Somehow this seemed the best of all. Toward the end we were having a real conversation, going back and forth the way we like to do. Finally I told him an anecdote in which Eakins took off his pants to show a woman student some point that escaped her about the masculine package.

"He did?" said Nick, incredulous. "Mr. Jesus dropped his drawers?" That struck me as incredibly funny, and once I started laughing I couldn't stop. It wasn't *that* funny, but it had been a long time since Nick and I had been able to laugh over anything at all, and soon Nick started laughing, too. We laughed and laughed, from sheer relief that we were laughing.

"Shh," said a guard, rushing in from another gallery. But we kept catching each other's eye and laughing some more.

"If you can't be quiet, I shall have to ask you to leave," said the guard stiffly, so we left. I would be back on Friday to give my talk; and Nick, I now knew, would be with me. We were leaving via the exhibit entrance, so the last painting we saw was *Max Schmitt in a Single Scull*. I looked over my shoulder at Max, who was looking over his shoulder at me.

"How about that, Max?" I asked him silently, holding Nick's hand. "We're good!" Max just sat there in his undershirt, soberly sizing things up. For him, it would always just be 7:20 P.M. on a day in early June (or mid-July), 1871.

July 2. Nick has this strange tie in sharp, expressionist orange and green. Sometimes it seems witty and delightful, but sometimes it's just bad. Last night it figured in a dream that began with Bob and me watching Eakins skate on a river at evening. In real life Benjamin taught his son to make calligraphic tracings on the ice, and in my dream Tom was gloomily skating flourishes. I could tell it was late in his life when he had lost all his battles.

"My honors are misunderstanding, persecution, and neglect," he wrote bitterly. At nearly sixty he was offered an award by the Pennsylvania Academy, which could no longer ignore his significance. He appeared in his biking outfit to pick it up and took it straight to the mint to have it melted down.

It was a beautiful scene on the river, pussy-willow sky, slate-gray ice. Eakins stopped skating figures and came over to chat. Now Nick was there, too, in his tie. Eakins said to Nick, "Nice tie." I looked at Bob, who shrugged.

"Edwina likes it, too," said Nick distinctly, and they all looked at me. Snow was beginning to fall. The tracery left on the ice was already almost gone.

Do I? I thought, looking at the ground between my feet. When I looked up, Bob was walking up a hill but turning to smile as he went. I smiled back and waved.

"Yes," I said to Tom and Nick. "I do."

Works Consulted

The following are some of the most notable or useful of the works I consulted.

PLAYING HENRY

Chris Given-Wilson, trans., *Chronicles of the Revolution 1397–1400*
Uta Hagen, *Respect for Acting*
K.B. McFarlane, *Lancastrian Kings and Lollard Knights*
Sanford Meissner, *Sanford Meissner on Acting*
John Julius Norwich, *Shakespeare's Kings*
Nigel Saul, *Richard II*

IN THE FOREST

Elliot Krieger, *A Marxist Study of Shakespeare's Comedies*

CLEOPATRA AND ANTONY

T. W. Hillard, "The Nile Cruise of Cleopatra and Caesar" in *Classical Quarterly* 52.2
Plutarch, *Plutarch's Lives*
Judith Thurman, *Cleopatra's Nose*

AN INCARCERATION OF HAMLETS

"Act V," *This American Life*, http://www.thisamericanlife.org/radio-archives/episode/218/act-v

Laura Bates, "'To Know My Deed': Finding Salvation Through Shakespeare" in Jonathan Shailor, ed., *Performing New Lives: Prison Theater*

Charles McGaw and Kenneth Stilson, *Acting is Believing*

Hank Rogerson and Jilann Spitzmiller, *Shakespeare Behind Bars* (film)

Amy Scott-Douglas, *Shakespeare Inside: The Bard Behind Bars*

Laurence Tocci, *The Proscenium Cage*

THE GROSS CLINIC

Kathleen A. Foster and Cheryl Leibold, *Writing About Eakins: The Manuscripts in Charles Bregler's Thomas Eakins Collection*

Michael Fried, *Realism, Writing, Disfiguration: On Thomas Eakins and Stephen Crane*

Lloyd Goodrich, *Thomas Eakins*

William Innes Homer, *Thomas Eakins, His Life and Art*

Elizabeth Johns, *Thomas Eakins*

Acknowledgments

Thanks to Chris Bullock, Jennifer Clarvoe, Ben Fountain, Frieda Gardner, Jonathan Haynes, Lewis Hyde, Amanda Powell, Jonathan Strong, Christina Thompson, and my editor, Susan Barba, for encouragement and suggestions along the way; to Jack Hitt, Derrick Hutchinson, Meg Sempreora, and Agnes Wilcox for conversations about Shakespeare in prisons; to Bob Long for emergency backup; and to my sister, Patsy Vigderman, for taking what she likes and fixing up the rest.

Prisoner A's account of his parole hearing in "An Incarceration of Hamlets" was inspired by Amy Scott-Douglas's excellent exploration of Shakespeare in prison, *Shakespeare Inside*.

Earlier versions of stories in this collection have appeared in the following places:

The Harvard Review: "Cleopatra and Antony"
The Kenyon Review: "The Gross Clinic" and "In the Forest"
Ploughshares: "Time to Teach *Jane Eyre* Again"
Southwest Review: "Casting Call"

About the Author

Linda Bamber is a Professor of English at Tufts University. A poet and critic as well as a writer of fiction, she is the author of *Metropolitan Tang: Poems* (Black Sparrow Books/Godine) and the widely reprinted critical work, *Comic Women, Tragic Men: Gender and Genre in Shakespeare* (Stanford University Press). Her poems, stories, essays, and reviews have appeared in such places as *The Harvard Review, The New York Times Book Review, The Kenyon Review, The Nation, Raritan,* and *Ploughshares.*